The Marlows and the Traitor

The Marlows
and the Traitor

by

ANTONIA FOREST

illustrated by

DORITIE KETTLEWELL

FABER AND FABER

3 Queen Square

London

First published in 1953
by Faber and Faber Limited
3 Queen Square London W.C.1
Second Impression 1964
Printed in Great Britain by
Latimer Trend & Co Ltd Whitstable
All rights reserved

ISBN 0 571 06769 7

For
A.M.C.R.

Author's Note

To anyone who takes an interest in naval affairs, it will be plain that, as Peter Marlow was only just fourteen at the time of this story, the happenings described must have taken place between September 1946 and May 1949. This in no way affects the story itself, and no one need trouble to discover why if they don't know already.

Contents

1

Encounter in a Thunderstorm

It was five o'clock in the morning and raining steadily. At St.-Anne's-Byfleet, where the four younger Marlows and their mother were staying, the empty promenade stretched out, black and shining, the lights on the standards pale in the dawn twilight. The only living thing in sight was a ginger cat, who had curled up for the night in one of the shelters, and was still profoundly asleep, one orange paw curved across his nose.

Farther down the coast to the east, where the open country began, the sea curved in behind the land, making a stretch of water like the seaward end of a broad river. At the landward end of this water, a pram dinghy was tied to a post on the bank and in the centre of the channel a small cutter, the name *Talisman* painted on her hull, lay on a mooring. For a time the only creatures to be seen were the gulls sleeping on the water and the curlews flying and crying as they skimmed and swooped low over the fields. Then a man in oilskins appeared at the end of the lane which ran through the water meadows. He walked down to the bank, stepped into the dinghy and pulled over to the cutter. After a few moments the sails were

13

set, the mooring-buoy splashed into the water, and the cutter began to ghost down channel, past the sedgy fields, past the mudflats, towards the open sea.

Far down on the horizon, a bank of bruised-looking clouds began to spread slowly across the sky.

A rumble of thunder, though it was only just audible ashore, woke Peter Marlow in his bed at the hotel. He rolled over sleepily, not knowing what had wakened him, and saw that the wind had sucked the net curtains outside and draped them over the window frames. There was also a large pool of water on the floor, just below the window, where the rain had blown in. Peter yawned hugely. Then he had a proper look at the weather, decided he didn't think much of it, reached sleepily for the three biscuits beside his bed, pulled the blankets over his head, and began to munch, curled up in a warm, crumby lump. It was just ten past six.

He finished the biscuits and any crumbs he could find, and went on lying snuggled under the bedclothes. He had meant to go to sleep again, but instead he had begun to think about last term, and by now he was properly awake. However much he tried to think of other things, or better still, nothing at all, his mind kept on coming back to the episode he thought of privately as the boat thing. He hadn't told his family; he felt too bothered about it for that.

He grunted crossly. He was tired of going over the boat thing in all its gory detail. If it hadn't been for that, it would have been a rather successful term. And sometimes he pretended that it had been; quite often he talked to himself as if the disaster of the boat had never happened.

But of course it had, and this morning he knew it; and the awful thing was that though nothing of the kind had ever happened before, there was no telling when something like it mightn't happen again. Because it wasn't the sort of thing you could guard against; a crisis blew up, and either you coped or you didn't; and if you were in the Service you *had* to be the sort of person who coped: Peter quite saw that. And it would be appalling—the worst thing that had ever happened, or could ever happen to him—to be kicked out of Dartmouth because he was a useless worm. (Not that the authorities had suggested this yet, but one never knew.) And besides, apart from the quite scorching humiliation of being thrown out, he would have to go back to being an ordinary schoolboy at an ordinary school; and that, after being a naval cadet at Dartmouth, would be too boring for words.

Peter stuck his hot face out of the bedclothes. It was no use fussing. Next term would have to take care of itself. In the meantime it was the middle of the vac, and he and Ginty and Lawrie and Nicola were spending it in a really lush, luxury hotel. Like his mother, Peter thought it an excellent idea to spend Great-Aunt Alice's small but opportune legacy on being thoroughly luxurious while they had the drains up at home. He was sorry for the elder members of the family who weren't there, either because they were foolish enough to be at sea or because they had gone visiting: as a matter of fact, he might have gone visiting too, for part of the time; but he told himself, and it was very nearly true, that the only reason he had turned down several quite promising openings was because he wanted to spend the vac in luxury and idleness—no bed-making, for instance; no turns at the washing-up; (but also, as he knew quite well, he hadn't wanted to spend the vac with anyone who had heard that blistering ticking-off on the hard.) Peter kicked savagely against the sheet: *he would not think about it any more.* It *was* because of the hotel; anyone would want to stay there.

All the same, he did rather wish they'd been staying at an inland place. The hotel itself was marvellous, but St.-Anne's was a very ordinary seaside place with a promenade and a beach and a tamed, tidy sea. And he didn't like the sea much, anyway. Although he had only been at Dartmouth for a couple of terms, he had already acquired a professional dislike of the beastly thing.

A sudden rumble of thunder rolled overhead and he plunged out of bed and across to the window to have a look. As a way of silencing his thoughts, a freak thunderstorm in April was an excellent idea. He watched for a time while the sky turned a dull coppery colour and fork lightning began to split the clouds away on the horizon and the rain fell more heavily than before. Then it occurred to him that it would be fun to go out; he liked thunderstorms. So he leaned dangerously out of the window to rescue the curtains, mopped the floor with the bath towel and began to hurl himself into his clothes. He thought he'd go along and see if Nicola would come too. She would certainly be awake, but she generally went out by herself before breakfast. Her family supposed she went off to St.-Anne's-Oldport, where she probably had friends among the fishermen: Nicola's passion for the sea and ships (preferably naval ships, but if not, any that were handy) was in the nature of an old, well-crusted family joke. Still, no one had asked her directly if that was what she did. As a family, the Marlows were rather good at minding their own business.

Nicola's room was just across the corridor. He found her shoving her head through the neck of her jersey, her bobbed, yellow hair tousled and on end, while she read, with a startled expression, the really rather depressing end of *A Ship of the Line*, which was lying open on the bed. She looked up as he came in, exclaiming: "Oh, Binks! Does Hornblower really get captured?"

"He does," said Peter, grinning. After Giles, who was the eldest, he liked Nicola, the youngest-but-one, the best of the family: and after Giles, Nicola liked Peter the best too, which made it even. She liked Lawrie, her twin, very well too, but Lawrie was so much a part of her that Nicola had never considered whether she really liked her or not, and if so, how much.

"Oh dear," said Nicola, reading fast and finding that Peter was not just being funny. She had never read a book before which ended in the apparent defeat of the hero, and though it was a very glorious defeat in every way, she didn't think she liked it at all. Peter waited till she had finished and then said in a maddening way: "But as a matter of fact, it's all right in the end, you know. In the next book——"

"Don't tell me," shouted Nicola, properly exasperated. "I want to read it myself. Did you know there's a storm going on?"

"Of course I know. That's why I came. Shall we go out?"

Nicola looked rather caught. Of course, it was a good idea to go for a walk in a thunderstorm, but at the same time, she had, as her family supposed, a prior engagement at St.-Anne's-Oldport. Still, it would probably be easier to go with Peter than go into long explanations about why she couldn't; so, "Yes, let's," she said, rather muffled because she was grubbing in the cupboard for her gumboots. "Only buck up and get your mack and things, or there won't be any storm left to go out in."

The hotel was barely awake. They saw a porter in shirt sleeves as they went softly down the main staircase, but he was hurrying away in another direction. The main doors were still bolted, so they let themselves out through the french windows of the sun-lounge which opened on to the drenched and dripping garden. The rain pelted down, flattening the daffodils.

It was still thundering by the time they reached the promenade, but the lightning seemed to have stopped. By rights, the tide should have been only just on the turn, but the sea, which never went out very far at Byfleet, was already slopping, churned and yellow, across the road.

"This is super," said Nicola, sloshing hugely through a wave which was spreading itself round their feet. "Oh, Binks, look! There's the fishing fleet."

Far out to sea, the smacks were returning to St.-Anne's-

Oldport, their sails black against the bright white band of light which was beginning to show above the horizon. Peter looked and then thought he saw another sail out of the corner of his eye; he walked backwards, his eyes screwed up against the white light which was flaring across the wave-tops and making it difficult to be certain whether there really was a boat wallowing slowly through the heavy seas away to the east or not.

"What are you looking at?" asked Nicola, walking backwards too.

"A boat, I think. Quite a small one. *There*——"

Nicola saw her too, clawing home through a head sea far outside the bay.

"She looks *very* small."

"I expect she's all right, really," he said doubtfully. "I suppose she was out night sailing, and got caught. I mean, no one but a lunatic would go out in weather like this for fun, would they?"

"*We* have," said Nicola, grinning.

"I mean sailing, you goop." Peter watched as the little boat dropped behind a ragged-edged rise of sea, waited until the tip of the mast showed again and the hull rose slowly to the crest, and then said with a shiver: "I wouldn't be in that cockpit now for anything."

Nicola glanced at him. "If I didn't like the sea as much as you don't seem to," she said in a complicated way, "I don't think I'd want to be in the Navy much."

"It isn't the same."

"What isn't?"

"Being in the Service and liking the sea." His colour rose suddenly and he added quickly, covering his instant thought that whether he liked the sea or not, he mightn't be in the Navy anyway: "Besides, this is a rotten coast for pleasure sailing. I had a look at one of the Thorpes' charts the other night —Mr. Thorpe showed me. He knows a lot, though you

wouldn't think so, just looking at him. They went right down
the Spanish and Portuguese coasts to Gib, last summer. *And*
those awful Miss Thorpes and Mrs. Thorpe too."

"*Gosh!*" said Nicola, impressed, thinking of quiet, bald Mr.
Thorpe and his cheerful noisy wife and two daughters who all
wore trousers much too tight and too brightly coloured for
their various shapes. "Did Johnnie go too?"

"You betcha!" said Peter, being Johnnie Thorpe rather suc-
cessfully. All the Marlows could—and did—imitate Johnnie
Thorpe on occasion. It wasn't kind or mannerly, but he was
the sort of person who invited mimicry: just seventeen, lanky
and overgrown, with a loud voice, a constant guffawing laugh,
and a violent, blundering clumsiness. Worst of all, he was
afflicted by sudden descents of shyness which crimsoned his
ears and made him hoarse-voiced and garrulous. Because
there was no one of his own age staying in the hotel, he would
have liked to have been friendly with the Marlows; but the
Marlows, in the politest possible way, would have nothing to
do with him, even though, as Mrs. Marlow pointed out,
Johnnie was really an extremely nice boy, much nicer than
his mannerisms would lead one to suppose.

But the Marlows were unconvinced. As Lawrie had pointed
out: "It's his mannerisms we'd be with," and really, in spite of
their mother's disapproval, there was nothing more to be said.
They agreed they were behaving badly; they agreed that it
wasn't at all kind to go off, leaving Johnnie Thorpe (who was
much too sensitive not to know when a polite excuse was a true
one, and when it simply meant he wasn't wanted) throwing
darts against himself in the games room; but there are some
people, as Ginty said guiltily, that you simply *can't* like, however good and nice they are, and Johnnie Thorpe was one of
them. So Nicola quite understood the odd note of hesitancy in
Peter's voice when he said:

"Mr. Thorpe said he'd take us out in the *Fair Wind* if we'd
like to come and Mummy didn't mind. If it wasn't for Johnnie,

I'd like to. But I don't see how we could go out in his father's cruiser and then not let Johnnie tag on. Do you?"

"No," said Nicola firmly. And added sadly: "And I couldn't, anyway." For Nicola, who loved ships and the Navy and the sea, was inevitably seasick on the shortest, calmest voyage and no pleasure to anyone. It did not matter so much if it were just her own family, but she certainly couldn't sail with strangers. As Giles had once remarked, this was obviously the reason why Nicola's heroes were Nelson and Hornblower: they were seasick too. She said: "But if you *want* to go, I could bear it. And she is lovely, the *Fair Wind*. Though I must say, I think it's a putrid name for a boat that hasn't a scrap of canvas anywhere."

Peter, who had never wasted time regretting, as Nicola did, that the Navy had changed from sail to steam, said: "What would you call her, then? *The Jolly Crank Shaft?*" Which made them both giggle.

The ginger cat, which was just waking up in its shelter, stretched gloriously fore-and-aft and yawned as they went by, his pink tongue curling. Naturally, they had to stop and talk to him, and rub him behind the ears; but the cat was prepared to be petted longer than they wanted to pet him, and at length Peter said: "Come on, Nick. It looks as if it were going to clear."

"And then we shall look *jolly* silly in our mackintoshes and our sou'-westers and our gumboots." Nicola who had been rubbing the cat's stomach found that he had suddenly curled himself round her hand and was kicking hard at her sleeve with his hind feet. She withdrew her hand gently and said: "Shall we walk along the Undercliff as far as we can? There's years before breakfast."

Peter nodded. Really, there was nowhere else much they could walk unless they went through the town and struck inland and there wasn't time for that. The Undercliff Road, which was the continuation of the Promenade, went on for miles, hugging the side of the cliffs once the hotels came to an end, and serving as a link between three or four small seaside towns. It wasn't bad once the cliffs began. Except, of course, that it was supposed to be impassable in a storm. He wondered whether he should mention this, and then, idiotically, thought he wouldn't. He didn't want to sound as if he were afraid of getting his feet wet, particularly now the storm was practically finished. He shrugged off the thought and decided to talk about something else.

"This Fancy Dress Dance thing at the hotel next week, Nick. What are you going as? Tweedledum and Tweedledee with Lawrie?"

"No, we're not. Nor anything twinnish. It's a thing we're tired of being. And anyway, Lawrie's going as Charlie Chaplin."

"How jolly odd."

"That's what I think. But she says she's been dying to be him ever since they took us to *The Gold Rush* last term. And she can look like him, Binks. It's awfully queer, but she can."

"I wish I'd seen that play of yours at school last Christmas. I'd like to know what all this is about Lawrie and her acting that everyone keeps on about."

"Well, so she is good. You'll see when she's being Charlie Chaplin." Nicola chuckled. "She bought a bowler hat for tuppence at a second-hand shop in the town yesterday, and a little cane."

"And what about her suit?" said he suspiciously.

"Yes, I know. She was going to ask you. Because yours would be just right and baggy on Lawrie. And the house-keeper's found her some old blackout material to make tails of. So we thought you might, 'cos you won't be wearing it yourself that night. You'll be in fancy dress too."

"I suppose I shall," said he rather gloomily, for though he wasn't over-keen on dressing-up, he knew that naval officers were supposed to join in festivities in foreign ports. "I shall be a pirate, I should think. Something harmless like that."

"That wouldn't be too bad. Mummy could lend you a hand-kerchief for your head, I expect. And Lawrie wants Ginty to be a mermaid, but I don't know how."

"And what about you?"

"I simply don't know," said Nicola gloomily. "The trouble is I don't *look* like anything."

"How d'you mean?"

"Well, dark like a gypsy. Or plaits would be useful. Or fluffy like that little beast who keeps telling everyone she's going to be a powder-puff."

He began to chuckle. "But you do look like something. You look like Lawrie. Go on, Nick. For a joke. Go in Lawrie's red and white caterpillar jersey and say you've come as Lawrie Marlow."

This struck them both as very funny indeed. And suddenly, in the afterglow of a good joke shared, he began to tell her about last term; not the edited version, suitable for parents: the things that were really important. The boat thing, for instance.

Briefly (and Peter wasn't brief: there were a great many *So you sees*, *Well and thens* and *actuallys*, all of which made a quite short story into a quite long one) what had happened was this:

They had been out in the boats; he had had the tiller and, because this was something he knew from A to Z (he thought) he hadn't really been thinking what he was doing. So that eventually, of course, the boat had gybed when he was least expecting it, and Brian Webber had been caught by the boom and knocked overboard. Even then it wouldn't have been so bad if he had brought the boat round at once and picked Webber up. But he hadn't; for two or three awful moments his mind had gone as blank as a cinema screen when the film breaks, and he had forgotten everything his father and his brother Giles—not to mention Lieutenant Foley—had ever taught him; and by the time he had got himself and his boat in hand, Lieutenant Foley had brought his own boat up and was yanking the dazed and spluttering Webber out of the water. It had been a dreadful few minutes. Far worse, really, than the tremendous rocket he had had from Lieutenant Foley as soon as he came ashore, with everyone being very busy within earshot, pretending not to listen, but actually with their ears flapping like—like *microphones*, thought Peter resentfully.

Nicola was a good person to tell. She listened and asked quite sensible questions and, when the story was finished, didn't pretend it had all been nothing. Somehow, it made him feel better to know that she looked at it much as he did. Feeling much more cheerful, he went on to talk about other things.

"And how's Selby?" inquired Nicola at length.

Selby was regarded as rather a freak by the rest of Peter's family; not because there was anything odd about him, but simply because he was a perfectly ordinary, clean, intelligent, well-mannered sort of boy. And this was the first time Peter had ever had a friend like that. All his life, he had had a talent for taking a fancy to the most unpleasant people, from his very first friend at the local kindergarten, who had been an angelic-looking little boy called Esmond who bit people without provocation and ran at them with open knives, right down through Roger, Hugh, Arthur and Paul, all quite horrid in their various ways, to Dickie Randall who, in Peter's last term at prep school, had been expelled for stealing: Peter's watch had been only one of the things the matron had discovered when she came to pack for Randall at the end of term.

So Selby, who was so nice and ordinary, was an enormous surprise to everyone. Lawrie had wondered afterwards if he had noticed how they had all watched at first to see what he would do next. And he didn't do anything next, unless you counted lying on his stomach for hours to watch the frogs and things by the pond. And that was something they had all done when they were younger, before they got used to them.

"Sel's all right," said Peter, but he said it doubtfully.

"Oh, *Peter*."

"No, I don't mean anything like that. But——"

"But *what*?"

"Well, a queer thing happened. At least, Sel says it was queer." Peter kicked at a pebble.

"Well, go on. *What*?"

"Well, Sel had leave out with his mother. And she kept him late, which is something you'd think she'd know not to do when his father's a Captain, wouldn't you? Anyway, Sel was belting back, and Lieutenant F-Foley", Peter stammered suddenly, "went past in his car with another bloke, and pulled up just ahead. And the other bloke got out and Sel was rushing past and Foley called after him and said he'd give him a lift."

"Wasn't that all right?"

"Well, of course. Sel was jolly thankful. And he says Foley was awfully decent and quite human and laughed a lot—not about anything, but as if he was tremendously pleased about something. Only then——"

"Then what?"

"That's what I don't know, not exactly. Sel says it all sort of changed. He—Foley, I mean—was still being decent, only *too* decent, if you know what I mean. All boys together and let's diddle the Captain and I've done this for you, what'll you do for me? Sel didn't like it a bit. And there was a terrific lot about naval discipline being excessive and a lot of things would have to be changed——"

"But isn't he Navy? Foley, I mean?"

"Yes, of course. That's what made it so queer, Sel thought. Anyway, he got in in time and that was all right, only then he wondered if it was. Because he didn't want—this is what Sel says—to have Foley blackmailing him about it."

"How could he possibly?"

"That's what I said. It wouldn't be enough. I mean, even official cuts wouldn't be the end of the world. But Sel wondered if p'raps it was an awful crime to have come up in an officer's car or something like that. And anyway, he thought

24

Foley had been so odd—all this discipline-is-bunk stuff. So in the end he rushed off to Bethune—that's our house officer—and told him."

"Told him what?"

"Well, not everything. Not the real Foley part. Just that he'd got a lift up, and that if he hadn't he'd have been late from leave, and was it all right?"

"And what happened?"

"Well, Bethune thought he was mad of course. And Sel says it did sound pretty harmless, put like that. Anyway, Bethune was quite decent about it. Said there was nothing to stop Sel using his initiative, and not to start developing an outsize conscience because it wouldn't *do*. So that was all right. But Sel thinks Foley must have heard about it, because the next day he said something about could Sel do something-or-other or wouldn't his outsize conscience let him?"

"Oh. And what happened then?"

"Nothing. Except, I mean, Sel looked as if he felt a feeble ass. But ever since then *he* says there's been a—a stirring sort of feeling. As if things ought to be all right, but aren't really."

Nicola considered this. "What's Foley like?"

"He's all right." Peter began to colour and to look very nonchalant. Nicola, who knew him rather well, knew that this meant he was really rather keen on Foley. "I don't think there's anything in it really—Selby's thing, I mean. *I* think he got a bit rattled and thought Foley meant a lot when probably he was just having him on."

" 'Mmm," said Nicola dubiously.

"You don't mean you *believe* Sel's thing?"

"I know it sounds odd." Nicola kicked a pebble in front of her. "P'raps not. But if it *were* true, it would be *jolly* odd."

"That's why it can't be. How could Foley blackmail Sel? And what *for*?"

"His pocket money," suggested Nicola, not very seriously. "Goop."

"Or he might think he could make him do things."

"What things?"

"Well—things Foley wanted done. Like the fag in that book at home who had to break bounds to buy beer for the prefects."

"Oh, *really*, Nick!"

"I don't mean *Foley* wanted his beer bought. I mean——"

"But Foley's a perfectly ordinary sort of person. Of course he wouldn't muck about like that."

"I expect not," said Nicola, sadly. "But I do think it's a pity, sometimes, that one never does come across people like that. None of our prefects would want beer bought for them either." Nicola giggled, thinking of the Sixth Form at Kingscote. "But of course——"

"Of course what?"

"Well, you're awfully wrong about people most of the time. Selby could easily be right."

A clap of thunder almost immediately overhead distracted Peter's attention from the really tremendously crushing retort he had been about to make. He had known for some time that he had been wrong about the weather; he had heard the thunder coming closer and had watched the sky turning copper colour again for quite a while. If it hadn't been for what he had heard Mrs. Thorpe say about the Undercliff Road a couple of nights back, he would have been delighted; as it was —he glanced at Nicola, but she was looking out to sea, watching the sheet lightning which kept lighting the horizon like the flash from hidden guns. The air felt very thick and pressed down, except that every now and then icy gusts came in from the sea; and he thought, rather uneasily, that it had been pretty low of the storm to hold off until now, when they were well along the Undercliff: and almost as he thought this, there was a brilliant flash of lightning, an enormous thunderclap, the rain came down in a rush and the sea came over the sea wall in a cascade.

They tucked down their chins and ploughed on determinedly for a few steps, Nicola because she was rather enjoying it, Peter because he couldn't bear to be the one to suggest that it would be sensible to wait till the weather was less violent. And at length it was Nicola who shouted in his ear: "I keep sliding towards the edge, don't you? Shall we wait till it stops a bit?"

He agreed with some relief, feeling rather a fool, now he had stuck it out, that he had left it to Nicola to point out the perfectly obvious fact that the sea water dragging at their feet made it increasingly difficult to keep their balance. They backed against the cliff face, feeling a good deal safer with something to lean against, even though the cliffs themselves gave no real shelter, since they were covered with concrete to about ten feet up from the road. In a startled sort of way, he saw that for the moment they were trapped between the cliffs and the sea. If the waves rose any higher and either he or Nicola lost their footing, they could easily slide beneath the rail and be swept out to sea or battered against the sea wall. They had run themselves into the most idiotic sort of danger.

He blinked the spray and rainwater out of his eyes, knowing that if he allowed himself to think about it, he was thoroughly scared. Legitimate danger was one thing; you could cope with that. But this sort of thing—despite himself he managed a sort of grin, thinking how furious Daddy would be if he and Nicola managed to drown themselves in this particular way; for few things made Commander Marlow more angry than people who bathed near groynes, or walked under crumbling cliffs in spite of perfectly clear DANGER notices, and were killed because of it.

He glanced at Nicola, but she was gazing out to sea with a calm, interested, very blue-eyed look. Quite obviously, their situation held no terrors for her at all. And really, the storm was so spectacular that after a bit he forgot his apprehensions and simply stared breathlessly at the sky which was being continuously cracked by fork lightning as if it were a china bowl.

"I'm soaked to the skin," shouted Nicola in a pleased way above the noise the thunder was making. "I've always wanted to be and now I am."

"How can you be through your mack?" he shouted back.

"I don't know, but I am. At least it feels like it. Aren't you?"

He wriggled his shoulders experimentally, and decided that perhaps he was. The rain streamed down their waterproofs and the sea creamed round their gumboots, while the sky grew steadily more copper coloured as if a fire had been lighted behind it. And then, suddenly, the sky cracked open above their heads, and a ball of light rushed along the horizon and fell into the sea: the thunder bellowed, the hail came down like a white wall and the sea swirled about their thighs.

He could feel himself slipping and sliding towards the rail and he could do nothing. He tried to see what was happening to Nicola, but the rain and spray had blinded him. Something struck his thigh a tremendous blow and he gasped, clutching the rail and feeling his legs dragged out on the receding wave; and then something else was swept against him and he grabbed at Nicola's arm, let go, and then held on again. And then, abruptly, the rain slackened: the thunder rumbled from far inland; the sea still left the road awash, but not so badly as to make walking precarious. He pulled his legs back on to the solid earth and heard Nicola say from somewhere below him: "It's all right. You can let go now. I've got hold of the rail. Can you give me a pull up?"

He yanked at her arm and, hampered by her gumboots, she half-scrambled, half-rolled under the rail back on to the road. The next moment she was standing beside him, streaming with water and looking rather white, but saying composedly: "You've lost your sou'wester, did you know? So've I, too."

"They must be half-way to France by now," he said, trying to match her manner and almost succeeding. He leaned against the concrete and began to tug off a gumboot to empty out the seawater; but the thunder muttered distantly, and he gave up the attempt, saying hurriedly: "Come on. Let's get back before anything more happens."

Nicola nodded. She felt very wet, and, though she wouldn't think about it much, rather shaken. She stuck her hands in her waterlogged pockets and said: "I suppose that was a thunderbolt, wasn't it?"

He said curtly, over his shoulder: "I suppose so."

"Well," she said, "that's something."

He saw what she meant, and though he still felt furious with her for frightening him by being so stupid as to be sucked under the rail and out to sea, it was quite true that at least they had had a thunderbolt. Though as a matter of fact, thought Peter, beginning to grin inside where no one could see, that

29

was something he'd swop with anyone. He took out his hand-kerchief to wipe his face and found that it was sodden. Inside his gumboots, his feet squelched horribly.

The promenade, when they reached it, was still deserted. The sea had rushed over the road here too, and the surface was strewn with sand and pebbles. The ginger cat, washing its paws on the seat in the shelter, stared at them with blank yellow eyes as if it had never seen them before. With one accord they sat down on the seat beside it, dragged off their gumboots and held them upside down. But they felt so revolt-ing when they came to put them on again, that they decided to go barefoot. Peter looked at his watch, shook it, held it to his ear and looked relieved: "Just half-an-hour till breakfast," he said.

"Good," said Nicola. "I think I shall have everything."

Peter sat bolt upright suddenly, looking out to sea. "I say! Nick!—what d'you suppose happened to that cutter?"

"I don't know. P'raps she got in before the second storm."

"P'raps," he said uneasily. "I wish we knew, though. I won-der where she was making for?"

"She could have run into Oldport, couldn't she?"

"She might. I don't know. I wonder if we ought to tell the coastguards?"

"But they'd have seen her, wouldn't they?"

"I suppose so," he said worriedly. A small boat, a treacher-ous coast and a sudden violent storm—suppose there were a man out there now, beyond the bay, clinging to the mast of a waterlogged boat or sitting on the keel of an overturned one?

"Besides, the fishing fleet are out—oh, look Binks! Passing the Limpet. Isn't that her?"

He thought, and then was sure, that it was. The little tan-sailed yacht was creeping sluggishly in, past the high towers of the black rock called the Limpet, into the shelter of the point which marked the bay of St.-Anne's-Oldport. So that was all right. And at that moment the rain stopped altogether.

Patches of clear sky appeared and a watery sunlight made the sea difficult to look at. And then the sun came out, full and strong, and the surface of the road began to steam.

With one accord, they took off their waterproofs.

"Perhaps we'll dry before we get back," said Nicola, eyeing her soaked navy shorts and jersey much too hopefully. "Or p'raps we won't meet anyone *before* we've changed."

"P'raps. But I think", said Peter cautiously, "that we'd better put our macks on again before we get to the hotel. Then we'll only look wet on the outside and anyone might be that."

" 'M. Yes. But what about our sou'westers? I mean, how much are we going to tell Mummy?"

"It's all right, isn't it?" he said, surprised. "She won't fuss, will she?"

Nicola felt suddenly at least ten years older than Peter, instead of a year younger. Mrs. Marlow might be the most unfussy mother in existence, but even she was likely to take a pretty dim view of the morning's happenings. She suggested something of this.

"Well, all right. If you *really* think so, we needn't actually say you were man overboard. We can just say we got caught on the Undercliff and got swamped."

"We did that all right," said Nicola, tugging at the front of her jersey. "It does feel mad to be so wet, with all one's clothes on."

"It looks mad too. I do hope", he said dubiously, "that we don't meet too many people. When we get to the hotel, I mean. It isn't only that we look wet. It's that we go on dripping."

"We're going to meet someone now," said Nicola. "Look. Along the promenade as far as you can see."

The little black dot did seem to be coming towards them; it was growing larger every second. "Better put our macks on," said Peter, struggling into his. "Ugh! It feels beastly. All cold and clammy." He looked her over and said gruffly: "Can't you do something to your hair? It's all little wet strings."

"So would yours be if it wasn't short. And I don't see what you're in such a flap about. You're being as bad as Lawrie. We're wet now, and we'll just have to stay wet."

Peter shut up. He thought himself that he was making a lot of fuss about something which couldn't be helped. But he couldn't help feeling rather shaken and savage. If Nicola had been drowned it would probably have been his fault, just as it would have been with Webber, and he was thoroughly tired of things that might have been his fault. He emptied the water out of his pockets and, looking up, saw that the little black dot was now near enough to be thought of as a man and a man with something familiar about him.

"I say! Nick! It looks exactly like Foley!"

"How could it be?" she said, as if Lieutenant Foley might be anywhere in England except St.-Anne's-Byfleet.

"I don't see what he thinks he's doing here, if it is," muttered Peter, equally unreasonably. "Oh, *blow*." He kicked a pebble out of the way, and said furiously: "It *would* be him, when he was the boat thing too."

Nicola, who understood this peculiar-sounding remark instantly, sympathized at once. She wouldn't have wanted to meet one of her own school staff, looking as she did now; particularly if it had been the particular member of staff who had seen her make a most tremendous fool of herself and had told her so. And even in the ordinary way it was tiresome meeting them when you had a relation they didn't know with you. She suggested consolingly: "P'raps it isn't him. Or p'raps he won't recognize you."

"It mayn't be, but I'm sure it is. Yes it *is*. Oh, *well*."

He had turned scarlet. As they came closer, his hand began to go up in an automatic salute, before he remembered that he was not in uniform, and put it down again. As they passed he stammered hurriedly: "G-good morning, sir. Are you——?"

But the man, after a brief glance, had gone by without recognition. Peter flushed deeper crimson still. Nicola, staring over her shoulder, saw that the man never looked back. She saw that Peter felt the most awful fool, and said nothing.

But as they got nearer to their hotel, he muttered at last: "I suppose I did look fairly unrecognizable. He must just have thought he didn't know me."

Nicola picked up a pebble and flung it out to sea. She didn't know whether to tell him or not. And then, because it was quite the oddest thing that had happened that morning, she burst out: "But he *did*, Binks. That's what's so funny."

"What d'you mean, he did?"

"Like in *The Thirty-nine Steps*. The First Sea Lord. Don't you remember? The one who couldn't have known Hannay and did."

"You mean the one who passed him in the hall?"

"And his eyes flickered. So Foley's did, too."

"P'raps he just didn't want to, then."

"It would be beastly rude. Is he rude?"

"No-o. Well, I mean, not in that sort of way."

And then they were at the hotel. And there were hundreds and hundreds of people on the terrace and on the steps, waiting for breakfast and looking on with amusement at Nicola and Peter Marlow, coming home from a nice walk before breakfast, barefoot, bare-headed, carrying their gumboots one in either hand, and soaked to the skin. Their cheeks tingling, they dashed up the steps and ran straight into their mother and Lawrie and Ginty and Johnnie Thorpe.

"Fancy going out and not telling *us*," cried Lawrie and Ginty. "*Beasts!*"

"I say, you *have* got soaked," guffawed Johnnie Thorpe cheerfully.

And their mother, who never held family inquests in public, said merely: "You'd better run along upstairs and change. We shall be going in to breakfast in five minutes."

2

The Hidden Sea

Peter, munching steadily through his breakfast, a stolid expression on his face, thought how absolutely extra-ordinary it was that it was always the very people you thought you could depend on absolutely who were always the ones who let you down. There was his mother—his gay, casual, accommodating mother—who hadn't turned a hair the time he'd broken his collar-bone playing football, nor the time he and Giles had been caught at sea in a fog and hadn't got home till the next morning, nor the time a beastly cousin's beastly hard-mouthed pony had run away with him in the New Forest, so that a branch had knocked him off and con-cussed him—there she was, sitting across the table and being in a perfect flap and all because he and Nicola had got a little wet. Peter stuck a lump of sausage in his mouth and felt thoroughly aggrieved.

"But Nicky, *surely* you heard Mrs. Thorpe telling us the other night that two men were swept off the Undercliff in a storm last winter and drowned? It really is too idiotic——"

"But, Mummy, I didn't! Truly not! I've never been near Mrs. Thorpe, not any night, ever."

"Well, Binks was certainly there. Weren't you, Binks?"

"Yes," muttered Peter in a sulky, sausagey voice. He *had* been there. He *had* known. It would have been altogether his fault if—

"And I don't believe for a moment that even that down-pour could have soaked you like that," said Mrs. Marlow, who had followed Nicola upstairs when she went to change and had exclaimed in a horrified way at the sodden state of her evasive offspring's garments. There had been a time when the twins had been delicate and much subject to ailments like bronchitis. And though they had now survived two terms at school and Nicola was looking very pink and healthy, Mrs. Marlow still thought instinctively in terms of rheumatic fever and similar consequences where Lawrie and Nicola were concerned; for though, as the mother of eight children, whose father was more often at sea than not, she did her best to be a tough, unharassed parent, her heart was in her mouth a great deal more often than she would have liked any of them to know. So as Nicola did not answer, but went on eating her bacon and eggs with a rather pinker face than usual, she said resignedly: "Well, Nicky? What else happened? Besides the rain being so very, very wet?"

So Nicola told her. And then, thought Peter (who was really very fond of his mother), there was the most wowing kind of flap. Simply frightful. Jaw, jaw, jaw, natter, natter, natter, thought Peter, feeling more and more guilty and more and more cross; as if he'd ever think of going along the Undercliff again, even in a flat calm. . . . He was so sunk in his crossness that he was quite surprised to hear Lawrie speaking to him, and about something that had nothing to do with storms or Undercliff Roads or pneumonia. When he didn't answer, she rapped on the edge of his plate with her knife to attract his attention.

"Did Nick ask you, Binks? And can I have it?"

Peter came out of his abstraction, grunted and remembered that Lawrie wanted to borrow his suit. He said ungraciously: "S'pose so. S' long as you don't cut it or anything."

"Of course she won't cut it," said his mother in her ordinary light, quick voice. "Bring the suit to me some time on the Saturday afternoon, and I'll sew the tails on myself."

"Good," said Lawrie with deep satisfaction. She loathed sewing.

"But you're to make the tails yourself," said her mother warningly. "If you don't, you'll have to be Charlie Chaplin in a monkey jacket. So I warn you."

"Oh, yes," said Lawrie. She thought privately that she could probably persuade the housekeeper to do them for her on her sewing machine. Lawrie had great faith in her powers of persuasion, allied with her ability to look about nine years old and pathetic at that. "And what about Ginty? What's she going as?"

Ginty, who had been sitting silently absorbing a large breakfast, while the various storms raged about her, stated firmly: "Not a mermaid. I can tell you that."

"Oh, but *why*?" wailed Lawrie. She thought it a terrible waste of Ginty's face that she should make this silly fuss about the difficulty of tails when she was much the best-looking person in the family. They all had very fair hair and dark blue eyes and the kind of skin which browns at once in a salt wind or a hot sun, but Ginty's pale silky hair curled just enough to turn up at the ends, and her eyes, which tilted like a squirrel's, were a dark, greeny-blue, with very long lashes. Lawrie, regarding Ginty sadly, said with a professional sort of interest: "Though, of course, mermaids do have long hair. You'd have that to make as well as the tail."

"Long hair to comb while she sits singing on the rocks, luring passing sailors to their doom," murmured Nicola, eating toast and honey.

"Ginty could do that all right," snapped Peter. "If any sailor heard her sing he'd jump straight into the sea and drown himself."

Ginty grinned cheerfully, not at all put out. She knew she couldn't sing; she had always been the one who turned over

36

for the accompanist so that she shouldn't put the rest of the class out. She said offhandedly: "I'll think of something," and helped herself to honey.

But Lawrie wasn't satisfied. Acting was the thing she liked best in the world, and though a Fancy Dress Dance wasn't really much of a substitute, it was something. And in much the same way that she would have fretted over the casting of a part, she badly wanted to see Ginty's face in its right setting. She chewed a piece of toast and marmalade, staring concentratedly at Ginty's face and said at last, her mouth full: "Then p'raps you could be whatever those girls in long ballet frocks are called."

"Sylphides?" suggested her mother.

"With little wings? Yes, I expect that's what I mean."

"I don't think, my lamb, that a long ballet frock is going to be a great deal easier than a mermaid's tail."

"You needn't worry, Momma," said Ginty calmly, "because I shan't want one. Wings! A Christmas tree fairy is exactly what I'd feel like."

"*No*, Ginty. Mum if you like and must, but Momma I won't have."

"All right, Mum. And actually I've just thought what I'll be," said Ginty who didn't like acting and wasn't specially keen on dressing-up.

"What?" demanded Lawrie.

"A nurse. That'll mean my black shoes and stockings, a dress and apron from Molly," (their corridor maid, who liked the Marlows because they opened their beds properly, left their rooms reasonably tidy, and one wet day, when she was short-handed, had helped her make up the beds with clean sheets) "and a napkin for my head. Oh, and a bit of ribbon to make a red cross of."

"But that's so *dull*!"

"I don't care. I shall feel comfy and not a fool. Which I should with a tail and wings. See?"

Plainly, Lawrie wasn't going to see; she was obviously prepared to argue the matter for hours. But the dining-room was
emptying, so Mrs. Marlow said hurriedly: "Have you all had
enough? Because, if so, I think Louis would like to clear."

Louis, their waiter, smiled and said there was no hurry, and
Nicola bolted another piece of toast and honey. Then she said
she really had finished, and Mrs. Marlow went upstairs and
the four children went out into the garden. The sun was
bright and hot now, and the sky had only a few soft-looking
clouds in it.

"What happened to you?" asked Johnnie Thorpe in his
hoarsest voice, as he strolled up behind them. "Fall in the sea,
or something?"

"Oh, mind your own business," said Peter furiously. Of all
the people he knew, he wasn't going to talk to Johnnie
Thorpe about it.

There was a shocked, appalled silence. Ginty and Nicola
tried desperately to think of something to say, and Nicola was
just about to say in her friendliest voice: "As a matter of fact,
I did," when Johnnie, addressing Ginty, said with an unexpected dignity: "You and your sister are playing in the
table tennis tournament this afternoon, aren't you? I'll see you
then, I expect," and walked away back into the hotel.

There was another silence while Peter kicked industriously
at a pebble in the path, and the other children, feeling sorry
for him, looked anywhere but in his direction. Then Nicola
said to Lawrie: "What are we doing this morning?"

"Well, nothing much, we thought. I mean, we've got this
tournament thing this afternoon, Gin and me, so we thought
we'd better take things quietly this morning."

"Why? You can't possibly expect to win," muttered Peter,
"so I don't see that it matters."

"We might," said Ginty quickly, before Lawrie could ex-
plode in a passionate denunciation of Peter's manners and
Peter's opinions. "We might be lucky. And anyway, we don't

want to win. The first prize is a breakfast set—cups and things. We want to come second with the camera."

Peter said nothing. Lawrie said: "So we thought we'd read in the conservatory. But you don't have to come. You can go and be frightfully energetic somewhere else."

"I'll come," said Nicola, thinking of Hornblower and *Flying Colours*. Besides, for some funny reason she didn't feel frightfully energetic. She thought she must have eaten too much breakfast. And the conservatory was rather fun. No one seemed to know about it but themselves. The only other person they had ever seen there was the gardener watering his ferns, and he didn't seem to mind them being there, once he was sure they wouldn't be taken funny (as he put it) with his flower-pots. So the Marlows had stowed their travelling rugs there, and with a cushion or two from the basket chairs, it was really very comfortable. And if there were any sun at all, it soon became gloriously hot under the glass.

Nicola fell asleep almost at once. Peter, slouching in a little later, slid *Flying Colours* from under her hand and went off to a corner of his own where, to his immense surprise, he promptly fell asleep also. Waking up to the sound of the warning bell for lunch, he was relieved to find that he felt much better-tempered again. Indeed, once he had eaten his lunch, he felt quite back to normal.

"Do you want to watch the ping-pong?" he asked Nicola, who was loitering in the entrance hall, waiting for Lawrie and Ginty who had rushed upstairs to get their plimsolls, and being as careful not to see Johnnie Thorpe asking for letters at the reception desk as Johnnie was careful not to see him.

"Not *specially*. Ought we to stay and cheer Gin and Lawrie, do you think?"

"I shouldn't think they could mind so frightfully if we don't. Anyway, we can ask. Lawrie," as Lawrie shot past again on her way to the games room, "d'you mind if Nick and I just wish you luck and go?"

"Go? Go where?"

"Anywhere."

"Well," said Lawrie doubtfully. But then she changed her mind and said: "No, not really. Let me borrow your knife for luck then, Nick. That's really what I wanted you there for."

A little dazed, Nicola searched in her pocket and handed over the knife. Lawrie dashed away.

"Lawrie is a funny kid, sometimes," said Peter critically, as they went out.

"Yes," said Nicola uneasily, feeling the emptiness in her pocket where the knife had been. "And I must say I wish I hadn't lent it to her. Suppose something happens like this morning, and it's here with Lawrie instead of out with me?"

"It couldn't really make any difference, I suppose."

"It could. It's lucky. Besides, I'm used to having it."

"I know. When I go to sea properly," once again Peter flushed scarlet and stammered suddenly. It was awful the way he kept forgetting. He could have kicked himself with annoyance, but he went on quickly in a haughty sort of voice as if no one could possibly think he had said something out of the way: "I'm not going to have any sort of mascots about. If anything happens to them one feels so awful."

"Like the pilots in the war. I wonder if anyone refused to go up ever, because they hadn't got their thing with them?"

"I shouldn't think so. But I think one might want to. That's why I'm not going to have one."

They had left the hotel and its grounds behind. "What now?" said Nicola.

"A bus to the world's end?"

Nicola nodded. "Let's take that funny little one. The one that goes to a place called Farthing Fee. D'you think the fare might be only a farthing?"

"No, but it ought to be. It would be jolly useful. Where does the bus stop?"

"By the church, I think. Come on, Binks. That's it, turning round now."

They need not have hurried, for the little single-decker waited ten minutes by the church before it moved off again, and in that time it had filled itself to the brim. Peter and Nicola had to get up and stand and, since no one can talk comfortably standing in a full bus, they had to amuse themselves by looking out of the windows, though there wasn't anything very exciting to be seen. The bus went through the back streets of the town, and then along roads lined with bungalows. In spite of its name and the number of people who seemed to live there, it didn't seem as if Farthing Fee was going to be a specially good place to go to. Nicola rather wished they'd gone into St.-Anne's-Oldport again and looked at the boats; and then they could have seen if the little yacht was still there.

And when at last the bus reached the end of its journey, she wished it more than ever. For Farthing Fee seemed to be just the end of an unmade road with bungalows on either side and a wireless shop and a pillar box. She was so disappointed that, as she got off, she asked the conductor: " 'Scuse me—but why is this Farthing Fee?"

" 'Twas the name of a field, m' dear. But don't ask me for why. Nor where 'tis now. Might be any of they, hereabouts."

"Oh," said Nicola. "Thank you very much." And she joined Peter, who was waiting in the road.

"What was all that about?"

"I was only asking what Farthing Fee is. But he says it's just a field and even that's lost now."

"It isn't much of a place, is it? What did you think Farthing Fee would be?"

"I didn't know. That's why I wanted to come."

"I thought it might be a cottage. Peppercorn rents and all that. And I suppose a field is much the same thing."

"Oh, well." Nicola stared about her at the open country

beyond the bungalows. "Where now? North, south, east or west?"

"South-west," suggested Peter. "I should think that would bring us out somewhere near Beeches Hill and then we could walk back."

But Nicola, who had strolled a few yards away to look at a one-armed signpost, was signalling excitedly. "Come and look at this! 'Footpath to Mariners.' We must go there."

"It may be just as bad as here," said Peter cautiously. "And we do know Beeches Hill is all right."

"We can go to Beeches Hill any day. Come on, Binks. We shan't want to come here again, and then we shan't know. And the lane looks all right."

He supposed it did. The grass had grown high, and covered the pathway as if the lane were very little used. Quite obviously no carts or cows had been driven down it for a long time. And stepping into the lane was almost like stepping on to the enchanted ground of the fairy tales he had had read to him when he was a very little boy, for the lane bent away almost as soon as it left the main road, and there seemed to be no world at all but the grass before and behind and the high hedges on either side.

"Isn't it quiet?" said Nicola, making it less so.

He agreed, speaking softly. "It doesn't look as if anyone bothers about this place. All the hedges along the main road are slashed back, but no one's done any hedging here for ages. Mind that bramble, Nick."

"*Ow!*" said Nicola, for his warning was too late, and the long arm of the blackberry had slashed her leg. She disentangled herself and said: "Lucky I don't wear stockings. I say."

"'M?"

"I was thinking about Foley."

"What about him?" he said gruffly, for the memory of the morning's encounter still made him feel red in the face.

"Suppose he was twins?"

42

"Suppose he was *what*?"

"Twins, like me and Lawrie. Or suppose he had a double."

"What on earth for?"

"Well. If sometimes he's all right and sometimes he's peculiar, that would explain it."

"So have I read *The Prisoner of Zenda*," said Peter sceptically. "And *The Prince and the Pauper*."

"That's what I mean."

"Yes, but those are books. How could Foley possibly have a double who went in and out of Dartmouth teaching seamanship?"

Nicola looked stubborn. "He could. If Lawrie and I swopped who we were one morning, how would you know for sure?"

"Easy. You'd start talking about ships and Lawrie about a film she wants to see."

"Supposing, then, Lawrie talked about ships and me about a film. What then?"

He thought a moment. "I can tell you one thing. Lawrie's always hitching at her stockings even when she isn't wearing any. And you put your hands in your pockets."

Nicola looked hurriedly at her hands and found that he was right. She took them out of her pockets, and, without noticing, at once put them back again. She said: "But those are things you know because you know us. If Foley had a twin or a double, and Foley talked about ships and his double talked about films, you wouldn't know he wasn't Foley because of that. You'd think that just to-day he was talking about a film."

"I suppose so," said Peter doubtfully when he had worked this out. "I mean, it's possible. But not really awfully likely."

"Then why d'you think he's so funny sometimes?"

"People *are* funny sometimes," said Peter wisely. "P'raps he has a thing about not knowing cadets in the vac."

"Would that be like him?"

"Dunno. I don't know him all that well. P'raps."

Nicola picked up a stick and began to slash about her impatiently. "Oh, Binks, don't be so stuffy. I think he sounds frightfully queer. What about the Selby thing?"

"I think that was mostly Sel in a flap. Really, Nick, he's not a bit mysterious. He's perfectly decent and ordinary."

Nicola looked sad. She thought of Foley's face as she had seen it that morning, an ordinary, sunburned man's face and supposed Peter must be right. The only thing she could remember especially were his eyes, a light, clear grey surrounded by very thick black lashes.

"What's his name?"

"Foley? I don't know. He signs himself L.P."

"Oh, well." Since Peter wouldn't play, Nicola abandoned the subject. The hedges were much lower now, not much more than banks, and they could see the surrounding country, a flat stretch of fields dwindling in the distance into mud flats and sea. A row of willows marked a small stream, and in a nearby field a pony came trotting up and put his head over a gate.

"Oh, Binks, what a lamb. Have you brought your sugar?"

This was not as unreasonable as it sounded, for all the Marlows, from Giles down to Lawrie, always carried sugar on walks in the hope of meeting friendly horses. After all, if they met no horses, they could always eat the sugar themselves. This particular animal, however, had no intention of leaving them with even a lump. He crunched all they had and blew hopefully in their pockets for more.

"I wish we could ride him," said Nicola longingly, hanging over the gate. "Could we, d'you think?"

Peter grinned. Then he climbed over the gate into the field, and stood still, watching the pony who had backed away, suspicious and wary.

After a while: "He's not going to be caught," said Nicola, who thought that this, though disappointing, showed excellent sense on the pony's part. "P'raps he's not broken."

Peter, who had just wheeled the pony into standing still while he, Peter, walked very quietly and slowly towards him, gave her a quick glance. Then, with an obstinate expression, he redoubled his efforts. Nicola, sitting on the gate to watch, was suddenly reminded of something which had happened at the swimming sports at Peter's school the year before she went to school herself. She remembered watching Peter climbing up to the topmost diving-board and a master standing behind her saying in a resigned voice: "Here we go again. Here's young Marlow all set to break his neck, just to show us all how easy it is. Why doesn't someone tell him it would be quite reasonable to be alarmed by that board at his age?"

She had wondered what on earth the man meant, and then forgotten all about it. But now, watching Peter and the pony, it was suddenly quite plain to her. And the pony *was* unbroken. Nicola was sure of it. She jumped off the gate into the field and said loudly, swinging her stick as she went towards them: "Oh, come on. It'll take hours to catch him. We can't spend all day."

At her first movement the pony had jumped sideways. Then he kicked up his heels and galloped off to a safe distance, where he stood, swishing his tail and looking knowing and impudent.

"I nearly had him," shouted Peter angrily. "What on earth did you want to do that for?"

"Sorry. But he didn't look as if he was ever going to be caught."

"I nearly had him," repeated Peter. But it was obvious that all hope of catching the pony had gone and he added: "But he'll never come now."

"Oh, well. . . . Shall we go on and see where the lane comes out?"

The pony watched them go. When they were out of the field he dropped his head and began to crop grass again.

They were walking between water-meadows now. Flocks of

curlews flew low over the rank grass, crying loudly. There seemed to be nothing but a deserted open countryside, leading at last to the sea. And then, suddenly, there was the house.

They were taken completely by surprise. They stared at the battered brick gate-posts, the heavy wrought-iron gates hanging askew on them, and the dilapidated board, half-hidden by an overhanging beech, saying: *This Desirable Residence. To Be Let or Sold,* as if it might be a mirage.

"But how did it happen?" said Nicola at last, almost whispering, as if she were afraid of being overheard. "It wasn't there before."

"It must be those trees hide it," said Peter matter-of-factly, strolling forward. He peered at something and said: "Hey! We've arrived."

"Arrived where?"

"Footpath to Mariners, you goop. This is Mariners."

"This?" And then Nicola also saw the name cut into the brick of the gate-post. "Oh, Binks, how heavenly! Oh, I do wish we lived here. Think of all that lane, just specially for one house."

"I suppose it's been empty for ages. That's why the lane's so overgrown."

"Then let's go in. No one could possibly mind, could they?"

Like the lane, the drive was overgrown with grass. It deadened their footfalls, so that they hardly knew when they stepped from the drive on to what had once been a lawn, but was now covered with dead thistle-heads and docks. The house, a long façade of dark blank windows, faced them across a terrace edged by broken urns, to which a flight of curved steps led from the lawn. They swished their feet through the brown thistle-stalks and dead stems of sorrel, and ran up the crumbling steps to wander along the terrace, pressing their noses to the windows.

"D'you think there's a way in?" asked Nicola.

"We can try. But it looks rather well shut up to me. Let's go round to the back."

They walked round the house, testing all the likely doors and windows, and at last found a wooden trap-door let into the yard near the kitchens. It was so warped and rusted that the bolts broke and the two halves of the door swung loosely downwards, as soon as Peter pushed it. "It's the coal cellar, I think," he said, peering into the darkness. "Shall I jump? Though it may be locked inside, of course."

"Oh, come on," said Nicola impatiently. "If it is, we can always climb out again."

Peter looked doubtful. He couldn't see how deep it was, and he didn't think it would be much fun to find themselves in a place they couldn't get out of. But while he was still considering this, Nicola had sat herself on the edge of the hole, like a paratrooper about to leave a plane, and had pushed off. He heard a thud and a squeak, and then a lot of sliding and slithering.

"Are you all right?" he shouted.

"I think so," said Nicola's voice, a little shaken and doubtful. "It's further down than it looks."

Peter waited, lying flat on his stomach, hanging over the edge of the hole. His first thought had been that he ought to jump after her. His second and more sensible one, that if Nicola had damaged herself, or if the door on the inside wouldn't open, he would be more useful where he was. He heard Nicola begin to move about and felt relieved. At least he hadn't got to cope with a sprained ankle or something cheerful like that miles from anywhere.

"Can you get into the house?" he shouted down into the darkness which, as he got used to it, was beginning to look grey instead of black.

"I don't know. I think there are some steps. I'm just going to see."

He waited: then Nicola's voice sounded again, but further away. "It's all right. We can get in. Are you coming?"

He shouted back: "Yes. Nick, wait a minute. What's underneath?" But she did not answer, and he supposed she had gone on into the house. He would cheerfully have smacked her head if she had been within reach. As it was, he let himself down through the trap, hung for a moment by his hands and then dropped, trying to fall limply, like a sack. He didn't want to drop stiffly on to a lump of coal and break a leg if he could help it.

He found himself lying uncomfortably on the pile of logs Nicola had scattered in her jump. He felt a bit bumped in places, but nothing to count. He scrambled to his feet and made for the flight of steps.

"Oh. There you are," said Nicola, peering down. "I wondered where you'd got to. I've just got a window open. I thought it would be easier."

"Then why on earth didn't you say so, you great goof?"

"I don't know. Sorry. I thought you'd know."

"How on earth could I?"

"Sorry," said Nicola again and humbly. "I suppose not. Have you damaged yourself?"

"No," he said crossly, though as a matter of fact his leg was beginning to ache where he had banged it on the rail that morning; and though he didn't at all want to have broken anything, at the same time he thought it would have served Nicola right if he had. "And what are we going to do now we *are* in?"

"Just look round," she said, surprised he should still be cross. "This is all kitchens, I think. Simply huge. I saw when I went to look for a window. Wasn't it lucky it wasn't coal in the cellar?"

He began to grin a bit. He thought really it was a pity it hadn't been: Nicola would have made a very good Little Black Sambo. They went along dark flagged passages with doors on either side, and at length reached a baize-covered door which opened on to a great entrance hall.

It had been a rather splendid house once. Not beautiful or

48

elegant, but handsome in a cold, symmetrical sort of way. Nicola and Peter looked into a succession of empty, beautifully proportioned rooms and felt rather chilly. Then they went upstairs without saying much, as if they hoped the bedrooms might be more comfortable.

But they were all empty and handsome, with the dust thick everywhere, rising and falling through the shafts of sunlight. There was a floor above that, and then the attic floor, where all the ceilings sloped and a small wooden stair, almost like a companion ladder, ran up to a trap-door in the ceiling. Nicola was peering through a round window which looked back the way they had come, so Peter went up alone, wrestled with the bolts, and stuck his head through. The next moment he had pulled it back and was yelling: "Nick! Come here!"

His voice echoed in the silent house; so did Nicola's feet as she came running out of the attic.

"What is it?"

"Come up here."

She scrambled up the ladder and the next moment was standing beside him on the roof. The countryside was so flat that they could see for miles, but at the moment neither was much concerned with the view; for above them rose another ladder, which ended at the top in a platform, complete with telescope, rather like a glorified crow's-nest.

"*Peter!*" shouted Nicola rapturously.

"No, *wait*," he said firmly. "It may be rotten. It must have been here for years. Let me try."

But possibly the ladder had been renewed at some time; in any case it seemed safe enough. Peter went up rather slowly, testing the rungs and then the platform before he hallooed to the impatient Nicola. He wasn't terribly good at heights; looking down always made him feel a bit giddy and idiotic. And he had wondered once or twice on the way up what would happen if some of the rungs *were* rotten; there was nothing, really, between the platform and the terraced garden below. He pulled his gaze away from the dizzy prospect under his feet and stared firmly ahead to the long line of blue hazy sea which lay beyond the green coastline, wondering whether it was Nicola or the wind which made the platform sway as he clutched at the rail.

"What a place!" said Nicola beside him. "Oh, *Peter*, wouldn't you like to live here?"

He nodded untruthfully: obviously any house that had its own crow's-nest would be wonderful, if you didn't happen to mind heights.

Nicola, who had been gazing rapturously around her, said: "We ought to go and have a look at that river before we go. Look! There's a mooring buoy in it. D'you think anyone has a boat here?"

Peter looked down rather carefully and said: "I don't expect so. I expect it belonged to the people who had this house before it was empty. Besides, I don't think it is a river. It doesn't go on inland."

"Not a river?"

"I don't think so. I think it's the sea. Look, you can see the line. Past that big rock and then that rather weedy channel and then it spreads out j-just below." He looked quickly out to sea again.

"Truly? A hidden sea?"

"Well, I don't suppose it's hidden much. Probably all the people round here know about it."

"But there isn't anyone round. D'you think they might have been smugglers, the people who were here first?"

"I expect they could have been. It would be an awfully good place. Or they might have been wreckers. It's a beastly coast."

"Smugglers are all right, but I loathe wreckers," said Nicola, who was now gazing through the telescope in proper naval fashion with both eyes open. "I say. I didn't know there were any lighthouses near here."

"Nor there are. There's a lightship, I think, but that's miles further down. Why?"

" 'Cos I can see one."

"Oh, nonsense."

"Not nonsense. Look for yourself."

He looked. Far out to sea a grey pin stood up against the skyline. He shut his eyes and looked again. But it was still there.

"It must be something on the glass."

"Bet you it isn't."

"But if it was a lighthouse we'd see it at night."

"P'raps it's a disused one, like the old Beachy Head light." Nicola had another look. "I'm sure that is what it is. A lighthouse, I mean."

Peter had found something. In front of the tripod which held the telescope was something he had vaguely supposed must be a sundial. Now he saw that what he had taken for the markings of the hours was a compass face; and on the outer rim were written the names of the various landmarks: "Limpet," he read aloud, "Old Harbour, Landfall, Carberry, Burden Reef——"

"Go on," said Nicola impatiently.

But for the moment he could not go on. When he did, it was to say in a queer flat voice that hardly seemed to believe what it was saying: "Foley's Folly Light."

"*What?*"

"It says so."

She looked where his finger was pointing and saw that he was quite right.

"Then he lives here."

"Nobody lives here."

They looked at one another. The wind from the sea sang coldly past their ears and the platform swayed beneath their feet.

"I mean—perhaps his home is near here."

He squinted through the telescope. But there was no denying that grey pin on the horizon. It seemed odd that Foley had never mentioned it. Not, of course, that you expected officers to chatter hugely about themselves, but all the same, if you had anything as unusual as a family lighthouse, surely the Ship was the place where you might talk about it without seeming to swank? Without at all knowing why, he had begun to feel vaguely uneasy.

Nicola said suddenly: "D'you think *they* were wreckers? The Foleys, I mean?"

"Why should they have been?" Peter went on staring through the glass. He had swung it a little to the left and was watching four yachts sailing outside the bay.

"Because of the lighthouse."

"Why because of the lighthouse?" Peter swung the glass back.

"Oh, *Binks*! Don't you *see*? It would be better than a fire on the cliffs, even."

"You mean, show a false light? But people would get to know."

"But if it was a very stormy night—and besides, you could imitate one of the other lights."

"S'pose so," he said gruffly. But he didn't want to talk about it any more. The thought of the false light and the ship driving in to have the bottom ripped out of her on Burden Reef was suddenly unbearable. He took his eye away from the glass and said: "We ought to be getting back, I should think," and began to climb down into the attic again. For the life of him he couldn't have run down the ladder in proper naval fashion if someone had been standing at the bottom with a fortune.

Nicola followed reluctantly. She would have liked to have stayed on the platform for a long time yet, but she recognized that Peter was suddenly in one of what she and Lawrie privately called his upsets. When he was in an upset he got rather white and angry-looking, and as Nicola knew from experience, it wasn't a bit of good asking him what the matter was. She followed him down through the silent house and out through the window she had opened. It couldn't be fastened again, but still, you couldn't tell that from the outside once it was closed; and now she had lifted the trap-door into place it looked much as it had done before they opened it. Nicola wiped her hands on her shorts; she didn't try to catch up with Peter who had gone on round the house, but followed at her own pace, feeling happy and rather sleepy after the strong wind on the roof. Presently she began to sing to herself in a clear, high voice which sounded rather like Peter's own had done before it began to break. Then, as she reached the gates, she thought of something.

"Hey!"

"What?" he called irritably.

"We must go and look at the hidden sea."

"You go and look at it if you want to. I'm going on."

"All right," thought Nicola. "I will. And you can jolly well go home alone if that's what you want."

She swung off down the lane, rather liking the feeling of being on her own for once. The lane ran past the high wall of the house, with water-meadows on the other side, and ended in an open space and a steep grassy bank. Nicola lay down on her stomach, dipped her hand in the water and sucked it. It tasted salt. So Peter had been right: it was the sea.

The bank ran straight down into the water, without shelving at all. The water, dark and weedy, looked as if it might be bottomless. A shoal of tiny fish turned and darted near the bank and Nicola tried to slip her hand into the midst of them. But they turned instantly and dashed away from the bank. She waited, her hand lying very still and innocent in the water, but the little fish had gone for good.

For a time she lay comfortably on her stomach, watching the reflections in the water, and telling herself secretly that she was a castaway. To her surprise, she found two pieces of toffee in her pocket and ate them hurriedly, the last of the rations she had managed to save from the ship before it went

down. All the same, she felt jolly hungry. A large, substantial
tea was what she most needed, with lashings of crumpets and
cake. But probably it was long past tea-time: it would be
nearly time for dinner by the time they got back to the hotel.

She knelt up. She was nearly ready to go, but still she
waited, not wanting to catch up with Peter too soon after the
way he had walked off. The mooring buoy twisted in the returning tide and she read the name on it: *Talisman*. A queer
name for a boat, thought Nicola, not sure whether she ap-
proved of it or not. Though, of course, you could call a ship
pretty well anything you liked and not all names made sense:
like *Fair Wind*, for instance. But she didn't want to think
about the Thorpes; especially Johnnie. So she thought about
Foley and the lighthouse and then her thoughts faded out
altogether and she knelt on the bank, almost as quiet, inside
and out, as the water in front of her. It was beginning to be
sunset. The clouds in the reflections were all dark gold, and
even the birds were still. There was no wind at all.

In the evening silence the quiet chug of the engine came
very clearly across the water and the fields. She scrambled to
her feet and looked about her. For a moment she could see
nothing, and then, as she shaded her eyes, she caught sight of
the tip of a mast moving through the fields near the coast.

Her cheeks tingled. She clasped her hands behind her and
watched the tip of the mast creep slowly in from the sea. She
thought it would be fun to wait, to be still there when the boat
tied up and anchored, perhaps to talk to the owner, perhaps
be helpful with a rope. . . .

And then, suddenly, for no reason at all, she knew it was
Lieutenant Foley coming from the sea. Her cheeks flamed
scarlet. She knew she could not possibly stay to be stared at by
the blank grey eyes which had looked so snubbingly past Peter
that morning, after the one betraying flicker. Like the fish a
little earlier, Nicola turned and darted away.

The entrance to the lane seemed miles away as she dashed

towards it across the grass. But when she reached it, the boat was still creeping through the fields, a long way from the main stretch of water. She was a little reassured by this, for whoever was on board could not possibly have seen her. All the same, the queer little tug of panic was still there, and she remembered suddenly, with a rush of fright, that her knife with the sixteen blades was at the hotel with Lawrie instead of safely in her pocket. She began to run again, along the lane, as fast as the long grass and brambles would let her. Her throat felt dry and choked, and she did not at all like the look of the trees and fields and hedges, standing motionless in their evening silence and seeming to watch as she ran by.

She had stayed longer than she had thought by the hidden sea. Peter was already hanging about at the top of the lane. When he had arrived there, the bus to St.-Anne's-Byfleet had been waiting at the corner, but it had long since moved off down the road. The conductor had said there would be half an hour to wait for the next. And of course he must wait. He slashed about him with a stick, oppressed by the empty fields and the approaching dark, and feeling furious with himself, as he always did when a hidden uneasiness made him kick out at whoever happened to be around. A fine officer he was going to make if he bellowed at his subordinates every time he got in a flap—if he ever was an officer. And anyway, it was one thing to be in a flap: quite another to behave badly because of it. And of course he wasn't cross with Nick. In a way, he didn't know what it was he was cross with, because you obviously couldn't be cross with a house or a lighthouse. And it was perfectly idiotic to mind being on that platform thing. He would have to come back the next day and spend the afternoon there. Nick wouldn't mind; she'd probably be frightfully pleased.

He wished she'd buck up. It was getting much too near half-past six for comfort. The next bus would be along any minute now. He wondered suddenly if she'd decided to go back to St.-Anne's another way—along the shore, for instance. It

would be an idiotic thing to do and exactly what Nick might do
except that she wasn't really awfully likely to go off on her
own, knowing he was waiting. Unless, of course—he stopped
slashing at the hedge—she was cross too, and had decided to
show him she wouldn't be yelled at for nothing. He felt tremendously fussed and jumpy suddenly. For quite apart from
anything else, their mother would be justifiably annoyed if,
after all the fuss this morning, he and Nick turned up for dinner late and separately. If only Nick would come—for in the
distance he could see the lights of the approaching bus. And
that wasn't any good, because he couldn't go off without making sure that Nick was nowhere around. He'd have to hare
back along the lane to make certain she wasn't still mucking
about at the hidden sea; or—and his stomach felt as if someone
had given it a sudden squeeze—that she hadn't gone back to
the house and climbed up to the crow's-nest again. At the
thought of going into the empty darkened house and searching
through the high empty rooms for someone who probably
wasn't there at all, of climbing that swaying ladder to the sky,
he felt himself turn quite green.

All of which was quite unnecessary; for as he dashed round
the first bend in the lane, he saw Nicola walking towards him,
hurrying with a sort of rapid stumble as if she had run herself
out. He put his hands to his mouth and yelled: "Bus!" and she
waved and broke into a stumbling run, not much faster than
her walk. When they reached the bus, it was nearly full. They
had to sit at different ends.

It was stuffy in the bus after the strong air outside. It made
Nicola feel yawny. She was rather glad they couldn't sit together; she felt much too sleepy to talk. Besides, she had begun
to wonder, now that she was in the dull safety of the bus, what
on earth had made her run like that. There was no reason at
all why the returning boat should have had Foley in it. No
reason at all why he should use that anchorage simply because
there was a lighthouse called Foley's Folly dead ahead. No

reason at all, if it came to that, why the St.-Annes should have any connection with Foley, either. That compass face had all sorts of names on it, and no one supposed that the people who had once lived at Mariners were related to the Limpet simply because the name was there. Nicola giggled. The stout woman with the shopping basket who sat beside her sighed heavily, and looked at Nicola as if she didn't like her much.

Nicola yawned and looked out of the window. She certainly wasn't going to tell Peter how the boat had come back and how she had thought Foley was in her, and how she had run because of it. For one thing, it made her sound such a fool. And she didn't care to sound a fool to Peter. She would probably tell Lawrie, of course, but that was different.

Lawrie met her in the corridor outside their bedrooms, half-changed and waving a hairbrush.

"Has Ginty told you?"

"Haven't seen Ginty. Told me what?"

"That Mummy's gone. Left us. Run away to sea."

"What *do* you mean?" asked Nicola patiently. "And you'd better come into my room while I wash. You can't charge about half-naked."

Lawrie, looking surprised at the idea that anyone should mind seeing her in her vest and knickers, came in and lolled on Nicola's bed.

"Daddy rang up at tea-time. He's at Farrant. Something to do with an exercise——" Nicola nodded impatiently: they all knew about that—"so he phoned Mummy and she's gone over. And she said if you and Peter weren't in by seven we were to let her know. But I should think you were—just. And we're all to be terrifically good and well-behaved and Ginty's to ring up each evening about seven and tell her we're all alive still. And she'll be back Tuesday evening or Wednesday morning, she isn't sure which."

Nicola sat on the floor to pull on her stockings. The only

nuisance about the hotel, she thought, was having to be so changed and clean and tidy for each meal. Of course, you expected it in term time, but the holidays ought to be different. She said: "I wish we could have stayed at Farrant instead of here. And then we could have seen the ships. Though I don't expect, actually, Daddy'd have taken us anywhere near them."

Lawrie was silent for a moment. Then she said: "As a matter of fact——"

"What?"

"Well, we didn't really mean to tell you. But actually, if you and Peter had been here, we were all going, because Daddy thought it would be fun for us to go over the Fleet."

Nicola turned cold. She sat on the floor, her stocking half-fastened, feeling as if someone had hit her hard in the chest. Lawrie rolled over and looked at her.

"Did you believe me?"

"Oh!" said Nicola furiously. For Lawrie often tried out what she called 'a voice' over some perfectly outrageous statement, and Nicola was always deceived.

"Did you? Good," said Lawrie, lying on her back and clapping herself, rather like a performing seal. "Because that's one you ought to have known. 'Go over the Fleet', indeed. As if Daddy would."

Nicola scrambled to her feet and took her velvet frock out of the wardrobe. She said coldly: "You're not a bit funny. And, as a matter of fact, you'd better go on getting dressed. It must be nearly half-past seven by now."

"Twenty past," said Lawrie, squinting at her watch. "I s'pose I'd better." She rolled over and put something on the bed-table. "So'd you better have this back."

It was the knife with sixteen blades. Nicola, looking at it, didn't bother to ask whether it had brought them luck. If it had, Lawrie would certainly have told her all about it by now. All the same, she put it firmly in her own pocket as soon as Lawrie had gone: she didn't mean to be caught without it ever again.

3

THURSDAY MORNING

*

Return to Mariners

[i]

Nicola slid off her borrowed bicycle, which she rode standing on the pedals because it was intended for a much larger person, and propped it carefully against the sea wall. It was just half-past six, a sunny blowy morning, with the sea sparkling as if it were covered with fishes' scales. The fishing fleet had just returned, and already there were some other early risers leaning against the sea wall waiting to buy their breakfasts. The air was full of the noise of the gulls which had followed the smacks in and now yelled and wheeled and swooped above the beach, greedy and ravenous.

Nicola sat on a bollard and snuffed the beautiful smells of salt and fish and tar. She was not a squeamish person and the sight of the gulls swooping on to the entrails and dragging them away over the pebbles as the men gutted the fish, did not turn her stomach as it would have done Lawrie's. Presently, for the catch was a small one, this part of the work came to an end, and she left the gulls and sauntered out to the end of the quay. She found the boat she was looking for, and called down:

"*Golden Enterprise*, ahoy!"

"Ahoy yourself. Oh, it's you, Nicola. Come aboard and make yourself useful."

Robert Anquetil was the local disappointment. Everyone who had known him while he was growing up and progressing by way of scholarships from elementary school to grammar school, and from grammar school to Oxford, where he had taken a Double First, had forecast a brilliant future for him. During the war, first in the R.N.V.R. and later in the Commandos, he had won the D.S.O. and bar; which, the local people had thought, would be such a help to him when the war was over. And then, as soon as he was demobilized, he had come back to be a good son, and help his father in the *Golden Enterprise*. But when his father died, no one could say that any more, because there was no one left for Robert to be a good son to. And soon it seemed as if Robert meant to spend the rest of his life as a fisherman at St.-Anne's-Oldport and not bother himself with being Prime Minister or anything of that sort. Only people like Nicola, and the small boys he took out in the *Golden Enterprise* so that they could learn at first hand what handling a boat was like, thought this showed uncommon good sense.

For a time Anquetil and Nicola worked in silence at swabbing down and cleaning up, coiling ropes and stowing sails. When everything was clean and tidy, Anquetil busied himself in the galley and they sat down to a breakfast of fried mackerel and fried potatoes and strong tea in the little cabin. Generally, they ate in a companionable silence, but this time, as soon as the edge was off her appetite, Nicola demanded through a mouthful of mackerel and potato: "D'you know Foley's Folly Light?"

"I do," said Anquetil. He looked at her meditatively across the table. "But as you don't go to sea in ships, how do you? It can't be seen from the shore."

"Well, do you know a house called Mariners? It's——"

"The Foleys' place? Yes?"

"Oh!" said Nicola, considerably shaken. Anquetil gave her another meditative look and went on with his breakfast. After a bit he said: "Well, go on. What about the Foley Light and Mariners?"

"We never thought Mariners *belonged* to him," said Nicola in a dismayed voice.

"Belonged to whom? It belongs to an old gentleman called Sir Charles Foley. He lives in London. Nicola, do tell your story from the beginning, and stop looking like a hooked cod."

Nicola, who was feeling rather like a hooked cod, shut her mouth hastily. Then she opened it again and said obediently: "Well, it was me and Peter. We found Mariners yesterday and went in."

"Trespassing," said Anquetil in an abstracted way.

Nicola blushed. "But it's empty. We wouldn't have if——"

"I know it's empty. No one's lived there for fifteen years."

"And there's a sort of crow's-nest on the roof with a tele-scope," said Nicola hastily. "We saw it from there, the light-house."

Anquetil went on with his breakfast. "Well. Why did you look so stricken when I said that Mariners belonged to the Foleys? Do you know them?"

"Not the one you said—Sir Charles. But we know another man called Foley. At least, Peter does. He teaches seamanship at Dartmouth. Lieutenant Foley does, I mean, not Peter."

"You mean Lewis Foley. He's the youngest son." Anquetil helped himself to some more mackerel and potato before he added: "We used to fish together."

"Did you like him?" asked Nicola anxiously. For some reason she very badly wanted the answer to be Yes.

He was silent for a moment. Then he said: "Lewis and I have been friends all our lives. But I wouldn't say I liked him."

"How d'you mean?" asked Nicola completely at sea.

"I don't think I can explain more than that. Well—sometimes you find yourself involved with someone with whom you have all the ties of affection and habit, but for whom you have no real liking. Just as you very often like people for whom you have no affection at all."

"I don't see that at all," said Nicola candidly. "If I like someone, I *like* them."

"Well, I can't get any nearer to it than that," he said. "You'll just have to take my word for it."

"But then—I mean, why didn't you like him?"

"Oh, various reasons. Probably it's just that he's a Foley. And you know what they say about the Foleys hereabouts? They say they're a sad, mischancy lot."

"Why do they?"

"Various reasons," said Anquetil again. "Mainly, I expect, because they've always lived very much to themselves. Look at Mariners itself, for instance; miles from anywhere; and they rarely had any friends staying there. Even as a family they went about separately. You never saw Lewis with any of his brothers."

"Has he got a twin?"

"A twin? No. Why?"

"He sounds as if he was so queer sometimes. As if there might be two of him."

Anquetil looked at her for a moment. "As a matter of fact, that's exactly how one always did feel about Lewis." He repeated reflectively: "As if there might be two of him."

Nicola looked shy and pleased.

"And I can tell you something else about the Foleys," said Anquetil rather quickly, as if he would rather discuss the Foleys in general than Lewis in particular. "It's a local tradition that they always die at sea. And, as a matter of fact, as far as anyone can verify, I think that's true."

"Is that why they built the lighthouse, do you think?"

"I suppose it might be. But, as a matter of fact, the first one was built in the eighteenth century. You know the temples eighteenth-century noblemen used to build in their grounds?

Well, Rupert Foley went one better. He built a lighthouse—
like the Pharos, I believe."

"The Pharos?"

"The Pharos of Alexandria. It's the first lighthouse of which
there's any real record—a square building of white stone, four
hundred feet high. Only the Foleys built theirs of black stone
and it only went up about a hundred feet. But they had the
wood fire at the top, to show a light by night and a column of
smoke by day."

"It doesn't look like that now," said Nicola, puzzled.

"Oh, it's not. That one disappeared during a winter storm.
And then Rupert's son, Humfrey, had a much better idea. He
built a proper lighthouse—a bit miniature, of course; it's only
eighty feet all told, and the light itself is a very primitive
affair; I shouldn't think it would carry further than four
miles, if that. Anyway, Humfrey built his lighthouse and lived
in it. And when he died, *his* son had a better idea still."

Nicola, who had been holding her breath, let it out in a
gasp. "*Wreckers.*"

"Yes," said Anquetil, surprised. "You're quite right. Who
told you?"

"I guessed."

"Well, it was a merry life, but a short one. The local people
resented it—this isn't a wrecking coast and there was no tradition for it. So one dark and stormy night, when young Fabian
was sending out his false flashes, they took the fleet out and
sailed to the lighthouse and broke their way in."

"And was he captured?"

"Dear me, no. He was a Foley, and Foleys always die at sea.
No, he climbed out on to the roof—which must have been
quite a feat in that sort of weather—and dived into the sea.
Only," said Anquetil, lighting his pipe, "he must have mis-
judged the place in the dark, because what he dived into was
three feet of water, and of course he broke his neck."

"*Ow,*" said Nicola, feeling the jar all along her spine.

"So after that, until the present lot, the Foleys rather fought shy of the place. And the fishing fleet keeps well clear of it, too, though what they think could bite them is more than I can tell you. But, of course, it's a filthy bit of sea round there—here, look." Anquetil shoved his plate aside and began to draw on the table: Nicola wriggled out of her place and came to look over his shoulder. "The lighthouse itself is built on a tiny island; you can only walk on it at low tide. There's a beach *here* and an outcrop of rock *here*, at the other end; that carries the lighthouse. North, south and west," he drew a series of jagged shapes, "you get the rocks sticking up out of the sea, like a defence in depth. And to the east, there's shoal water. That's the way the fishing fleet came to take Fabian. The rocks are impassable to anything but a dinghy. Of course, there's the short cut; but that's something that only the Foleys and I know about."

"Oo-oo," breathed Nicola.

But Anquetil grinned and shook his head. He said: "All the same, the light must have been kept in working order because the Mayor of Oldport got permission from the Trinity House people to light it during the Victory Celebrations. I think they strung it with fairy lights, too," added Anquetil, looking as if he didn't think that a particularly good idea; and then, after a pause, he said: "Lewis was tremendously proud of Fabian. Thought him no end of a lad. We had our worst fight over that."

"Did you fight much?"

"Oh, no, not often. He took it too seriously. After a bit he always wanted to kill one. But that time, *I* was angry." Anquetil looked rueful. "If you can imagine anything so ridiculous as being angry over someone's long-dead ancestor."

Since Nicola, from the age of nine, had had a passionate attachment to Lord Nelson, she saw nothing odd in this at all. She said: "We thought we met him—Lewis, I mean—yesterday. Could we have?"

"You might." Anquetil's voice sounded oddly abrupt. "I've seen the *Talisman*"—Nicola's heart gave a jump—"in the distance often enough the last week or so, but whether it's Lewis who's sailing her, or another of the family, I couldn't say."

The *Talisman*. So it had been Foley coming in on the evening tide. Nicola looked solemn.

"Would he be very furious if he found us there?"

"At Mariners? Yes, I expect so. No one likes having strangers traipsing over their houses, even when they're empty. At least I imagine not." Nicola grew pink. "Why? Are you thinking of going back?"

"There's the crow's-nest," mumbled Nicola. "It's such a heavenly place."

"But not yours. We'd better wash up. And then you'd better be getting back for your proper breakfast."

Rather subdued, Nicola piled the crockery in the little sink, washed up, and afterwards washed out the cloths in sea water, while Anquetil put everything back on its proper rack or peg. He began to hum to himself, a song Nicola had often heard him sing when he was working, which went to a jigging little tune and had apparently only one verse:

> *"Injuns on the railroad*
> *Russians on the Spree*
> *Sugar in the petrol*
> *And up goes she!"*

"I can see", said Nicola after a bit, and rather glad of an opportunity to begin a new subject, "that Injuns on the railroad are a bad thing, but why shouldn't Russians be on the spree? And what happens if sugar does get in the petrol?"

"They don't teach you Geography at your school?"

"They do. Average Mean Temperatures and Climatic Conditions and Horse Latitudes and things like that."

"Very erudite. But I meant Geography according to the maps. The Spree is a river in Germany."

"Oh." Nicola considered this. "Invasion, you mean?"

"Invasion or occupation."

"And what about sugar in the petrol?"

"As soon as the petrol gets warm the sugar melts. That thickens the petrol and that stops the engine. Or so I've been told. I've never tried it myself."

"Oh," said Nicola. She looked at what she could see of his engine. "Wouldn't you like to try sometime?"

"The night you come fishing."

Nicola grew pink again. Anquetil insisted that seasickness was mostly nonsense and that anyone could cure themselves if they gave their mind to it. But Nicola wasn't so sure. For after all there was nothing in the world she wanted to do more than be able to go to sea in any ship that offered itself, so that if it was just a matter of not wanting to be seasick, she would never have been sick, even once. And, liking Anquetil as she did, she could think of nothing worse than being seasick in his company; it was such a humiliating business, even with only the family to see. She put the last knife in the locker and said she must be going.

"Nicola," said Anquetil. His voice sounded loudly behind her. She stopped, rather startled, her foot on the ladder.

"Don't go back to Mariners. I know all about the crow's-nest. I've been there myself. But Lewis can be very unpleasant if he feels like it. Your brother especially doesn't want to fall foul of him. It really wouldn't be worth it."

He sounded so very much in earnest that Nicola said hastily: "No, all right. I don't expect we will." And at the time she meant it.

[ii]

Nicola came into the dining-room for breakfast, looking a good deal more dishevelled than her mother would have liked or allowed. But, in spite of the quantities of fried mackerel and potatoes she had eaten aboard the *Golden Enterprise*, she was

quite respectably hungry again, and, on the other hand, full
to bursting with information; the more she thought over all
Anquetil had told her of the Foleys, the more romantic it
sounded and she was dying to tell the others. In the circumstances, tidy hair, and a grey skirt instead of shorts, would take
far too long to achieve. So Nicola came straight into the
dining-room and started on her grapefruit.

Ginty looked her over doubtfully, and wondered uneasily if
she should say anything. In the general way, Ginty, being in
the middle of the family, was in the fortunate position of having no responsibility for anyone but herself. But it had suddenly occurred to her, as she was having her bath, that, with
their mother away, she, Ginty, was now temporary eldest and
the one who would be blamed if anything went wrong. This
was a quite extraordinary and frightful thing to have happened, for Ginty loathed responsibility and always looked the
other way at school when there were new girls to be taken in
tow or anything of that sort. Because she was intelligent,
charming to look at, good fun and excellent at games, no one
ever seemed to have noticed this, except her eldest sister
Karen, who was also head girl and in that capacity had once
told her disparagingly that she was really a very light-weight
sort of person. The criticism had stung so badly that Ginty had
put it out of her head at once and rushed off to play tennis.
And now, here she was saddled with this awful business of
being eldest. But almost at once she remembered that Peter
was there too. Being a boy, any responsibility that was going
would probably be his job. Ginty decided comfortably that she
wasn't going to do anything about being eldest unless someone
else thought of it too. So she said nothing about Nicola's appearance and asked her in an ordinary conversational way
where she had been.

"To the harbour. I've been finding out about the lighthouse."

Peter looked up. "Have you? Who from?"

"One of the fishermen." Nicola wasn't going to enlarge on Anquetil and her early morning breakfasts. You had to have some privacy.

"Go on," said Lawrie, wriggling interestedly. She and Ginty had heard all about Mariners and the lighthouse and the hidden sea the night before and she thought it sounded an excellent sort of place.

Nicola needed no urging. She scraped up the juice from her grapefruit and told them almost everything Anquetil had told her. The only bits she left out were the bits about Foley himself. She didn't quite know why. She had a vague idea Peter might prefer to hear them privately, because in a way, Foley was his property, partly because he taught him, partly because of the boat thing, partly because he so obviously liked him. Nicola thought this a pity. From what Anquetil had said, Foley was evidently rather a beast, and it was a nuisance for Peter that the people he liked should so often turn out to be awful.

For quite a time they listened properly; but after a bit, as generally happened when one of them was trying to tell the others something, the conversation became distinctly confused, and while Nicola was still talking about the Victory Celebrations and the fairy lights, Peter was saying: "Well, look here, Gin. If you and Lawrie want to come too, why don't we ask for sandwiches and walk there over Beeches Hill? The bus is so madly dreary."

Nicola listened, dismayed. Before her visit to Anquetil, she had wanted to go back to Mariners at the earliest possible moment, but now Anquetil's warning was much too clear in her mind. She burst in, saying: "Oh, must we? To-day?" which was all she could think of for the moment.

"Why not to-day?" demanded Ginty.

"Well—we went yesterday," said Nicola rather wildly. "It's so dull to go to the same place two days running."

"It's not two days running for us," remarked Lawrie in a prim little voice. "My Nicola must learn not to be selfish."

"Who are you being now?" asked Nicola, momentarily distracted.

"Anyone but me. A dear old aunt, I think, probably."

Nicola looked exasperated. Ginty said: "If you don't want to come, you don't have to. I'll ask for sandwiches for three."

"Oh, I'll come," muttered Nicola. If they were going to be caught by Foley, and if there should be a frightful row, she thought she would rather be there than not. She added crossly: "And anyway, it's trespassing."

"So it was yesterday. You didn't mind then."

"I didn't exactly think of it then."

"I don't see what harm we can possibly do to a perfectly empty house. We needn't even go into the house if you're really in a flap about it."

Nicola looked relieved. But the next moment Peter said stubbornly: "If we don't go into the house, how can we get up to the crow's-nest? You are an ass, Gin."

"We don't *have* to sit in the crow's-nest," said Nicola uneasily.

They looked at her in astonishment. Then Lawrie asked in a spirit of pure curiosity: "Are you frightened, or something?"

"No, of course I'm not frightened," said Nicola furiously. "How can you be so stupid sometimes?"

"It sounds to me very much as if you were," said Lawrie, in a grave and disapproving voice. "I can't think *what* Hornblower would have said."

Nicola's face flamed scarlet. She said again, furiously: "Of course I'm not frightened of the crow's-nest. No one but a—a lily-livered loon could be, possibly. It's nothing to do with that. It's—well, that it's trespassing, and there's Foley——"

"What Foley?"

Nicola looked at Peter. Peter, in a level, indifferent voice, remarked that there was a Lieutenant Foley who was an officer at the Ship who seemed to be staying somewhere near.

"But he's not living at Mariners. You said it was empty."

"His boat's there," muttered Nicola.

"He can't eat us even if he does find us," said Peter coldly. All the same, he was crossly aware that he might have seen some sense in what Nicola was trying to say if she hadn't started talking about lily-livered loons.

"But he might," cried Nicola. And she tried to remember exactly what Anquetil had said about Lewis Foley. Somehow, it didn't sound as convincing as it had done when Anquetil was talking: that he had admired Fabian Foley—that it sometimes seemed as if he were two people—that when he fought he always wanted to kill his opponent after a bit. . . . She knew it sounded lame and exaggerated as she told it, and she wasn't really surprised when Lawrie said complacently:

"So do I sometimes seem as if I were two people."

"So should I like to have Fabian for an ancestor," said Ginty. "It would be almost as good as having a pirate in the family."

"So does anyone want to win a fight," said Peter coolly, getting up from the table. "If that's all you're worried about, Nick, I should think we might ask for sandwiches. But, of course, if you don't want to come, you don't have to. You can always stay here and play a nice safe game of sand castles."

"Of course, I'm coming," muttered Nicola sulkily. She knew she had made a fool of herself and she didn't like the feeling. And she thought gloomily that she was going to feel a lot more of a fool when they all got back that evening and nothing whatever had happened.

[iii]

She was still feeling rather silent and apart from the others when they reached Beeches Hill. By then it was twelve o'clock and, by their reckoning, time for lunch, and they lay sprawled on their macks to eat the sandwiches and the fruit. There was always a strong, steady wind pouring along the crest, and Nicola, munching meat-roll, lay facing into it, and tried to stop remembering the things Anquetil had said. But she couldn't help remembering how she had run the previous evening from the bare chance that it was Lewis Foley coming in from the sea, long before Anquetil had had a chance to say anything. Especially she remembered his eyes, grey like those of the sea rat in *The Wind in the Willows*. The sea rat, thought Nicola, had been a frightening animal, too.

She was surprised to find that the idea of Foley frightened her. Without thinking much about it, Nicola generally took things and people as they came, not finding any of them particularly alarming. She tried to think why Foley, whom she didn't know except at second-hand, should make her feel so odd, and, after thinking hard for a time, could only suppose that it was because he had refused to recognize Peter when they met on the promenade. Which was idiotic. It was a most peculiar thing to have done, but no one could call it frightening.

Ginty chucked her an apple. Nicola turned over on her back, her knees humped, and lay crunching it. She had the most curious feeling that she would like to stay here, on the top of Beeches Hill, and wait for the others to come back. But, of course, she couldn't do that. She lay silently listening to the others talking, and, when lunch was finished, threw her mack over her shoulder and went down the hill towards Farthing Fee, still walking a little apart from, and in front of, the rest of them.

By the time they reached the entrance to the lane she was several yards ahead. She walked straight into it, without waiting for the others; she wasn't going to wait for them and have them asking if she was sure she wanted to come or if she would rather stay behind. She knew they thought she was sulking, but she couldn't help it and she didn't care. She could hear them behind her giggling about something, and thought it was probably herself. Well, thought Nicola, swishing about her with a stick she had picked up, she didn't mind about that either.

It seemed very warm and quiet and still between the hedges

after the wind on Beeches Hill. Nicola stalked on, hoping the pony would remember them from yesterday and be friendly; and if Peter wanted to try to ride him and break his neck at the same time, Nicola wasn't going to stop him. He could just go ahead.

But the pony wasn't there. Nicola hung over the gate, making the most coaxing noises she could think of, and then climbed the gate into the field, which ran up in a slope towards the centre and then dipped again. But he was nowhere to be seen. Disappointed, Nicola stuck a lump of sugar in her own mouth. She thought it was being the most beastly day; and yesterday (most of it) had been such fun.

"Are you coming?" called Peter.

"In a minute," retorted Nicola crossly, without turning round. When she was sure they had walked on, she ran back again down the slope and followed.

She saw they had passed the gateway as if they had decided to look first at the hidden sea. Nicola felt relieved. If the *Talisman* were there, or better still, just coming in and tying up, even that imbecile lot wouldn't think they could go tramping over Mariners. Of course, if Foley were there they might ask . . . there would be no harm in that . . . and if he was beastly about it, it would serve them jolly well right. . . .

But the stretch of water was empty, save for the dinghy lying to the mooring buoy. Under the blue sky and the afternoon sun it looked a cheerful, friendly spot; not at all like the still place of gleams and shadows which Nicola had run from the previous evening. She began to feel a little less uneasy. Her hands in her pockets, she strolled forward and stood beside Lawrie, staring down into the water. She said: "There are the little fish I saw yesterday."

The whole thing began to seem more friendly. Ginty took a bar of chocolate out of her pocket and divided it up. After a bit, still munching, they all sauntered back up the lane towards the house.

Mariners looked exactly as it had done the day before. The window at the back was still unfastened. Peter pushed it up and they all climbed in. Ginty, who was last, stayed to shut it; but when she caught up with the others who had gone on along the passage, she exclaimed breathlessly: "Don't go off like that again. It all echoes so."

"I thought we'd go straight up to the crow's-nest," said Peter rather loudly. "We can look at the rest of the house afterwards."

It was pleasant up on the crow's-nest in the sun. There was a little wind from the sea, but not enough to make the platform sway as it had done yesterday. Peter, who had felt rather sick, thinking about it, in the wind on Beeches Hill, felt enormously relieved. He lay down flat on his back and stared up into the blue sky at a small dissolving cloud: there must have been quite a lot of wind up there, for in no time at all the cloud had shredded away, leaving the sky quite empty and blue again. Above him he could hear Lawrie and Ginty and Nicola swinging the telescope to and fro, identifying landmarks, picking up ships and yachts at sea. He shut his eyes. He wasn't really asleep, for in a way he could hear their voices, and the squeak the telescope made as it was turned, and a piece of wood creaking beside him. . . .

"Binks! Wake up!"

He sat up, his heart bumping. Nicola was prodding him with her toe. Startled, only half-knowing where he was, he scrambled to his feet. The platform seemed to lurch and he grabbed at the rail.

"What's the matter?"

"Nothing dreadful. But there's a fog coming up. You can't really see anything much any more."

He saw that she was right. The air felt cold and the sun was pale behind a high drifting mist. The outlines of the nearest rocks were only shadows. The Limpet had disappeared altogether. Even as he looked the mist rolled inland, covering the mooring buoy and the dinghy; in a moment more, it had swallowed the trees at the bottom of the park.

"Let's go down," said Peter. In another moment the fog would have covered them too and he saw himself climbing down the ladder to a roof he could barely see. "Hurry up. We don't want to be caught."

"It's all right," said Nicola, a little surprised at his urgency. "It's not as thick as all that." But fortunately for Peter's feelings, Ginty was already climbing down and Lawrie was preparing to follow. Only Nicola still stood with her eye to the telescope, trying to feel what it would be like at sea with a fog rolling towards one, swallowing the ship from bow to stern. . . .

"*Nick.*"

"Yes, all right." Nicola began to climb down. "Hey! Binks! That's my head you're standing on."

"Sorry," he muttered shamefacedly. The fog was wreathing over him, but it wasn't, as Nicola had said, really as thick as all that. He took a deep breath and finished his descent in a slower, less panicky, fashion.

"Now what?" said Ginty, when they were all standing in the attic passage again.

Lawrie said: "Let's go into absolutely every room from top to bottom. And see if there's a smuggler's passage. There ought to be."

"I don't think there could," said Peter, wiping his hands on his shorts and peering out of the window beside him; but the fog pressed against the glass and he could see nothing at all. "Because I don't see where it would come out. There aren't any cliffs, and you couldn't tunnel in mud. Besides, it's so lonely here anyway. I don't see that there'd be any point in a tunnel when you could just as easily bring the stuff in from the sea by the creek."

"Oh, well. Let's look, anyway," said Ginty. "At the rooms, I mean. Only if there's a passage, you can go in, and I'll keep guard or something."

They accepted this without comment. They all knew that Ginty hated the feeling of being shut up underground. Years ago, when their house was bombed during the blitz on London, Ginty had been trapped in the cellar. She never talked about it, but those four hours had left her with a natural dislike of being underground, or in narrow, closed-in places. When she and Peter had stayed one holiday with cousins in London, she had had to go everywhere by bus and never travel by Tube at all. Really, Peter thought, it was lucky for him that it was heights he minded. It would have been awful to have been in the Navy and to have minded being below decks.

Methodically, they looked into every room. It was only half-past three, but the fog made a sort of twilight, so that the rooms looked even higher and more shadowy than they had done the day before. "And that's all," said Peter, when at last they stood in the circular tiled hall with the high dome above their heads. "I don't think it's really worth looking for a smuggler's passage, and this fog mayn't lift for ages."

"Oh, but we must," said Lawrie. "Look for a passage, I mean. And even if we don't, there are all the kitchens and places to look at. Come on, Binks. We said *every* room."

"Oh, all right." He supposed it was all right. Even if the fog held, they couldn't very well get lost, following the lane. And then they could take the bus from Farthing Fee. Ginty added, echoing his thought: "Only we must leave by five, if we're going to ring Mummy at seven. It would be awful if she thought she'd got to come rushing back or something."

"She shan't, she shan't," sang Lawrie in a cheerful sing-song, pushing at the leather-covered door behind the staircase. "Come on, come on, my children dear, your fairy godmother is here."

The flagged kitchens and sculleries were cold, but somehow, with their enormous chimneys and black, time-dulled ranges, more interesting than the rest of the house. "If only there wasn't this fog," said Ginty, standing directly under one gigantic chimney, "this is the sort of chimney one ought to be able to see stars through in the day time. Isn't it a waste? I've always wanted to, and when it's fine there's never the right sort of chimney and now there's the right sort of chimney——"

"There's a fog," said Peter. "Foley would say that that was one of life's little ironies."

It seemed queer, speaking his name aloud in what had once been his home; particularly as none of them had thought about the Foleys for quite a while. Ginty came out from under the chimney without speaking, and Lawrie and Nicola went off to explore on their own. After a minute Ginty said tentatively: "What d'you think he was like when he was young, your Foley? D'you think he'd ever have come down here much?"

"Getting currants and things?" Peter made an effort to imagine Lieutenant L. P. Foley, R.N., at eight years old. "I don't know a bit. I can't think what he'd have been like as a kid."

"It must be beastly to have one's house still there and not able to live in it," observed Ginty reflectively. "I mean, if it was burnt to the ground or something, that wouldn't be so bad. But I'd hate it—wouldn't you?—to have to think of a lot of other people living in my house."

"Someone's been sleeping in *my* bed," said Peter, being Father Bear rather well. "Yes, I think I would. Is that Nick yelling?"

They went out into the passage. For the moment neither twin was visible. Then Lawrie stuck her head round the corner crying impatiently: "Come on!" and they dashed after her.

"*Look!*" she said proudly.

Peter and Ginty squeezed past the opened door and looked. A long flight of stone stairs went down between damp bricked walls. They could not see the bottom.

"Nick nearly fell down," said Lawrie with relish. "Are you coming? We've got our torches."

Ginty shook her head, flushing a little.

"I'll wait for you," she said quickly, "I'll——" she looked round. "I'll sit on the backstairs or something. Only don't be too long."

"It isn't really a secret passage," said Lawrie, who wasn't particularly imaginative where other people were concerned and hadn't much patience with Ginty's dislike of going underground. "It's only a cellar."

"I know," said Ginty, backing away. "I'll wait on the stairs. But don't be too long."

"We won't," said Peter. "Put on your torch, Lawrie. Is Nick down there?"

A light appeared at the foot of the stairs and Nicola called impatiently: "Do get a move on. I want to show you something."

"Show me what?" called Peter. "Lawrie, do for goodness sake stop playing Tinker Bell with that torch and shine it on the stairs. I can't see where I'm going."

"Something very queer," said Nicola, her voice sounding nearer. Peter hurried, felt his heel slip on something slimy, nearly sat down, and finished the descent cautiously. Nicola appeared out of the darkness, looking smudged and cobwebby.

"We don't need both torches on now," said Peter. "Save yours, Lawrie. One never knows how much is really left in the beastly things. What is this place?"

"I think it must have been the wine cellar," said Nicola, her voice echoing a little in the damp vault. "Anyway, there are a lot of bins, and it looks as if there are some bottles right at the end. But that isn't what I wanted to show you. Do buck up."

"What is it, then?"

"I think there's someone living here," said Nicola over her shoulder as she led the way down a wide passage lined (as she had said) with empty wine bins. Then, abruptly, the passage widened into a room. The light from Nicola's torch fell on a very ordinary kitchen chair and table.

Peter, who had been prepared for a bed and a body at the least, got his breath back.

"You chump, you. I expect that was always there."

"I expect it was," said Nicola. "And I'm not at all a chump. If you'll just look for a moment, dear boy, you'll see it's clean. So's the floor."

Peter looked. He looked at the bins, which were grey with thick, undisturbed dust, and at the table-top which was as clean as the one at home. He said huskily: "Can we open those shutters, do you think?"

It was not easy. The shutters, at least, had not been touched for years. Standing on the chair, Peter tugged; and at length, unexpectedly, the shutter gave, rending away from its hinges altogether. Peter staggered off the chair to the floor, still clutching it.

"Ugh!" he said, leaning it against the wall. "It's filthy."

Thriftily, Nicola switched off her torch. Lawrie said with a chuckle: "You do look funny, Binks. Like a not-quite nigger minstrel."

Peter ignored her. He was looking round the cellar for more signs of occupation, and he was hoping he wouldn't find them. But they were there. A spent match, the empty cover of a cheap, loose-leaved note-book, a screwed-up sheet of newspaper——

He picked it up, smoothed it out, and felt his heart thump. For it was the *Daily Mirror* comic strip: and it was only five days old.

There was a sudden blaze of light. Peter looking up, startled, thinking that the cellar's occupant had returned, saw that it was only Nicola, who had turned on a handlamp she had found, and was looking rather startled herself at the amount of light it gave. She recovered, however, and said: "Now we can look round properly. That window's too basementy to let in an awful lot of light."

Peter hesitated. He rather thought they ought to go away at once. Whoever it was who came here, and however little right they had to be here, they themselves had none at all. If it were a tramp—but a tramp would only use a place like this to sleep in: there was no sign of a bed or any sort of bedding. Someone of their own age, then, who had made a secret place for themselves—but that lamp didn't look like something which might belong to a person of their age. And then the solution came to him in a sudden blaze of relief. Of course! The Foleys themselves! Mariners was still for sale. They would have every right to come here and use any part of the house they liked. . . . Peter stopped feeling quite so relieved. In that case, it was very odd indeed that the only part of the house which showed signs of use should be a blacked-out cellar. . . .

"I say. Peter."

"Yes?"

"Come here."

Lawrie and Nicola were sitting on the floor at the far end of the cellar beside the bin which still held a few bottles. He went across to them.

"Look what we've found."

It was a deed box with a broken lock. The initials *F. de N. F.* could still be seen painted in white on the side. Nicola, the lid thrown back, was sorting methodically through the contents. Lawrie, deeply absorbed, was pressed close against her.

"Oh, look here, Nick——"

"What?"

"You can't go looking at old family papers."

"They aren't old family papers. They're not old at all."

"What are they, then?"

"I don't know," said Nicola in an odd-sounding voice. "Let's take it over to the table."

"Where did you find it?"

"Under that bin. Under a lot of sacking. Can you grab that handle?"

But Peter hesitated; he wanted to push the box back under the sacking, and clear out now—this moment——

"Look here, Nick——"

" 'Scuse me," said Nicola politely. She scrambled to her feet, still hugging the box, carried it to the table with a rush and dumped it. Lawrie followed with the lamp.

"Nick, if it's letters——"

"It isn't letters, I keep telling you. At least, not that sort. I wish you'd come and look."

"D'you know what I think?" said Lawrie.

"What?"

"I think it's a spy ring."

"Oh, Lawrie!" Peter was so relieved that he laughed. "What utter tripe!"

"It's not tripe. You look. There's masses of microfilm, and letters that don't mean anything, so they must be in code, and hundreds of notes. Notes in maths."

"*Notes* in *maths*?"

Nicola pushed a small sheaf of paper across to him. The sheets were four inches square and very thin. He picked them up and saw what Lawrie meant. He saw also that even though maths was his best subject, the formulae were far too complicated for him to have the slightest chance of grasping them. He stood staring down at them.

"Then there are these," said Nicola. "And these."

'These' were the letters, which were written on the same kind of paper as the formulae, and which, as Lawrie had said, didn't mean anything. 'And these' were the masses of microfilm. Peter pushed the letters aside and picked up the microfilm.

"D'you know what I think?" said Lawrie.

"What?" he muttered.

"*I* think we ought to call the cops."

Peter turned quite pale. "But——"

"I thought the police at first," said Nicola. "But now I don't." Peter looked at her hopefully. "*I* think we ought to take the whole lot over to Farrant to Daddy. He'll know we're not being funny, and the police mightn't. Specially if Lawrie began talking spy rings to them. It'll be much quicker in the end."

"But we don't *know*——"

"No, we don't, and I don't see how we can find out, just us. That's why I think Daddy ought to see it. He can."

"But suppose it's just——"

"Just what?"

"Well, just nothing. Just something from the war that's been forgotten. We'd look such fools."

"Only to Daddy." Nicola looked puzzled. "Do you really think we oughtn't to? Because even if it's only old stuff, I should have thought the Navy ought to have it back."

"Why the Navy?"

"Well, *look*, you goop. There's a sub on one of those bits of film."

That did make a difference. Peter, who wasn't at all keen to explain to his father or the police how they had discovered the deed-box (trespassing, housebreaking) and being told that they had stumbled on secret, official papers and that it would be better not to make nuisances of themselves in future, hooked a foot round the chair-leg and sat down. He picked up the microfilm and held it against the handlamp.

"Not there. Further on," said Nicola, leaning over his shoulder. "*There*."

"I don't think that's a sub," he said slowly.

"Don't you? What is it, then?"

He hesitated a moment before he said uncertainly: "I *think* it's a torpedo. Let me look properly," and pulled the strip of film through his fingers until he got to the beginning. Then, methodically, he began to study each negative. Some seemed to be photographs of letters, and that was no use to him, because they were too tiny and anyway they were backwards. But there were others which looked as if they might be photographs of charts and constructional drawings: another of an

M.T.B.; some which he couldn't make out at all; and the torpedo again. . . . Peter began to wonder if Lawrie mightn't be right. But a spy ring! It was too fantastic. And why should a spy ring operate in Mariners and keep its loot in a deed-box marked *F. de N. F.*? Ought the Foleys to be warned that someone was using Mariners for something very odd indeed? Or if they· could get hold of Foley before they did anything else, might he be able to explain the whole thing without any fuss at all?

[iv]

It was very quiet on the backstairs. Ginty, who had been waiting for some time now, hugged her knees and stared out at the fog which still pressed against the barred window at the end of the passage. She had been thinking about a good many things in a vague sort of way. The people at the hotel . . . Johnnie Thorpe . . . the *Fair Wind* . . . the sea . . . swimming . . . next term . . . the summer term was always the best, Ginty thought, simply because it was the swimming term. She loved swimming; it was one of the few things that was always as good as you thought it was going to be. Hockey and tennis and cricket were all very well in their way, but if you were off your game you could make an awful fool of yourself. Ginty wound the end of her shoe lace round her finger and wondered if she might win the middle school diving cup. She badly wanted to: her elder sister Rowan would almost certainly win the senior. She imagined the end of term: Miss Keith standing behind her table with all the cups and shields and colours on it, reading from a list: *Senior Diving Cup—Rowan Marlow. Middle School Diving Cup—Virginia Marlow*; and then herself getting up and squeezing along the row of her form with people whispering *good show* and biffing her on the back. Ginty shut her eyes and shut off her thoughts at the same time. It wasn't lucky to imagine one's success. It made the thing almost certain not to happen.

A soft chug-chug broke the silence. Ginty supposed it was a motor-cyclist bumping slowly down the lane. But when it stopped the house seemed almost more silent than before. Ginty wondered what on earth was keeping the others so long. Her feet sounding very loud on the bare boards, she went along the passage and looked down the steps. There was a greyish sort of light coming from somewhere and a faint sound of voices. So they were still alive. She called down the steps, meaning to call loudly, but somehow, in the silence of the house and the twilight of the fog, her voice sounded barely audible. No one answered her. She waited a moment, and then went back to the stairs.

But now, for no special reason, she had begun to feel nervous and uneasy. Not just bored and impatient because she had been left alone so long, but a sort of eerie apprehension that the house was much too still inside and much too lonely outside. And the fog was so thick you couldn't see a yard from the window: anyone—a whole gang of people—could be creeping up to the house and you would never know it till you stepped out into the ambush.

Ginty clenched her hands desperately. Being underground wasn't the only thing that frightened her. Ever since that time in the cellar (which, curiously enough, hadn't seemed nearly as frightening at the time, with people talking to her through a hole in the wall, and pushing in chocolate and cups of tea, as it had been afterwards, remembering) she had always been liable to become suddenly terrified for no very good reason. All sorts of things could become frightening if you began to think about them—travelling in trains, sitting in the gallery of a theatre, thunderstorms—all manner of things. It wasn't reasonable, and she did her best to hide her panics, for she was very much ashamed of them. But there was no denying they existed, or that one had caught up with her now.

Whenever Ginty was frightened, a little sharp pain started under her ribs. It was there now, beastly, like a dozen pins stuck in all at once. Ginty told herself she was a fool. It was idiotic to sit here and frighten herself with stories of things that couldn't possibly happen. It was only that she was cold and wanted her tea; and that the fog was so thick and muffling; and that the house was so silent——

But the house wasn't silent any more. Upstairs, a door had closed.

Desperately, Ginty choked down her panic. One of the doors they had opened must have closed by itself. Or rats. Rats, people said, made very human-sounding noises. . . .

Her heart was banging so hard that she couldn't tell whether she heard footsteps or not. She told herself she didn't —that it was all imagination. She sat perfectly still, holding her hands together, trying to keep them from trembling. But it didn't help much. Swallowing hard, she got up. And as she did so she saw something move. On the landing above, two legs walked silently behind the balustrade.

Afterwards, she thought of all manner of sensible and resourceful things she might have done. At the time she did none of them. She felt so weak with terror that she thought she would never be able to move or think coherently again. And then she did the silliest thing she could possibly have done. She bolted headlong along the passage and down the cellar steps, calling loudly: "Aren't you coming? Haven't you finished yet? You've been simply ages."

They were surprised but pleased by her appearance. They said Hullo, and What was up? and then started to explain about the cellar's inhabitant and the deed-box. Ginty, keeping her head down and pretending to examine the sheets of paper, barely heard what they said: there was a horrible roaring noise in her head and she couldn't breathe properly.

"So we're going to take the whole lot back to the hotel," finished Peter in a doubtful but determined voice, "and then, in the morning——"

Lawrie made an odd noise between a gasp and a squeak. It startled him.

"What *are* you doing?" he said impatiently.

"By the bins," whispered Lawrie.

For a moment they all stood petrified: and then a man moved into the circle of light. Peter took one look and then said, with immense relief: "Oh, thank goodness. Look here, sir, I know we shouldn't be here, but it's this stuff we've found——"

He pushed the small wads of paper and the coils of micro-film across the table as if they ought to be able to speak for themselves; and as he did so, saw the revolver in Foley's hand, pointing directly at him.

After that, everything seemed to become violent and hurried and confused and yet to take an enormously long time to happen. The papers and the microfilm were vanishing into Foley's pocket: they were hurrying up the cellar stairs and into the passage, with Foley behind them: they were hurrying through the small park which surrounded the house, feeling the fog like wet, sea-smelling wool in their faces, half-losing one another, stumbling over irregularities in the ground, colliding with tree-trunks, feeling invisible arms of blackberry whip painfully across their legs and arms, always with the sense that Foley and his gun were at their heels. And then, just when it seemed that the park must go on for ever, they reached a wall. Foley jerked open a small door and they were standing on the foreshore; the dinghy was tied to the bank only a few yards away.

"Get in," said Foley. "Quickly. Hurry."

They got in. The dinghy moved beneath them. Ginty stumbled towards the bows, Nicola and Peter sat on the thwarts.

"Hurry up," said Foley into the fog.

But nothing moved. Foley came across to the dinghy and looked down at them.

"Where's the other one?"

They looked at one another. They looked back towards the house. They listened. But nothing moved and there was no sound. Lawrie had gone.

Lawrie Runs for it

Lawrie recovered her wits sooner than the others: to be exact, they returned to her, a bit shaken, but intact, as they were being herded up the cellar stairs. Perhaps this was because Lawrie, though she was neither as brave as Nicola nor as matter-of-fact as Peter and Ginty, was not at all surprised at meeting a spy in real life and finding it was someone she knew. Like the others, she thought of spies and gangsters as people you met with chiefly in books and plays and films; but then to Lawrie, films and plays were never quite pretence; they were something, so Lawrie thought privately, which went on with a particular life of their own, even when the last performance was ended at the cinema or the curtain came down on the last act. When people burgled and spied and murdered in real life, it was, so Lawrie thought secretly, because the special life of the cinema and the theatre had overlapped the ordinary, safe, school-and-home life that she and her family lived. So to meet a man with a gun in an empty house seemed to Lawrie a perfectly possible thing to happen. Really, when you remembered the number of times it happened in films, it was only surprising that it hadn't happened sooner. She was, she found to her annoyance, a bit

scared, because even though spies and gangsters always came
to a sticky end in the last reel, the innocent people quite often
came to stickier ends before that. All the same, in spite of
being scared, Lawrie, in an odd way, was rather enjoying herself. She kept thinking: "This is how it feels—this is how my
feet go—when I'm in films I must remember this."

They all stumbled through the foggy park, and Lawrie kept
expecting something to happen. What ought to happen, of
course, was that Peter should knock up Foley's gun, hit him a
tremendous thump on the chin, and then they would all
leap on Foley and bring him to the ground and truss him up.
Then three would stay on guard while the other one rushed
back to civilization to call the cops. But nothing of the kind
seemed to be going to happen. So far as Lawrie could see—
and the mist, as they entered the little wood near the end of
the park seemed thicker than ever, so that Foley and the
others looked almost like ghosts—they were all going to trot
obediently in front of Foley until he told them to stop. And
suppose, as they scurried along, Foley shot each of them in the
back, one, two, three, four, and dropped them in the sea? A
nice thing that would be, thought Lawrie, not so much
alarmed as indignant. Even if Foley *were* caught by the cops and
brought to justice several reels on, it wouldn't help *them* any.

It was while she was thinking this that she fell into the little
hollow. It was a fairly shallow hollow and it was full of leaves,
so Lawrie fell soft, but all the same, it knocked the breath out
of her. For the moment she simply couldn't get up. And by the
time she was able to sit up, still rather breathless, she was
alone. She was just going to shout "Hi!" when she stuffed her
fingers into her mouth to stop herself. As it was, a stifled little
crow got out, but luckily there was no answering shout. Lawrie lay down flat on the leaves and waited, counting up to two
hundred.

Still nothing happened. Lawrie sat up. She was almost prepared, because she had seen it happen so often, to find herself

looking into the muzzle of Foley's revolver, or to find that two perfectly strange men—other members of the gang—were standing over her. But nothing like that happened. The only things in sight were the trees and the fog.

The trees and the fog. Lawrie's heart sank. Trees were bad enough: she had heard plenty of tales of people walking in circles among trees until they collapsed from exhaustion and the snow covered them. Not that there was likely to be any snow at this time of year; and, of course, once the fog lifted, she could probably find her way out easily enough. She remembered the little wood as they had seen it from the crow's-nest earlier that afternoon. It hadn't really looked like more than a fair-sized belt of trees.

But at the same time, Lawrie didn't think she ought to wait. The fog was partly enemy, but partly friend too; if Foley were to come after her, it would be the best hiding-place of all. Lawrie looked at the little hollow and at the place where her head had been lying: she knew where it was, because there was a rotten tree-stump directly ahead: very well, then. If she turned her back on that she would be facing towards the house.

Lawrie turned round. And at that moment, just for an instant, the fog lifted like a curtain. It showed the house—not quite where she had expected it, rather more to the left—but much more important, it showed her a high wall only a few yards away. A high wall. The wall, probably, round the property. If she were to follow that, she couldn't possibly get lost.

A better idea occurred to her. If it was an old wall like the one at home, it was probably a bit worn and climbable. And if she could get over the wall and into the lane she wouldn't have to pass the house again. That would be very useful. If Foley and his gang were up at the house waiting for her—Lawrie's heart bumped—she would slip by in the fog and miss them altogether.

The fog had come down again, but by now Lawrie was standing under the wall. It was a good fifteen feet: Lawrie wondered if, once she had climbed to the top, she would ever be able to get down again. She didn't think she'd care to risk a jump and the possibility of a twisted ankle. When things hurt Lawrie, they hurt her a lot. Mrs. Marlow said that Lawrie made more fuss over a routine visit to the dentist and a tiny filling than all the rest of the family put together. Running for help despite a sprained ankle, like all the best school-story heroines, wasn't something Lawrie had ever felt she'd be able to do, however many lives depended on her. But this bit of wall looked climbable—up or down. She wished she were Ginty, who was the best climber in the family, and who would have been at the top in two twos, but as it was, she supposed she'd just have to make do with being herself. It wasn't too difficult—rather a lot of toes and fingers and a nasty bit where she had to lie flat to the wall and hold on, like a fly, by suction almost. But after a while, a bit grazed and grubby and breathless, she got to the top and looked over. Then she grimaced. The other side of the wall was quite smooth. She'd have to crawl along the top for a bit and see what she could find.

And then she saw she couldn't. Indeed, if she hadn't chosen that particular bit, she probably wouldn't have been able to get up at all. For as far along as she could see, the top of the wall was protected by broken glass and a single coil of barbed wire. It was only here, where the top had crumbled away, that one could get over. Whoever had told Nicola that the Foleys weren't friendly people had been right.

Still, there wasn't much point in climbing down again. Lawrie pulled herself up and worked her legs round so that they dangled over the lane. She still didn't think she could jump—indeed, when she looked down, the wall looked much higher than when she had looked up. She wondered if she could hang by her hands and then drop—but there were only about four feet of Lawrie and a good fifteen of wall. That still left eleven feet—no, a bit less because her arms would lengthen her——

Lawrie had an idea. She wriggled out of the woollen cardigan her mother had made her promise to wear when she
went out, and looked about her. Just beside her hand a loop of
iron stuck up out of the broken piece of wall. Lawrie doubled
the cardigan sleeve round it, and tied it with what she hoped
was a round turn and two half-hitches. If Peter or Nicola had
been there it would have been a round turn and two half-
hitches without any question at all. But Peter and Nicola had
other things to think of. Lawrie gave the sleeve a tug and
hoped for the best.

Then, very gingerly, she took hold of the cardigan and let
herself over the wall, trying to brace her feet against it as she
had seen mountaineers do in photographs. She couldn't really
manage it very well. She went down in a series of jerks and
thumps, clutching desperately at the cardigan until she
reached the other sleeve. And then the knot, which was really
rather a poor imitation of what she had intended, gave way.
Lawrie fell the last few feet into a ditch full of nettles and
brambles.

Nettles are beastly things: so are brambles. Lawrie, bumped
and grazed and scratched and stung, scrambled out of the
ditch, not crying, but feeling as if the swollen, hiccoughy feeling in her throat might mean tears at any moment. Lawrie
cried much more than anyone else in the family, and the rest
of them took it so much for granted that Lawrie never
bothered very much: if she felt like crying, she did. But just at
the moment it didn't seem as if tears were going to help much
or get her any sympathy at all. Silently, desperately, Lawrie
hunted for some dock leaves. But even when she had found a
clump and scrubbed the leaves over her arms and legs, they
didn't seem to do much good. The cold, stinging irritation
went on just the same.

It was cold and wet with the fog all round. Lawrie struggled
into her cardigan, barely noticing that it was badly torn and
stained. She started off along the lane and then remembered

that the wall ought to be on her left. She was about to turn round and go back when she heard the sound Ginty had heard earlier—a quiet chug-chug, muffled by the fog. Lawrie stopped. She remembered what Nicola had told her about the boat coming in the previous evening. If Foley had gone—if he had left the other three gagged and bound on the bank—it would be only sensible to free them at once so that they could all dash back to the hotel and tell the police. Lawrie went stealthily forward, remembering that it might, without any difficulty at all, be a trap. But no one waited round the corner of the wall with a cosh. The boat had gone. Even the dinghy had gone. There was no one left at all, though Lawrie searched and searched, scurrying anxiously up and down the bank like a dog at a station who has mislaid his owner. The only sounds now were the water whispering against the other bank and a seagull crying sharply once as it flew through the fog far above her head.

It was then, as she stood peering into the fog bank as if, if only she looked long enough, it must surely clear and show her something comforting, that the whole thing stopped being something out of a film and became dreadfully, frighteningly real. The boat had gone; Nicola and Peter and Ginty had gone; there was only Lawrie and the fog and the emptiness of the surrounding fields which might, for all anyone knew, contain hordes of enemies, waiting to leap out on her.

It was lucky she happened to be standing on the small trodden path which was the continuation of the lane, for she simply turned away from the water and ran. She ran blindly, sobbing in a desperate panicky way, just aware that she was running back past the wall, past the gates and into the lane between the hedges. Then, as she ran on, not noticing the blackberry thorns which snatched at her, she heard the footsteps. When she stopped, so did they. When she ran on, so did they.

Lawrie put her fists to her mouth to stop her crying. She was more frightened than she had ever been in her life, but she could still think. It occurred to her that if there were really someone following her, he had only to run fast between the hedges and he would catch her without any trouble at all. The sensible thing to do would be to get through the hedge into the fields and then the fog would help.

It was no use trying to break a way through the hedge, for it was far too thick and thorny. Lawrie walked quietly, almost on tiptoe, licking up her tears as they fell, and wiping her cheeks with her hands. At last, after what seemed a fearfully long time, she came to a gate. She looked back into the fog, but nothing moved, so she climbed over quickly, dashed under the shelter of the hedge, lay flat, and waited. She waited for what seemed like a long time, but no one went past on the other side.

She got up and began to run again. Some of the fields were grass, some ploughed with crops growing in them. After she had crossed each she had either to find a gap in the hedge or the proper gate. She began to feel very tired; and at last her foot, not looking where it was going, caught itself on a half-buried piece of iron and tripped her up.

She fell on grass. It was so lovely to lie still that she didn't think she'd ever get up again. For the moment, she simply couldn't get up and go on. She looked at her watch and saw that it was just five past five. It seemed odd that it could still be a perfectly ordinary time like that when such extraordinary things had been happening. For that matter, were still happening. She had no right to be lying here on this lovely soft soaking grass. Lawrie counted ten slowly and got up.

The mist was thinning. It blew past her in long drifts, and the trees and hedges became first dark shapes and then their proper selves again. The sky overhead was a soft twilight blue with long golden mares' tails sweeping across it. Lawrie tried to run and found that it was as much as she could do to walk fast.

Suddenly she pushed her way through the last hedge and found that she was on rough, open ground. Then, farther away, she saw a street lamp. She was at Farthing Fee.

It was twenty-past five. Lawrie looked over her shoulder. She supposed no one had really been following her at all—the footsteps had just been imagination; the sensible thing to do would be to wait for the half-past five bus. But she didn't think she could. It was too lonely—all the downs and fields and trees and things. Lawrie started to trudge along the unmade road, thinking she would pick up the bus when it passed her on its return journey to St.-Anne's-Byfleet.

After a while the little bus went by, going towards Farthing Fee. Lawrie trudged on. She was very tired and in a queer, jumpy sort of mood when every bush behind every gate seemed to lurk like an enemy. Lawrie began to think she wouldn't phone from the hotel. You couldn't tell, when it was a matter of spies and gangsters, who mightn't be in league with the enemy. Suppose the hotel manager was? Suppose by now Foley had got in touch with him through his secret transmitter? Suppose they were waiting for her when she got in and pretended to let her telephone and then drugged her or something? Lawrie had seen plenty of films where that sort of thing happened and she wasn't going to be caught like that. She would get off the bus in the High Street and telephone from the post office. She hadn't any money on her, but that wouldn't matter: Mummy had said they were to reverse the charges.

She heard the sound of the bus jolting along behind her. She turned round thankfully and held up her hand. And it didn't stop. It was full to the brim. It simply bucketed past her, leaving her behind on the pavement.

Tears rolled down Lawrie's cheeks. She was so tired and unhappy that she could have opened her mouth and bellowed like a baby. Only you couldn't in the street, not at Lawrie's age. Much embarrassed by the inquisitive stares of two passing children a year or so younger than herself, Lawrie licked up her tears and trudged on.

Sometimes she tried to run, particularly when the street was empty. But her legs were tired, almost with a tiredness of their own, and they weren't much good at it. She found herself looking enviously at the snug bungalows and small houses as she went by, with their trim, bright gardens in front and bright-lighted rooms behind. She felt dreadfully forlorn and outcast trudging along by herself, in the middle of a perfectly horrid happening, with no one at all to talk to. In all the other awful things that had happened in Lawrie's life, there had always been someone else. Generally Nicola. Fearfully, Lawrie wondered where Nicola was now.

She turned a corner and found herself in a main road. And there were buses passing all the time. Lawrie saw the back of one with *St.-Anne's-Byfleet* on the destination panel, which had just been held up by the traffic lights. Lawrie made her legs run, saw the lights change to amber and scrambled aboard just in time.

The conductor was on the upper deck. Lawrie saw a seat in the front beside a fat woman with a basket, and, with a lovely feeling of relief, sat down on it. It was wonderful to be back, just for a moment, in the ordinary world of lights and buses and shopping baskets and 'Fares, please!' . . .

"Fares, please!" thought Lawrie, horrified.

But she hadn't got any money. At least, she didn't think so. Surreptitiously, Lawrie put her hand first into one pocket of her shorts, then the other. Panic-stricken, she decided to sit very still and look as if she wasn't there. She wouldn't cheat the bus company. She'd pay a double fare next time she was on a bus. But she simply couldn't face all the business of name and address or, almost worse, some strange grown-up offering to pay for her.

Luckily, the conductor hadn't noticed her scramble at the traffic lights. He thought he'd taken all the lower-deck fares.

He stood on the step, making up his time-sheet and checking the numbers on his tickets; Lawrie could see his reflection in the glass screen behind the driver's compartment. As each stop jolted her nearer to St.-Anne's, Lawrie relaxed. It wouldn't be far to walk, even if she was turned off now.

But she wasn't turned off. The bus turned into the High Street and the fat woman beside Lawrie got up. The post office was just across the street. Lawrie got up too, and followed the woman down the bus. As they stood on the step, the woman turned and looked at Lawrie. Lawrie smiled politely, not much liking the look of her—she had a tight, thin little mouth and too much lipstick on it, thought Lawrie critically—but wanting to be polite. But the woman didn't smile back. She said sharply, loudly: "Well, and aren't you going to pay your fare? Or did you think you were going to get away with a free ride?"

Poor Lawrie turned scarlet. The conductor looked at her. So did all the people who had been near enough to hear what the woman had said. The conductor said: "Didn't I give you a ticket then, m' dear?"

Dumbly, Lawrie shook her head.

"Where'd you get on, then?" The conductor took up his rack of tickets, and the bus pulled up at the stopping place.

She had to say something. "I haven't got—any money," she muttered desperately, feeling all the eyes around her boring into her like spikes.

"Thought she'd have a free ride, I daresay," said the woman triumphantly, looking round for applause. "These children are up to anything these days—wangle this, get away with that——"

"Can't afford free rides, m' dear," said the conductor, winking cheerfully. "Company'd be broke in a week. What's your name, now? Where d'you live?"

"I'm in a frightful hurry," burst out Lawrie desperately. "Won't it do if I pay double next time?"

"Oh, yes, I'm sure," said the woman nastily. "That's a likely one."

"Just your name and where you live," said the conductor. "Makes it easier, like, than having to remember."

"But I *would* remember—oh, well, then, it's Marlow. And we're staying at the Majestic Hotel. On the front." Lawrie tried to jump off.

But the conductor caught her arm. "Hey!" he said. "Don't give me that, now. Majestic Hotel?"

"*Really!*" said the woman. And there was a titter of laughter from the other passengers and from the waiting queue.

Lawrie looked bewildered. But if she could have seen herself—scratched, grubby, her shorts and cardigan torn, her jersey stained green—she wouldn't have wondered. She didn't look in the least like the sort of child whose parents might be staying at the Majestic.

"Now, see here, m' dear——" began the conductor.

"Aw, get a move on, Fred," said a workman who was waiting, fuming at the delay. "Can't stand here all night. Forget it, can't you? Likely her dad'll give her a good hiding when she comes in, as it is. My missus would if one of ours turned up, looking like that."

The conductor looked over Lawrie's head and prepared for argument: "Now see here, Charlie, m' dear——"

Lawrie saw her chance and took it. She wrenched herself free, darted through the crowd by the steps, heard a roar of laughter behind her, and dashed out from behind the bus. She never saw the motor which swerved and braked in a frantic, unsuccessful effort to avoid her and came squealing to a standstill ten yards farther on from where she lay face downwards in the gutter on the far side of the road.

"Right under my wheels, officer," stammered the driver of the car which had knocked Lawrie down. "I hadn't a chance, not in a thousand. She ran out from behind that bus——"

"It was her fare, m' dear," said the conductor, who looked as green as the unfortunate driver. "Tried to make a bolt for it, she did. 'Tis right what he says, 'n you can take my word for it. Never looked to right nor left. Just went slick across——"

"Yes," said the policeman, writing stolidly. "Now, if you'll give me your name, sir—and yours, too, Fred. Anyone know who she is? Joe, have you telephoned the ambulance?"

"Chemist's done that," said Joe. "He's bringing a rug."

"Put it over her, then. Best not try to move her. Wasn't no one with her, then?"

"By herself, she was," said the fat woman. "There now, what a terrible thing to happen. Seems like a judgment almost, doesn't it? It's their poor mothers I'm sorry for, that's what I always say."

Fred muttered something about judgments being more use-fully visited on meddlesome matties who couldn't keep their tongues to themselves.

"She said", said the woman, ignoring this after an offended silence, "that she was staying at the Majestic. But that sounds a likely tale to me, don't you think so, officer? Though I must say when I saw her on the bus last night—the Farthing Fee bus, officer—she looked tidier than she did to-night."

"Majestic," said the policeman, writing it down. "Never can tell. Did she say her name?"

"Something beginning with T," said the woman in her confident carrying voice. "What was it now?"

"Marlow," said the conductor stolidly.

"Marlow," repeated the woman. "Yes, that's right. It was something else I was thinking of. Yes, Marlow, she said."

Robert Anquetil, easing his way through the outskirts of the crowd, heard her. He stopped, and then began to push his way gently through. He looked at what he could see of Lawrie and then touched the policeman on the shoulder.

"Yes, sir?—Oh, hullo, Bob. Pretty mess, isn't it?"

"Did you say the child's name was Marlow?"

"Fred, here, says she said so. Why? D'you know her?"

"I can't tell without seeing her face. Is she——?"

"She's not dead, but I'm not trying to move her." A bell rang urgently in the distance, and came rapidly nearer. "There's the ambulance now. You'd best wait and see."

The crowd parted and let the ambulance through. The attendants sprang out, lifted Lawrie on to the stretcher, and turned to slide it back into the ambulance.

"Just a minute," said the policeman. "There, Bob. D'you know her?"

"Yes," said Anquetil after a moment, his face rather white. "Her name's Nicola Marlow. She's staying with her family at the Majestic. But I think the mother's away at Farrant for the week-end. Look here, can I go with her? If she comes round in the ambulance, I'll at least be a familiar face."

The policeman nodded. Anquetil followed the stretcher inside. The policeman dispersed the crowd, and then, getting on his bicycle, pedalled slowly along the road towards the Majestic Hotel.

5

THURSDAY NIGHT (1)

*

Midnight Conference

In a dingy room at the back of the police station a man sat leafing through a file. He was a tall, bony man, dressed in tweeds, with features that looked as if they had been slapped on while the reddish clay was still wet. Occasionally he glanced at his watch; now and then he drank a mouthful of tea from the oversize cup beside him. After a time, as a distant clock was chiming one of the quarters, footsteps sounded along the passage and Anquetil came in, looking tired.

"Oh, there you are, Robbie," said the man at the desk. "What's been keeping you? Sit down and have some tea."

"I've been up at the hospital, sir," said Anquetil, drawing up one of the hard chairs, "waiting for that child to come round. I thought she might talk to me more easily than to a strange policeman. But she isn't round yet, and her mother's arrived, so I thought I might as well come away."

"What did you tell Mrs. Marlow?"

"Nothing, sir. At least—I said I was plain clothes, and that we wanted to know what had happened as soon as possible, so that we could begin looking for the other three in the right place: so, if the child came round, would she please tell us *exactly* what she said, even if it sounded like nonsense."

"Did she believe the plain-clothes bit?"

"Oh, yes. She wasn't really thinking about me at all. What with the one in hospital and the three missing, I don't suppose she cared if I was the man in the moon. There was one thing, though."

"Yes?"

"She didn't think the child was Nicola—the one I know. She says she thinks it's much more likely to be her twin, Lawrie, because the child Lawrie would be more likely to forget her bus fare."

"Does that make any difference as far as we're concerned?"

"I don't think so. Except that it does make the Foley possibility that much more likely."

"Why?"

"Because the *Talisman* is gone. Nicola wouldn't have gone in her for fun, because she insists she's always sick. But I don't know, sir," said Robert gloomily. "Now I've had time to think it over, I don't know that I haven't been jumping to conclusions without a shred of real evidence. It's quite likely I've brought you down on a thorough-going goose-chase."

Commander Whittier sat back and lit his pipe. When it was well alight he said: "Well. Let's see what we have to go on. What are the possibilities as you see them now? You've been down to Mariners?"

"Yes. I went as soon as they took the child into the operating theatre. According to the doctor she's come off more lightly than she had any right to, but it sounded fairly fierce to me."

"What's the damage?"

"Concussion and bruises. Two cracked ribs and a bone broken in her arm. And her leg's fractured, they think."

"Hm. Then I don't suppose we'll get much out of her for a while. When she does come round and if she does mention Foley, you'd better talk loudly about drug smuggling. That'll explain our rather excessive interest. Well, go on, Robbie. You went along to Mariners?"

"Yes. It was dark, of course, and I couldn't do much about lights in case it was a false alarm and Lewis was still around. But I'll swear the place was empty when I went over it. The only thing I found was in the cellar—this piece of paper, sir," said Robert handing it across. "It was lying in a corner as if it had fallen out of something. And there was an empty deed-box, open, on the table. There was nothing else at all. Except that the *Talisman* and her dinghy are both gone."

"As if whoever had taken her didn't mean to come back? 'M," said Whittier, studying the paper in his hand. "I think the Special Branch people had better look at this. It may be a code, or it may be a formula of some sort. Either way, it's beyond me. Well, go on, Robbie."

"*A*," said Robert firmly, "it's just coincidence: Lewis has gone in the *Talisman* and the children have disappeared in-dependently—fallen into the quarry, or lost themselves in the fog; the police have search parties out. *B*, the children made off in the *Talisman*, and because of the fog and the gale, have had to stay at sea; or, of course, they may have tried to get back and wrecked themselves. In that case, I suppose we can assume that Lewis is still ashore. Or *C*, they went back to Mariners as Nicola said they would, discovered something, were caught by Lewis and taken off. Those are the only alter-natives I can think of, sir."

"And which d'you think the most likely?"

"*A* and *C*," said Robert promptly. "I don't think they're the sort of children who'd think it clever to make off in someone else's boat. And as I said before, if Nicola's one of the missing, I don't think she'd have gone just for the fun of it. Unless, of course, she went to find out if she could sail without being sea-sick. It's just possible."

Whittier sat doodling thoughtfully on the cover of the file in front of him. He said at length: "Even if your first two alterna-tives are correct, they're no use to *us*. For the time being, we may as well concentrate on *C*. If things are coming to a head with Foley and his lot, we may be able to get a real lead on him. You'd better tell me the whole thing from the beginning. I only came in on it a week ago, and I can never make anything of these wretched reports. They're always meaningless."

Anquetil, who had first met Commander Whittier when they were both working for Intelligence during the war, remembered that familiar complaint and smiled faintly. He got his pipe going, collected his thoughts and said at last, abruptly:

"I got into this because of that job we did in France—the Abbeville business. About a year ago the Admiralty began to have reason to believe that there was a leakage of information somewhere—nothing very vital, but nothing they could put their finger on. After a bit, they had a stroke of luck and narrowed it down to one of their clerks—a girl called Ida Cross. So they planted some information in her way, just to make sure, and settled down to discover how it was leaving the country."

Whittier said "Ida Cross", nodded, and went on doodling heavily.

"After a bit, one or two things began to add up. One of our M.T.B.'s reported the presence of a submarine during an anti-sub exercise—which wasn't particularly odd in itself, except that this sub was in a position which our own people couldn't account for. None of our subs had been in that particular spot during any part of the exercise. So they filed that away and went on looking. And then a series of reports came in from two of our agents in the Baltic that a number of Nazis, who were wanted for war crimes, had been given their lives on condition that they acted as go-betweens—carrier pigeons—you know what I mean."

"Yes."

"After a bit they got names and particulars. A couple of S.S. men, three guards from various concentration camps, a number of minor Party officials who hadn't behaved very nicely—that sort of person. And then one of our agents came

across with the information that all these people were collected together in a small port on the Baltic and were to leave
by U-boat on the night's tide." Anquetil began to light his
pipe again. "The Admiralty haven't heard any more from
him. They think he must be dead."

"Quite so."

"Well. There wasn't a lot they could do. It wasn't much to
go on. But they sent out a couple of destroyers with instructions to pick up if possible, and then shadow. And more by
luck than anything else, the destroyers *did* get on to her. And
they *did* shadow her for quite a way—enough to have some
idea of her course and destination. But then—they think—the
sub must have got suspicious because she suddenly went to
sleep on the bottom and in the end gave them the slip altogether. It wasn't entirely their fault—there was a full gale
blowing and they had their hands full and by morning, so far
as they could tell, she'd gone."

"Uh-huh."

"That was all for some months. And then she—the U-boat
—was picked up again. A young man who'd been out in a
sailing dinghy, tumbled into the coastguards' hut above St.-
Anne's, full of information about a whale which had surfaced
and nearly capsized him. The Admiralty got the report and
said yes, absolutely, it must have been a very large whale indeed, and where exactly did this happen? So the young man
produced his log, full of pride and excitement and a lot of
details he'd remembered afterwards—how it looked at him
and how it blew and what its name was and how it had told
him that the wife and children were up north but quite well,
thank you——"

Whittier grinned.

"So then the Admiralty got its file down and had a look
and tried to see how things added up so far. They were a bit
worried by now, because though all the planted information
was going out very nicely, other stuff, stuff that Ida Cross or

someone else had dug up for themselves, was going out too. They could have pulled in the Cross woman, of course, but in a way, she was their only real clue. They *knew* about the U-boat, but she was being darned elusive—they think she's probably one of the snorkel type. And they didn't know who was passing the information from Cross to the U-boat. They wanted, you see, to have as much as possible inside the bag before they pulled the string."

Whittier said "Quite so", and blew a long and thoughtful cloud of smoke. His pencil scratched across the surface of the file.

"Well. They sieved through everything they'd got. And they came to the conclusion that the U-boat's stamping-ground was somewhere near the St.-Annes. That's when I came into it. They knew I knew this coast, and they thought a fishing-smack would be less obvious than a destroyer. But what *I* couldn't see was why a U-boat should choose this coast for the meeting-place. The tides are bad, the shoals are bad, there's a lot of traffic one way and another—anyway, I told the Admiralty what I thought and they said they knew all that, and they agreed it was mad, but there it was. They'd keep open minds, but until they got another lead, they wanted this coast watched."

"Quite so."

"Well, I mulled it over, and gradually it began to seem as if it might not be such a mad idea on the U-boat's part as I'd thought. After all, if you want to hide, it's best to choose either the *most* obvious place, because that's where no one will look for you, or the least obvious, because that'll take the searchers a long time too. And then I had another thought: that it might be something to do with their shore contact. Perhaps, for some reason, he or she had to be here. So I kept a look-out for the U-boat, but I watched the natives too. It was none of the fishermen—or at least, I was fairly sure it wasn't. There never seemed to be any stragglers—or at least, not regular ones; and no one seemed to be in the *habit* of taking their boat out at odd times. And then I had a stroke of luck. I saw Ida Cross."

"Go on."

"She's one of those plain creatures. Stringy hair, and a pale thin face, and rather thick glasses. They'd pointed her out to me at the Admiralty. Anyway, there she was, walking down the High Street in full hiker's kit—rucksack, walking-stick, shorts, stout shoes and ankle socks, and looking as if she had a blister on her heel. So I followed. We both took the bus to a dreary little place called Farthing Fee, and I went into a shop to buy a torch battery while Ida looked at a map." Anquetil was silent for a moment, staring at the doodles on the file cover. "When I came out she was just turning down the lane labelled 'Footpath to Mariners'. And then of course I knew. It was Lewis Foley."

Whittier looked up. "You're quite sure in your own mind about Foley? Remembering that he is a naval officer, and that his war record was spectacular, if rackety?"

"Quite sure, sir."

"Why, Robbie?"

"Because Lewis has no loyalties, only enmities. I don't think for a moment he's an ardent Communist. I think he's only in it, because he gets a peculiar kick out of being on his own against the rest of us. He always did." Robert met Whittier's eyes. "I may be taking a lot for granted, sir, but when I saw Ida Cross go down that lane, I could have kicked myself for being so slow. Anyway, I caught the next bus back and wrote a line to the Admiralty. The next thing I knew was a wire telling me to come up immediately. Some imbecile had left a Top Secret file within Ida's reach and it had been tampered with."

"Go on."

"That was last Tuesday. This morning"—Anquetil looked at his watch—"*yesterday* morning, Nicola Marlow told me that she and her brother, Peter, had seen Lewis and that they'd been into Mariners. Oh no," as Whittier looked up in some surprise, "not as burglars. Mariners has been empty for years. And they didn't know it was in any way connected with the Foleys—they only wondered, afterwards, if it might be. Nicola said they thought of going back and I warned her off. But when she (or what I thought was Nicola) turned up like that, the first thing I thought was that they'd gone back after all, that Lewis had caught them and that Nicola had come back for help. I didn't know about the other child—Lawrie—then. But it all adds up much the same. That's why I waited at the hospital. Because if she came round and remembered, it might save so much time."

"So it would," said Whittier, drawing a complicated portrait of a sea-serpent, "but we obviously can't count on that. We'll get on to Special Branch and get them to send their people down to look over Mariners as soon as it's light. If the children were there, we'll soon know from their finger-prints. Foley, too. Tell me, now. If Foley did find the children there —what's he likely to have done?"

Robert hesitated. But he said at length: "I don't think he's likely to have hurt them. I should *think* he'd take them with him in the *Talisman*. Of course, he may have left them tied up somewhere, which would be rather terrifying, but not lethal. But then, if the reason they haven't turned up *is* because Lewis caught them, it *can* only be because they'd discovered something. And then he couldn't afford to leave them behind. If they were just cheerfully sitting in the crow's-nest taking it in turns to look through the telescope, he need only have bawled them out for trespassing and sent them home."

"Crow's-nest? Telescope?"

Anquetil explained. Whittier said: "If you hadn't been down to Mariners, I'd suggest that the crow's-nest had given way and they'd fallen. But I suppose you've covered that?"

Robert nodded. Whittier doodled some more and then said: "Why can't Mrs. Marlow say for certain which child it is? Aren't the clothes any clue?"

"No. Because they both wore the same. And as they're home clothes, not school, they aren't marked."

Whittier went on doodling. He said: "Coming back to Foley. Why shouldn't he have hit the children on the head and pushed them over the side?"

"Well," said Robert, looking rather white, "I suppose he could have done. But if he was going to do anything of that sort, I think we'd have found the—the——"

"The little corpusses?"

"Yes—by now. He has a shocking temper for about thirty seconds at a time. But in the ordinary way, he's rather a gentle person."

"I see. You know Foley rather well, don't you?"

"Pretty well. In a sort of way, we've been friends all our lives."

"Yes. Look here. D'you want to go on with this? I daresay I could get you out of it."

"I did wonder," said Robert candidly, "the day I saw Ida Cross galumphing down the lane. If there'd been anyone handy then, I think I would have chucked it. But by the time I'd had time to think it over, I decided I'd rather know for certain—what happens in the end, I mean. All that."

"All right. And of course, we may be too late all round. Supposing your theory is right, they may all be aboard the U-boat by now."

Robert stared at him appalled. He said violently: "Oh, for heaven's sake, no. Look here, sir. For one thing, I don't think, Lewis would willingly hand them over to thugs like that. He's quite irresponsible, but he's not callous. And for another thing, this must all have been a quite unexpected complication for him. He wouldn't have had time to arrange a rendezvous yet. And if they were at sea when the storm blew up, they certainly won't be able to transfer from the *Talisman* to the U-boat until the gale blows itself out."

"Quite so. Very reasonable. But I just mention it."

Robert opened his mouth, shut it again and said nothing. He got up, pulled back the blind and saw that it was just beginning to get light; the rain was clearing and the clouds were beginning to roll away and leave patches of clear sky. Even the wind was less violent than it had been an hour ago. Perhaps by breakfast time, the missing trio would have been found, rather damp, perhaps, and hungry, but quite safe and more than ready to chatter about the night's adventure. Perhaps in an hour or so, Lawrie—Nicola—would regain consciousness and be able to say what had happened. Rather desperately, Robert set himself to try to believe all this.

But by midday none of these things had happened. Lawrie was still unconscious. And the men of the Special Branch who had come down to look over Mariners, had told Anquetil that not only the majority of the finger-prints they had found in the house compared with those in the children's bedrooms (the

children's were all over the house; Foley's mainly in the wine-
cellar): but that four mackintoshes had been found in one of
the ovens (where Lawrie had dumped them the day before,
acting on some primitive notion of tidiness). As for Anquetil
himself, he had walked down to Fitton's Creek (the local name
for the hidden sea) while the Special Branch people searched
the house, and had found that the *Talisman* and the dinghy
were still missing. It seemed certain, thought Anquetil, with a
curious sense of personal loss, that if it *were* Lewis who had
taken the *Talisman*, he had gone and did not mean to return.
They would have to search the sea for the boat. The *Talisman*'s
engine was capable of perhaps three knots and she would have
put to sea—when? There was no means of telling until that
child came round. Not then, perhaps. For even though the
children had been at Mariners, the alternatives remained: the
children need not necessarily have encountered Lewis: they
could have "borrowed" the *Talisman* and Lewis might still be
ashore. . . . Or Lewis might have set sail from Fitton's Creek
long after the children had left. . . . From what the hotel
people had said, the children *could* have reached Mariners
about eleven-thirty the previous morning. And by eleven-
thirty that night the *Talisman* was gone. The margin was enormous. Anquetil, who had been making calculations on the
back of an envelope, stuffed it, rather hopelessly, into his
pocket. In any case, it hardly mattered. A 'plane could quarter
the sea far more speedily and efficiently than a ship.

He walked back up the lane to the car and found one of the
men in the act of scrambling down from the wall with a torn
piece of knitted material in his hand.

"Where the child climbed over, I suppose," said Anquetil.
"She was wearing a navy cardigan. It lends a bit of colour to
the escape theory, I suppose, but after all, children do climb
walls for fun. I don't think it helps us very much, except that
we'd better search the grounds. They could have gone through
the park to the creek."

But the grounds yielded no clues. Driving back, Anquetil called in at the police station before going on to the hospital, to see if news of any kind had come in that would put a more cheerful complexion on the matter. He badly wanted something comforting to tell Mrs. Marlow.

But when he got in, the only items awaiting him were a piece of wood and a life-belt lying on the sergeant's desk. The planking bore the letters "ISMA". The life-belt was more plainly marked.

Anquetil stared at them, shocked and silent. The sergeant looked at him lugubriously.

"Coastguard brought them in, not fifteen minutes back. Picked up near the Pot Hole. Looks bad, doesn't it?"

Anquetil nodded speechlessly; he felt in his pocket for his pipe. After a moment he said:

"Look here, Sid. Ring the hospital and ask for Mrs. Marlow. Ask if the child's come round, because if she has I must go up there. But if not, tell Mrs. Marlow that I asked you to tell her that we've discovered that the children *were* at the house and that's all we know for certain. But for pity's sake, don't tell her about this. If anything—if they have been drowned—we shall know soon enough."

The sergeant nodded, putting out his hand to the telephone. The Pot Hole was a great place for finding things; and not only wreckage.

6

Thursday Afternoon (2)

*

Shipwreck

[i]

The *Talisman* had been motoring over the oily water for nearly an hour. Peter and Ginty were in the cabin, Nicola, who had pleaded inevitable sea-sickness and been believed because her cheeks were already the colour of cream cheese, was in the cockpit. The tell-tale compass in the cabin roof still swung a little as Foley took the *Talisman* past a reef, but Peter wasn't watching it any more. He was sure now, without any hope of being wrong, that Foley was the enemy. Selby had been right.

He had put off believing it for quite a long time. After the confusion of the discovery in the cellar and the rush through the park, the whole thing had suddenly seemed to slacken back to normal. Standing on the bank, Foley had become quite ordinary again. He had pocketed his revolver and shrugged and laughed and said that Lawrie—if that was her name—was going to have a long walk home. She should have waited and sailed back to St.-Anne's with the rest of them. And then—and this was what had seemed so convincing while it was happening—in a quite pleasant-sounding voice, but with an edge to it which had shrivelled them (Peter had heard that voice before)

he had given them a fine tongue-lashing for prying and tres-
pass; there had been no spirit left in them by the time he remarked that if they had had a fright it was no more than they
deserved, and that if he ever saw them within a mile of his
land again he would hand them over to the police. When Peter
had protested huskily that they too could walk home, he had
been told that Foley preferred to have tramps like themselves
under his eye until they were well away from his property.
There had been nothing to say to that. They had climbed
aboard the *Talisman* and gone where they were sent in silence.

But that had been over an hour ago. There had been time
for Peter's cheeks to cool, and for him to remember the sheets
of formulae and the microphotographs and the expression on
Foley's face when he first found them. For a while he had still
tried to persuade himself that these might represent Foley's
own work, or that Foley might be engaged on something like
counter-espionage which would look frightfully suspicious, but
really be immensely laudable. It was, Peter found, practically
impossible to accept that someone who had been around the
Ship in a perfectly ordinary way for two whole terms, was a
traitor.

Only—they were not sailing to St.-Anne's-Oldport. If they
had been, they should have been sailing due south long ago;
and they had been, and were still, allowing for shoals and tide-
rips, sailing north-east.

He pressed his face to a port-hole and wondered what was
going to happen. The fog was still thick and from a long way
off he could hear fog-horns. Peter swallowed hard on an uneasy thought that the fog was thick, the *Talisman* small, and
just the right size for being trampled on if they struck one of
the shipping lanes. He wished the *Talisman*'s own fog-horn was
in use, instead of lying on the bunk opposite, beside Ginty.

He looked across at Ginty. She was sitting curled up on the
bunk, her face pressed against the port-hole, shivering like a
puppy. Rows worried her far more than punishments. She

would take lines or gating or stopped pocket-money quite
cheerfully, but even a quite mild talking-to reduced her to
shreds and tatters. It wasn't any use trying to talk to her yet.
Peter got off his bunk, and, moving very gently, tried the cabin
doors. They were locked. As in their own boat, the engine was
tucked away behind the companion ladder. But even so, there
was nothing much he could do. It would need a crowbar, or
something of that sort, and a much stronger person than Peter,
to do any real damage. Of course, it would probably be quite
simple to switch off the petrol; and perfectly useless too. Foley
would simply come down and switch it on again.

Peter went back and sat on the bunk again and tried to
think. If—he faced the prospect steadily, if shakily—if Foley
meant to knock them on the head and dump them over the
side, there was practically nothing they could do about it. He
could deal with Nicola first, being the handiest, then Peter
himself, then Ginty. They might put up some sort of a fight—
Peter felt rather sick at the thought of the inevitable defeat—
but it wasn't likely to last long.

On the other hand, if Foley meant to murder them, he could
easily have done so by now. So perhaps he wasn't going to.
Perhaps it wasn't as easy to kill people in cold blood as it
sometimes sounded. Perhaps—here Peter came fairly near to
Foley's present intentions—perhaps he meant to put them
ashore in some isolated place and let them get back to civilization as best they might. By the time they had told their story
to the police, he would have an enormous start, and to try to
find a cutter the size of the *Talisman* once she was in deep
water wouldn't be easy. Besides, Foley could abandon her
after a bit and get ashore in Spain, perhaps, or Portugal and
lose himself. There wasn't much they could do about that,
either.

Or was there? For one thing—this occurred to Peter for the
first time—whatever plans Foley had made for escape if he
were discovered (and Peter supposed that if you were passing

information to enemy agents, you must have a plan of escape) it wouldn't be likely to include three unwanted passengers. It would include—perhaps—one body on the cellar floor and no witnesses. It wouldn't take Lawrie, for instance, into account. Peter hoped fervently that Lawrie was being sensible, and not careering about the countryside telling a blood-curdling story to all and sundry. If only Lawrie would go straight to Daddy and tell him first, things might move quickly. It was a bit soon, perhaps, to hope that a couple of M.L.s were already steaming to the rescue, but it needn't take long, if only Lawrie showed some sense. It occurred to Peter that she might. It had been quite sensible to escape. It was a pity they all hadn't—it would have been easy enough—the fog had been as thick as a curtain in the little wood. . . .

But at the back of his mind he knew that though escape might have been easier and would certainly have been more comfortable, it was all to the good that they were here. At least they were a drag on Foley that he hadn't bargained for. The microphotographs and the formulae were still within reach. If only they could delay Foley until Lawrie could tell her story to someone who would believe it, until the pursuit had time to catch up with them—Peter had another look at the engine. Would it be a good idea to switch off the petrol? Or would it be better to behave as if they suspected nothing?

"Peter," said Ginty in a shaken voice.

He had almost forgotten her, she had been so quiet. "Hullo," he said.

"What d'you think's going to happen?"

"I don't know. I've been thinking——"

"We're not going to St.-Anne's, are we?" She nodded miserably towards the cabin roof. "I've been watching."

"No. I know."

"Is he really a spy, d'you think?"

Peter finally made up his mind. "Yes. I'm sure he is."

Ginty's voice shook. "Oh, Binks, *no*."

He decided it was no use trying to talk to Ginty at the moment; she was so obviously on the point of breaking down that he had to say something fairly calming. He said:

"Look, Gin, it's no good working yourself up. We can't do anything much for the moment. If we kick up too much dust, he'll tie us up or something, p'raps. We're much better free. At least we can——"

"What can we?" demanded Ginty in a frightened voice.

"Well—swim if we have to."

"*Swim?* But we must be miles out by now. We couldn't possibly."

"I've been thinking," said Peter carefully. "He may put us ashore somewhere soon. If we keep quiet and not seem to suspect anything, he may let us go, and then we can go straight to the police. So if he comes down, don't ask any questions. Pretend we haven't noticed the compass—pretend we still think it's frightfully wicked of us to have gone trespassing—all that."

Ginty nodded, clenching her hands tightly. "But—Peter—"

"What?"

"Do you—you don't th-think he's going to—to kill us, do you?"

"No. Because if he was, he could have by now. Look, are you hungry? Because if you are, there's sure to be something to eat down here."

But Ginty shook her head, and stared out of the port-hole again. Peter sighed. He felt pretty hungry himself, and he wished it was Ginty who was sitting sea-sick in the cockpit instead of Nicola. Nick would have been a much better companion. Together, they might have been able to plan something. . . . He really was frightfully hungry. . . . He decided to look for something to eat and to explore a little at the same time. There ought to be enough warning before Foley came down.

The lockers behind the bunks were full of food. It was mostly in tins, but there were also some slabs of Dutch chocolate.

Peter took a slab, broke it in half, broke some off and stuffed it in his mouth, and shoved the rest into his pockets.

The Ship's Papers and the charts were in the locker under the bunk. The Papers were in an envelope and looked perfectly ordinary. The charts. . . . Peter spread them out on the table, prepared to let them roll back at a moment's notice and fling them into the locker, and rifled through them. The North Sea, the Skaggerack, a large-scale chart of a section of the Norwegian coast, the Baltic, a very old one of the Channel. . . . Peter began to notice that they were marked with little red stars in odd places, and that each star was dated. Red stars in the middle of the sea . . . they certainly weren't lighthouses or lightships . . . and then he got it and his heart thumped unpleasantly. Another ship. An enemy ship. Perhaps he was wrong about their being put ashore. Perhaps they were being taken to this ship, whoever she was. But why? The answer was much too clear and probable: to be interrogated and then killed. Peter leaned on the table, staring at the chart. It was absolutely essential that they should stop the boat somehow. Switching off the engine was no good—but if he could wreck it—there must be tools—at least while the fog and the calm lasted they could do nothing but drift. . . .

Above his head came the sound of the cabin doors being unlocked. Peter let the charts roll themselves up and flung them into the locker almost in one movement. By the time Foley came into the cabin, he was sitting on the side of the bunk, staring at his hands. He did not dare to look up. He was afraid Foley might see from his face what he knew and what he meant to do if he could.

"Get up a moment, will you?" said Foley, quite pleasantly. "I want to have a look at the chart."

Peter got up, stepping towards the doors. Looking up, he could just see Nicola clutching the tiller. She didn't look especially sea-sick. If anything, she looked rather cheerful.

"Sit down, will you?" said Foley, without turning round.

Peter sat down. If Foley was going to work out a course, it didn't look as if a meeting with the other ship was particularly near. He wished he could think of something really clever to do—something like hitting Foley over the head and sailing the *Talisman* back to St.-Anne's. If only he had thought of it sooner, he would have tried to have a spanner handy. Now, while Foley was bending over the chart, it would have been easy. . . .

As if he felt his thoughts, Foley looked up and caught his eye. For a moment they stared at one another and then Foley looked down at the chart again. Peter felt his cheeks growing scarlet and his heart beginning to thump. Did Foley know what he was thinking? Had he shown much too clearly——?

But Foley took no further notice of him. He seemed to have settled down to something rather complicated. Peter wished he could eat another square of chocolate, but he didn't want Foley to know he'd been looking round the cabin. He shifted restlessly. He looked across at Ginty, at the companion, at the cabin roof—

He looked, and then looked violently away, in case Foley should look up and look with him. For the compass no longer pointed north-east. It had swung round south-west. Nicola was sailing the *Talisman* back to Oldport.

He nearly choked with excitement: if only there was something he could do to help. But he could think of nothing except to keep supremely still and silent and do nothing to distract Foley's attention from whatever it was he was doing. But sooner or later he would finish, and then he would see, and then—Peter thought frantically and to no purpose. His mind remained an obstinate, useless blank.

The minutes ticked past. The hands on the little cabin clock moved almost without seeming to move. How long had they been at sea? A little over an hour and a half? And some of that must have been wasted amongst the shoals so far as distance went. . . . Peter held his breath: five minutes . . . ten . . .

fifteen . . . twenty—Foley moved and Peter's heart sank, but
it was only to consult the mathematical tables beside him—
twenty-five, twenty-seven, twenty-eight, twenty-nine——

Foley rolled up the charts.

He got up, stooping under the low cabin roof and said to
Peter: "Move your legs." The *Talisman's* motion had become
a little uncertain. The cabin doors, which had stayed open,
swung to, almost closing. Just for a moment, as he moved,
Peter caught a glimpse of Nicola. She had let go the tiller and
was bending down. He wondered, edging towards the doors
and meditating a dash on deck, if she were feeling ill again.

The cutter was beginning to dance like a skittish pony:
Ginty was staring out of her port-hole with an expression that
seemed more astonished than anything else. And Foley—Peter
saw him check for an instant, the check of someone who knows
at last that something is wrong. He looked up, gave a queer
wordless gasp, and scrambled to his feet. Peter, his fists
clenched, the cabin doors swinging behind him, prepared to
be in his way. Somehow, he was aware that the engine wasn't
having much say in the direction the *Talisman* took any more;
there was a different feel to her—the compass was swinging all
over the place——

"Get out of my way," snapped Foley.

Peter retreated towards the ladder. He had vague thoughts
of scrambling up and kicking Foley in the face as he came.
Then he and Nicola would lock the doors (not much fun for
Ginty) and take the *Talisman* back——

And at that moment the engine coughed twice and died.

[ii]

Nicola made up her mind about Foley much sooner than
Peter. But then, she had had more opportunity. She had felt
dreadfully ill to begin with, for the warm smell of oil and petrol
added to the motion of the boat in the shoal water, had been
too much for her, and she been sick three times almost im-

mediately, hanging over the coaming and wishing she could die, now, instantly, for the engine didn't seem to be a particularly powerful one and it was going to take ages to get back to St. Anne's—ages of feeling absolutely awful—ages of being sick in front of strangers——

She became aware of a curious buzzing noise. There was the engine of course, and the sound of the sea round the boat, and a good many noises going on in her own head, but this was different. It was irregular, but it was firm. Nicola had heard it before, during the short time she had been a member of the school guide company: it was a morse buzzer.

She had been sick all she could be at the moment. She huddled back on the cockpit seat and looked at Foley. He was steering with his knee against the tiller and there was a thing which looked like a walkie-talkie on the seat beside him; and beside this, Foley was working a buzzer. Hazily, Nicola tried to read it, but she hadn't had time to become very expert with a buzzer; she made out a few isolated letters and then she had to be sick again.

When that was over, Foley was just finishing. Nicola made out a group of letters, because they were repeated three times as if they were a signing-off signal. And then he pushed in the rod, snapped the case over the buzzer, and put everything away in one of the lockers under the cockpit seat. Nicola shut her eyes. She felt icy cold, her head was full of cold cotton-wool, she seemed to be slowly floating away, and she was quite sure that Foley was a traitor.

She felt something being tucked round her, but though it felt thick and heavy, if it was meant to keep her warm, it didn't help much. And then Foley's voice, quite close and friendly, said: "You do look cheap. Here, try this."

Nicola felt something round and metallic pushed between her lips and something that tasted perfectly beastly ran into her mouth. She spluttered and swallowed, and swallowed again——

"Ugh!" said Nicola, getting her face away.

"Don't you like brandy?"

"Is that brandy?" Nicola's mouth was burning and the beastly taste was still there, but now that the brandy had hit her stomach it felt wonderful. A lovely warm glow. Nicola opened her eyes.

"That's better," said Foley. He was looking at her with a sort of rueful concern. "I thought for a moment you were going to pass out. You'd better have another swallow."

Gingerly, Nicola took the flask he held out to her, swallowed, shuddered, and began to feel more human. Even her hands and feet felt fairly warm again. She hugged Foley's coat round her, and handed the flask back. For the moment she felt quite friendly towards him. She looked about her, but the fog still clung to the surface of the sea and visibility was what Nicola supposed they called nil; it was almost like sailing about in a tent. If it hadn't been for the wake, no one could have told they were moving. She asked: "When we get in to Oldport, shall I ask Mr. Anquetil to keep your dinghy for you, if we're going to row ourselves in?"

He had been thinking of something else and he said "Oldport?" almost absently. Then, as he realized what she had said, he glanced at her with a queer little half-smile. Nicola felt herself become very still, almost as if she was bracing herself against a blow. But he didn't say in so many words *We're not going to Oldport*. Instead he said: "Are you a friend of Anquetil's?"

"Yes," said Nicola. "He said he," she hesitated: "he said he'd known you a long time."

Foley smiled again, still with that little half-smile. "So he has," he said. "A very long time. *Faithful* Robert."

Nicola said nothing. She wanted to ask straight out if they were not going to Oldport after all, but the words stuck in her throat as if she might not be able to speak without bursting into tears. She shut her mouth tightly and looked ahead to the bows. Whatever happened, she wasn't going to cry. To have been sick was bad enough, but that she couldn't help. Anyone could help crying if they gave their mind to it.

The little engine chugged on. It was a less powerful one than the one in their own boat, thought Nicola, but neither Giles nor Daddy cared about using one much. Generally, they only used it to get in or out of a very crowded anchorage, and then not if they could help it. Probably Foley, thought Nicola contemptuously, used it any time things got difficult. Somehow, it helped a bit to think contemptuous things of him, even if it was probable that they weren't especially true.

Also, it occurred to her that she no longer felt sea-sick. Perhaps it was the excitement, perhaps it was that no one had thought of treating Nicola's sea-sickness with brandy before, but she really felt quite well. She began to feel more cheerful. If she wasn't going to be sick again, nothing would be so bad. Not even sailing with a traitor to an unknown destination.

Nicola got up. She had to make sure about that. Moving as casually as she could, as if she was tired of sitting on that side and wanted a change of view, she edged her way across the cockpit, having a good look through the port-hole at the compass card as she did so. She sat down on the other side, curling her legs under her and not looking at Foley. She felt pale, and she didn't want him to know that she knew, or that knowing, she minded. But—north-east by east; and they ought to be heading due south. Nicola felt her stomach give a sort of squeeze. Not as if she was going to be sick, but the sort of squeeze one got before a match, even a form one.

She sat quite still, trying to see a map of the coast in her head, trying to think where they might be making for. But there were so many possibilities that after a bit she gave it up. There were hundreds of places and they might be making for any of them. Or none of them. Or the Baltic. She stared into the fog.

The engine sounded rather odd, she thought: as if it were

missing a bit. Foley heard it too. He said: "Damn. She must be getting dry. I should have filled up before we started, but", he gave Nicola that queer little grin again, as if she ought to see the joke too, "it was all rather a rush, wasn't it? Look here, can you take the tiller a minute?"

Nicola was up in an instant. He might be a traitor and goodness only knew where they were going, but she wasn't going to refuse a chance of actually steering a ship at sea.

"Gently," said Foley. "Don't clutch. Think you're riding a bicycle, and hold her lightly. That's right. Keep her like that. I shan't be a minute."

He was opening a locker under the cockpit seat and bringing out a can of petrol as he spoke. Then he opened a hinged flap in the cockpit floor, reached down, unscrewed a metal cap, and poured the petrol in. It took no time at all. Nicola relinquished the tiller sadly and went back to her seat. For the first time she remembered Lawrie.

She gave a sigh of relief. They weren't entirely cut off, after all. But it would probably take Lawrie ages to get hold of anyone who was likely to believe her: even with the microfilm and the rest of the stuff, the only person Nicola had had any hope of convincing was Daddy. And if Lawrie turned up alone, or, worse still, blurted it all out over the telephone, they might so easily think it was just Lawrie doing another of her voices. Perhaps they wouldn't believe her until the hotel people said that the rest of them hadn't come in. And in the meantime they were sailing steadily north-east by east as fast as the engine would take them. A couple of lines jigged through Nicola's head:

> And when Matilda shouted: "Fire!"
> They only answered: "Little liar!"

It sounded only too likely. Nicola made a mental resolve that Lawrie shouldn't be allowed to practise her voices ever again.

If only there was something they could do to delay things. If only the fog would lift so that they could see where they were. Besides, if the fog lifted and the wind came, things would be so much easier. There was a lot you could do to sails: cut the sheets, slash the sails perhaps—Nicola fingered the knife in her pocket and felt bold and piratical. But an engine— Nicola knew nothing about engines. She didn't see what you could possibly do to those.

Time passed. The fog showed no sign of lifting. If anything, it seemed rather thicker, though a long swell was beginning to make the *Talisman* lift a little. Far away, Nicola could hear something that sounded like a distant cow. After a bit, it oc- curred to her that this was probably a fog-horn. She wondered why Foley wasn't sounding, and then remembered that vessels under twenty tons weren't legally obliged to. And the *Talisman* was a lot under twenty tons. All the same, Nicola didn't think her father would have thought much of that for an argument.

"Look here."

Nicola jumped. "Yes?"

"Think you can take the tiller again for a bit?"

She thought she probably ought to refuse, because it was pretty stupid, really, to keep on being so helpful; but the idea of steering the *Talisman* was too tempting. Nicola wriggled over to where Foley had been sitting and took the tiller in both hands.

"That's right. Firmly, but not too hard. Can you see the compass card? Then keep her as she's going now. I shan't be long. Perhaps a quarter of an hour. Call me at once, though, if anything happens."

Foley nodded to her, opened the doors and ran down into the deep little cabin. Nicola kept her eyes fixed on the compass card and found that she wasn't doing too badly. Of course, it wasn't like real sailing, but it felt wonderful. Nicola wriggled happily, looked at the compass card and found she had come off course. She was just going to put the tiller over a little, when the sudden blazing opportunity struck her; of course she needn't go back on course; of *course* she needn't. The thing to do now was to bring the *Talisman* round on a course south-west by west and keep her there till Foley came back. And if only Peter and Ginty could think of something clever—something like jumping on Foley as he came down and hitting him over the head, they might get back altogether.

A flame of excitement swept over her. She was about to swing the tiller over when she saw how stupid that would be. Even in the cabin, Foley would probably notice if the *Talisman* came about like that. Very carefully, fretting at the delay, even though it was so necessary, Nicola pressed on the helm. Very, very slowly the compass card swung round. Even Nicola wouldn't have known they'd turned if she hadn't been watching it. But there it was. South-west by west. They were going home.

She suddenly felt immensely happy. She knew it wasn't a reasonable feeling, for in a very short time Foley would be back in the cockpit again, and the *Talisman* would be brought round on the right course once more. But just for the moment it was glorious to have done something that would at least bother him a bit. Nicola felt a bubble of happiness rise in her throat: she hummed a tune; after a moment she fitted words to it:

> *"Injuns on the railroad*
> *Russians on the Spree*
> *Sugar in the petrol*
> *And up goes she!*
>
> *Injuns on the railroad——"*

The thought hit Nicola like a blow in the chest. For a moment she sat perfectly still at the tiller, holding her course, the idea spreading and glowing in her mind. *Sugar in the petrol and—*

Yes. Nicola hung on to the tiller as if it was the only thing which kept her from wrenching up that little flap in the floor without wasting another second. But she had to wait. Foley couldn't have been gone long—not more than a very few minutes. The thing would be to sail back as far as possible, and then, as soon as she heard Foley coming out of the cabin, put in the sugar. Nicola's hand went into her pocket and found the six lumps she had put there after breakfast in case they met the pony again. Now. Open the little flap, reach down and unscrew whatever it was Foley had unscrewed—could the *Talisman* sail herself that long without giving the show away?

Better do it in two stages. Cautiously Nicola released the tiller, knelt on the floor and yanked the flap open. Then she scrambled back to the tiller. It was all right—barely a point off course. Nicola let go again, knelt by the open flap and reached down into the darkness. The smell of hot oil and petrol came up, a pungent, sickening smell. Nicola shut her eyes, groped wildly and felt for the cap. Better not unscrew it completely. Better loosen it just enough to be able to get it off quickly when she needed to. . . . Nicola scrambled back to the tiller, black spots jigging in front of her eyes and swallowing desperately.

But the wind of the *Talisman*'s motion and her own excitement fended off the sickness. In a moment or two Nicola felt all right again. Her heart thumping furiously, she clutched the tiller, trying to judge the time much as Peter was doing, more accurately, in the cabin. She seemed to sail and sail—it must be ages more than fifteen minutes—

She realized suddenly that the speed and the motion had increased. And there was sound ahead—dull and muffled, but something more than the chug of the *Talisman*'s engine and the chuckle of water past her sides. Nicola held on, peering ahead into the fog and uncomfortably conscious that it was much more difficult to hold her course than it had been. Something far stronger than herself was trying to take charge of the boat. She stood up to get a better purchase on the tiller and as she did so, the fog seemed to thin a little. The muffled roar came steadily closer. Nicola looked ahead, suddenly able to see much farther. And then, as the fog eddied and lifted, she saw the white tossing waste of shoal water straight ahead, and felt the current's tug on the boat grow stronger.

Nicola gasped. From the cockpit of the little *Talisman*, the breaking seas looked steeper and uglier than perhaps they were, and for a moment Nicola nearly threw in her hand and shouted for Foley; had she been a more experienced sailor, she would probably have done so. But then she remembered that if she called him up and he took them out of the shoals she would have achieved nothing but a half-hour's delay. And if she waited much longer, Foley would feel for himself that there was something wrong; already the cabin doors were beginning to swing; as they swung open again she saw him move. Nicola let go the tiller and let the current take the boat; feverishly, she unscrewed the cap, dropped in the lumps of sugar, screwed it back, stamped on the flap, and scrambled back. Whatever happened, it was done now. With a sensation of choked excitement, Nicola grabbed the tiller and drove for the shoal water. The next moment the air was full of spray. Through the swinging cabin doors she caught a glimpse of Foley standing up and Peter backing towards the companion ladder—

And at that moment the engine coughed twice and died.

[iii]

The *Talisman* was flung every way at once. Nicola clung to the tiller, but more to have something to hold on to than for any good she thought she could do. She had a moment's compunction when she thought confusedly that even though Foley was a traitor, it was probably rather mean to wreck his ship when she was still wearing his jacket and he had given her brandy and been really rather kind—Giles, when she had ruined a day's sailing for him by being sea-sick, had been far less sympathetic. And then she saw Foley grab Peter from the companion ladder and swing him behind him into the cabin. She heard the crash as Peter cannoned into something and felt sorry for Foley no longer.

And then he had wrenched the tiller from her and she had no time to think of anything except the questions with which he was pelting her; what course had she steered? for how long? and what the devil did she think she had been doing?

Somehow, his fury and the glimmer of panic behind his eyes, made her feel very cool and confident. The *Talisman*, caught between the current and the tide, was still being flung about like a bottle in a fast stream, but Nicola didn't care. She answered his questions briefly and truthfully, while Peter and Ginty came scrambling up the ladder into the cockpit, Peter with a swelling lump on his forehead. He didn't look at Foley. He had rarely felt so small and foolish as when Foley yanked him off the companion and sent him sprawling into the cabin. In a way this was lucky, for his rage swamped the alarm he knew quite enough to feel at the sight of the danger they were in; he looked at Ginty, but Ginty was never afraid at sea. She held on to the coaming and eyed the white crests around them as confidently as if she were the mermaid Lawrie had wanted her to be.

"What's wrong with the engine?" shouted Foley above the noise the sea was making.

But Nicola wasn't telling. If he knew, there might be a way of putting it right and then all her trouble would have been wasted. She shouted back: "I don't know," and clutched at the coaming as the *Talisman* gave a particularly vicious leap and a lot of sea sloshed aboard.

The current was sweeping them on at what seemed a tremendous rate. The fog, although they had barely noticed it in the last few minutes, was much thinner. Peter could feel a wind on his cheek, quite different from the one made by the *Talisman*. Foley, who had yanked up the flaps in the floor and was

E   129

doing things to the engine, hadn't noticed. Peter didn't know whether to tell him or not. If they had been in any other patch of sea they could have set the sails as a matter of course, but there didn't seem much hope of getting them up as things were now. The mainsail, perhaps, if she could be hoisted from the cockpit; but you would want to cram on everything you had to get steerage way against a current as strong as this; and the

Talisman was bucking like a stallion; anyone brave enough—or foolhardy enough—to crawl out along the foredeck would stand an excellent chance of being jerked off and into the sea before they had gone a couple of feet.

Suddenly the fog was gone, rolling away to make a brown smudge like smoke all along the horizon. And there before them, barely fifty yards away, was the lighthouse; black as the Limpet itself, towering, tremendous, lifted high above the sea on the highest point of the rocky island which was now

being laid bare by the falling tide. And at that moment, the
engine picked up again.

Foley flung himself on the tiller. He was trying to bring her
round to run her ashore on the shingle; and slowly, fighting
every inch of the way, the *Talisman* obeyed. But there was not
room enough; driven by the current and the engine, the *Talisman*
man closed the gap between herself and the island long before
she came round sufficiently to run ashore in comparative
safety. There was a jarring crunch which flung them to the
floor of the cockpit; and as they picked themselves up, the
dinghy which they had been towing now drew attention to
itself by coming up and banging heavily against the side.

7

*

The Lighthouse

[i]

Everything seemed so quiet and still all at once that they could hardly believe it. Grabbing at the coaming to keep themselves from sliding about the slanting floor of the cockpit, they braced themselves for something more to happen. But nothing did; the waves broke quietly on the shingle a little way away, the wind hummed in the rigging, the sky overhead was a quiet evening blue filled with combings of mares' tails. For a moment, no one moved. Then Foley groped in the locker under the cockpit seat for the transmitting set. As he climbed cautiously along the foredeck, he said over his shoulder: "You three had better come ashore too. Better bring some stores with you." He dropped over the bows, scrambled across the rocks, dropped on to the shingle with a crunch, and walked up the beach to a stairway cut in the rock. He took the steps two at a time, opened the door into the lighthouse and slammed it behind him.

The children looked at one another. Then Nicola said: "What d'you think he'll do now?"

"How should I know?" Peter looked at the expanse of empty sea, wishing for a passing yacht whose crew might come to the rescue and finish a job they had so far bungled pretty badly. "P'raps we'd better get the stores and bedding and stuff ashore. We shan't be sleeping in the *Talisman* to-night."

"Shan't we? D'you think we're going to stay here?"

"I don't see what else we're going to do. She won't float off much before high water, I shouldn't think. Besides, she may be damaged. I expect—"

He had been going to say *I expect Foley's gone to whistle up the other ship*, but he stopped himself. It sounded too ominous and frightening. He said instead in a muffled sort of voice: "I expect we'd better get the stores out," and went down into the cabin.

They found that the easiest way to deal with this was for Peter to hand things up to Nicola, for Nicola to scramble along the deck to the bows, and for Ginty to take them up the beach and dump them in a tidy pile at the foot of the stairway. When it came to the charts, Peter hesitated. In one way, he would have liked to destroy them; on the other hand, with those crimson stars on them, they were evidence of a sort. Peter left them for a bit, and handed up the primus and the cans of petrol and paraffin. By the time he had done this he had made up his mind. He tucked the charts under his arm and scrambled up the companion ladder, saying: "All clear below." Then he and Nicola edged along the foredeck for the last time and jumped ashore to join Ginty on the beach.

"He's still in there," said Ginty, who was looking white and miserable. "Peter, why—?"

But Peter had remembered something else and was taking off shoes and socks. Wading cautiously, for the stones were sharp, he waded out to the *Talisman*'s stern and freed the dinghy's painter. Then he waded back towards the shingle, the little dinghy bouncing behind him. The others helped him pull her up the beach.

"Peter, listen," said Ginty as they tugged.

"Listen what?"

"Why are we bringing everything ashore? Why don't we get away?"

"How?"

"Oh, *Peter*. In the boat. Can't we refloat her or something?"

"How?"

"With the engine. Oh, Binks, do for goodness' sake let's get away."

Peter looked as if he might be going to say "How?" again. But instead he said: "I don't see how we can. Even if the engine would take her off, the minute it started up Foley would be out here."

"Couldn't we tow her off in the dinghy? Like Giles did when we went aground that time in the Hamble?"

"We might. But she seems pretty fast to me. If you ask me, her bows are jammed between those rocks. It's not as if she were on mud. And I don't think we *could* row against that current, even though the tide'd be with us."

Ginty's face quivered. "Oh, Peter, don't keep saying why we can't. Do think of *some* way we can—we can——"

Peter kicked at a stone. "Look here, Gin. I don't think there's any way we can get away at the moment. And as a matter of fact, I don't know if we ought to."

"Ought?—why oughtn't we?"

Peter looked up with a worried face. "Because he's still got the microfilm and the rest of the stuff on him. If there's a chance of getting it away from him or stopping him handing it over, then I expect we ought to."

"But how *can* we do anything?"

"I don't know. P'raps we can't."

"But if we got away, we could sail back to St.-Anne's and get the police or someone. He can't get away if the boat's gone."

"N-no." Peter thought of that other ship of whose existence he was so certain. "But suppose he destroyed all the stuff before we got back. It would just be our word against his. And

134

his family's lived at Mariners for centuries. Why *should* anyone believe he's a traitor?"

"But *can't* we do anything?" Ginty's voice had begun to waver, rather like Lawrie's when something went badly wrong. "He'll just—he'll just——"

"You're forgetting Lawrie," said Nicola. "She knows what's happened, more or less. She must have told *someone* by now. And besides, we *have* done something. We're back here, instead of miles away at sea. It isn't much, but it's something against him."

Peter remembered something. "Nick, what happened to the engine? Did you do something to it?"

But Nicola had already made up her mind about that. She still thought it would be as well if it remained a mystery to Foley, and if she were the only person who knew, the more chance there was of its staying a secret. So she said: "Not a thing," and looked at Ginty. But Ginty had walked off. She had walked down to the edge of the sea, and was shoving rather hard at some limpets on the top of a large rock. Her back looked very miserable, as if she didn't much want to talk to either of them.

"Let's go inside," said Peter softly to Nicola, after a moment.

They went softly up the rock steps and into the lighthouse. A door faced them and from behind it, very faintly, they could hear the sound of the buzzer. Peter put his hand to the door-handle and turned it gently. But the door was locked. They turned their attention to the stairs which went curving up between the inner and the outer walls.

There were five stories with a room on each. The first was where Foley was; the second had chairs and a table; the third and fourth had bunks built against the walls; the fifth was the lantern itself. Nicola and Peter did no more than glance into each; they wanted to see what there was to be seen, but they didn't want to be caught doing it. They had left the lantern and were going down again, when Peter dashed back and reappeared with a key in his hand.

"Take them out of the doors as we go down," he whispered to Nicola, "and then we'll throw them in the sea. He can't lock us in then."

It was an easy thing to do, but nightmarish all the same. They scurried down the stairs, dragging the keys from the locks, seeming to take an appalling time and nervously terrified that Foley would finish what he was doing and catch them before they had finished. But when they reached the bottom of the stairs, the buzzer was still going irregularly behind the door. Peter dashed down the rock steps and ran crunching over the shingle to the sea's edge. He flung the keys, one at a time, as far as he possibly could. Then, since Ginty still didn't look as if she wanted to talk, he climbed back up the rock steps and sat with Nicola at the top.

"I'm hungry," said Nicola. "Aren't you?"

Peter remembered the chocolate in his pockets and handed her half. Neither felt much like talking, though both felt that what they ought to be doing was to be making some sensible and resourceful plan which would confound Foley for ever. But they both felt immensely sleepy, and Peter's head was aching badly where he had banged it when Foley flung him aside. So they just ate their chocolate, and watched the sea and wondered in a vague sort of way what was going to happen next. Both thought, though neither said so, that it was high time the rescue party put in an appearance, but the great curve of sea was empty of everything but waves and seagulls. After a while, they heard Foley come out of the lower room and lock the door behind him. He did not come outside, but went up the stairs into one of the rooms, where they could hear him dragging things about. They supposed they ought to go and look, and they both felt much too weary ever to move again.

After a while he came down again, and this time came out to them.

"We shall be sleeping here to-night," he said abruptly. "Better get the bedding ashore now, and then we'll have supper——"

"We have," said Peter, getting up. "I mean, we've cleared the boat. We thought," he tried to put it in a way which would make Foley tell them what was going to happen, "we thought we wouldn't be putting off before morning."

Foley made no comment on this. He looked at the pile of stores and equipment on the beach and said: "That'll have to be moved up here or the tide will get it. Better do that before we do anything else. What's your sister doing?"

Peter did not answer. He called to Ginty and she turned round and came back up the beach, looking very white and with dark smudges under her eyes, but not, any more, as if she were going to cry. In silence, she helped to carry the stores from the beach to the second room. There was a lamp burning on the table, and they all noticed that shutters had been fixed over the windows. But they said nothing: as for the stores they simply dumped them all together in a heap. It hardly seemed worth while being tidy about it, if they were going to load up again in the morning. Foley picked out a couple of tins of soup, some tinned meat and biscuits, cocoa and condensed milk.

"A horrible mixture," he said dispassionately. "But I daresay you can stomach it. Can any of you use a primus?"

Ginty could. Generally it was one of the elder girls who did the cooking if they were in their own boat, but if they were all doing something else, it sometimes fell to Ginty. She found the saucepans and a tin opener and set to work in silence.

They were all rather silent. Even supper, when it was ready, didn't seem to wake them up. No one spoke until, as they were eating the tinned meat and biscuits, Foley said: "About to-morrow. I shall be sailing as soon as the *Talisman* can be re-floated. That will be sometime on to-night's tide. I'm leaving you here, and you should have enough stores to see you through until you can signal someone to take you off. That should be fairly soon, I imagine. For one thing, as soon as your sister tells her story, they'll have people out looking for you."

No one answered. It all sounded so quiet and ordinary—and yet it wasn't, for as he spoke, Foley's hand went to his inner pocket as if to reassure himself that the little oilskin packet was still safely there. Peter clenched his hands under the table and tried to think of something—*anything*, from stabbing Foley to the heart, to driving holes in the bottom of the *Talisman*. But he knew he couldn't hope to match Foley if it came to physical violence; he still felt hot and ashamed when he remembered that moment when Foley had flung him aside as if he had been matchwood.

"And you know," Foley added in a gentle-sounding voice, "I shouldn't go telling a lot of wild stories when you get back. You haven't a shred of evidence, have you? You can't even prove I carried you off. For all anyone will know, you may have taken the *Talisman* out yourselves, and wrecked her. Oh yes," as Peter looked up, "she will be found wrecked. Enough of her, anyway, to make the theory convincing. And as no one knows I've been at Mariners, no one's going to miss me when I've gone. So whatever story you tell, there'll be no proof that you're not lying."

Nicola opened her mouth to speak and then shut it firmly. She wasn't going to tell Foley what she had told Anquetil, in case he thought of a way out of that too. Peter stared at the table-top. It all sounded perfectly reasonable, and he couldn't think of a way out. Not that Daddy would think they were lying, but in a way, that wasn't so important. What mattered were those formulas and the microfilm. If Foley were to get clear away—if no one were to believe them ever—Peter picked up his cup of cocoa and drank it, his teeth chattering on the rim.

"And now you'd better all go to bed," said Foley when all the cups were empty. "You two," to Ginty and Nicola, "in the room above this, and you," to Peter, "in the room above that. There are enough sleeping bags and you'll find bunks against the walls. It's not luxury, but I daresay you'll be relatively comfortable. And as we shan't meet in the morning, I'll wish you a speedy rescue—and not too much trouble from your parents when they get you back."

They felt very young and foolish and helpless. The only hope, thought Peter and Nicola, picking up the sleeping bags, was that whoever Lawrie had told was doing something about it now. But even if she had, no one, now, would expect to find them so near St.-Anne's. After all, thought Nicola wretchedly, it hadn't been a specially good idea to turn the boat back and sugar the petrol. She stumped up the stairs to bed and wished Ginty didn't look so relieved.

"I'm sorry," said Foley, as they went up, "that I can't let you have lights. You'll have to manage in the dark. But I think you'll get just enough light to see by if you leave your doors open."

They were so sleepy that they couldn't even think why they couldn't have lights. They took off some of their clothes, put the sleeping bags on the bunks and climbed in. In five minutes they were fast asleep. This was not only due to fresh air and exercise. It was partly that, of course; but chiefly it was because Foley had dropped his last three sleeping tablets into their cups of cocoa along with the saccharine; it was the best substitute he could think of for the keys they had so inconveniently thrown away.

[ii]

Lewis Foley glanced at the chronometer on the wall and got up. From the time the children had gone to bed, he had been sitting at the table in the lowest room, placidly smoking a pipe and playing himself at chess. Now, at slack water, it should be possible to see whether the *Talisman* could be refloated or if she had been too badly damaged. He had been very confident about his boat's probable condition in his radio messages to the U-boat, but, as he cheerfully admitted to himself, without much real evidence. He turned down the lamp and went out, closing the door behind him.

It was quite dark. Overhead the stars were clear enough, but the moon, which had only just risen, was hidden by a cloud-bank. He waited until his eyes became accustomed to the darkness and then went down to the beach.

There was no water under the *Talisman's* keel now. He moved slowly round her, feeling her with his hands. He could find no damage to her planking, but he was not too sure about the rudder. As for the part of the keel which was jammed between the rocks, he could tell nothing about that until she was afloat. Then, if she were holed, he would know it fast enough.

The moon had lifted clear of the cloud bank by now, but the sky overhead was beginning to fill with light, scurrying clouds and a fresh wind blew on his cheek. He turned up his coat collar, turned away, and stumbled against the dinghy. It was absurd to leave her there; the tide, which would rise to within three feet of the lighthouse itself, would float her away. She was tiny and very light: he dragged her across the island to the small natural harbour at the eastern end of the island, attached a kedge and tied her to a ring in the rock. The children might find her useful when it came to making their escape.

Foley grinned to himself. He had received his orders for the disposal of the children, but he had never taken kindly to obeying orders. This was fortunate, for the instructions had been perfectly clear and precise. The children were to be killed before he left the lighthouse, taken on board the *Talisman*, and left in her when the sea-cocks were opened; the quick dispassionate burrs in his head-phones had continued that it would be best to kill the children by holding them under water, unless their struggles made this impossible; then there would be no suspicion about the manner of their deaths. Foley had listened to this, had tapped out the signal which meant that the message had been received and understood, and signed off. At the time, he had thought that if they had given him his orders without quite so much criticism of his actions, he might have done as they wanted. But later, as they sat round the supper table, he had wondered what sort of a man they took him for, that they could instruct him in the best method of murdering three children with no more emotion than they showed in giving him the position of the rendezvous. That he worked for them—or rather, through them—did not make him the same kind. He was guilty of treason, and he had behaved in other ways of which people like his friend Anquetil would no doubt disapprove; but he had never had a bent for cold-blooded cruelty, and he did not see himself beginning now.

The wind was freshening and setting towards the north. The light, scurrying clouds of half an hour before had been the precursors of a solid mass which now covered half the sky. Foley observed this with some annoyance as he went up the rock steps into the lighthouse. And as he did so, the first scatter of rain was hurled against the windows.

Two hours later, he went out again. The tide had turned and there was enough water under the *Talisman's* keel to have shifted her. But she lay as he had seen her at low tide, only now with the sea breaking round her stern. When he put his hand on her, he could feel no movement beyond a lifeless, shuddering jar.

He went back into the lighthouse to fetch a crowbar. Standing knee-deep in the icy sea, he tried to force the crowbar between the rocks which held her, and break her free. But the rocks held fast. He thrust the crowbar in from every angle, but he could get no purchase on her. Because he could not believe in such a monstrous piece of bad luck, he continued to thrust and heave and strain, until at length, and suddenly, something gave and he staggered backwards. But it was not the *Talisman* which had moved; it was the crowbar which had broken in his hand.

He saw then that it was useless. He was up to his waist in water, for the tide, driven by the wind, was flooding in before its time and the sea was already breaking over the boat and pouring into her. He waded back to the beach, barely aware of the cold and the gale, of his soaked clothes and his bruised and aching hands. She was on a lee shore and he would have no second chance. She would be smashed to pieces by the morning.

He watched till the sea took possession of her and the rising tide drove him back to the lighthouse. There, he remembered the spare clothes in the locker, and, while he towelled himself, put some coffee to heat on the primus. He did these things mechanically, thinking that in a few hours, when the tide went down and revealed the wreck, he would have to call up the U-boat and report again. He looked at the oilskin packet lying on the table and remembered the mood of light-hearted arrogance in which he had compiled the formulae, only a week ago. But that, he remembered uneasily, listening to the gusts buffeting the outer walls, had been before the thunderbolt.

He shook himself impatiently, telling himself not to talk nonsense. It was quite true that when the thunderbolt had plunged into the sea two mornings ago, he had seen it as a sign that his mission was ended; and when, still shocked and shaken by the storm, he had made the mistake of walking past young Marlow as if he had never seen him before in his life, he had seen this as additional confirmation. He saw too—indeed, he had known it for some hours—that he should never have kidnapped the children. There had been another, far simpler, alternative: he had only needed to look over the microfilm and the formulae in a stern and interested way, put them in his pocket and announce that he would turn the package over to the police immediately, and he would have been safely at large on the high seas by now, instead of cooped up here, with three children on his hands, and his only means of escape a rag-tag pack of allies who would secure his safety only so long as he was of use to them.

And now, once he had handed over the oilskin packet, he would be no more use at all: as he poured out the coffee, he saw his death quite clearly.

Foley grinned to himself. Thunderbolts and fate were all very well, but he didn't really believe a word of it. He had been in corners as tight as this before, and had always escaped disaster. However bad things might look at present, something was bound to turn up. He had never known a time when his luck hadn't turned in the end. He decided not to wait till morning to call the U-boat. He would report his position now.

It was nearly two hours before the U-boat's signal came through. The quick burrs in his head-phones made one suave attempt to persuade him to dictate the formulae, but he grinned to himself, made a token excuse and refused. The burrs accepted this. He was to call them up in half an hour **to** hear the new instructions. It was hoped this would be the **last** time this would be necessary.

While he was waiting, he went out to see what had happened to the *Talisman*. It was nearly dawn, and the tide had cleared the greater part of the island. Driftwood was strewn among the boulders and seaweed, and littered the margin of the sea. Of the *Talisman* herself, nothing was left, except the bit of the keel which was still tightly jammed between **the** rocks.

He went back and listened to the U-boat. Because of the fleet exercises, it would be unsafe to take him off until 06.00 hours on Sunday. The children also would be taken on board. They would be disposed of later.

He signed off, and went out again. It was a fine morning, with a clear sky and a scudding wind. He was certain now that, rationally speaking, he and the children would not be alive by Sunday evening, and he knew too, that this could be avoided easily enough between now and Sunday morning. He had only to make a signal to a passing boat and they would be taken off. Whereupon he would be tried under the Official Secrets Act and imprisoned; for if he and the children were taken together their story would begin to carry weight.

And trial and imprisonment was something he would not face; the children's safety could not weigh against that. Foley shrugged and did not debate the matter. He had always told himself that he would prefer death at the hands of the people he had served to the justice of those he had betrayed; and now, always supposing the worst did come to the worst, he found, rather to his surprise, that it was still true.

8

---

*

Breakfast at the Lighthouse

Nicola woke up feeling very cheerful indeed. It was a fine morning, she had had a good night's sleep, and Foley would have gone. All they had to do now was to have breakfast and get themselves home. Ginty, who felt a little less cheerful than Nicola, was also relieved about this. Whatever Lawrie had told people, their mother must have been dreadfully worried, and Ginty had a beastly, nagging feeling that it was mostly her fault. She was the eldest, she ought to have put her foot down, she ought to have said they weren't going trespassing in anyone's house, however empty. If there was a frightful row, as there was practically certain to be, Ginty thought it was probably bound to be about that. Someone—possibly mummy and daddy, quite certainly Karen and Rowan when they came to hear about it—would be sure to say: "But Ginty, you were the eldest. Why didn't you stop them?" Ginty wished she had. It was only by the greatest possible luck that things had turned out as well as they had. If Foley had been a different kind of person—if the *Talisman* had been wrecked yesterday. . . . An awful thought struck her: suppose she had been the only survivor and had had to go home and tell them *that*. Ginty shivered. Whatever anyone

145

said to her, things might have been almost incredibly worse.

Peter, pulling on his shorts in the room above, was also, in spite of his long sleep and the fine morning, feeling pretty sick with himself. Naturally, he couldn't help being glad they were going home to-day—he supposed they'd have to signal a passing boat from one of the windows, or something of that kind—but there was no getting over the fact that he'd made a very poor showing. Foley had got away with the oilskin packet intact, and he'd done exactly nothing to stop him. Nicola, in spite of being sea-sick and not being used to boats, had done much better. At least she'd tried, even if nothing had come of it. Turning the boat back—with a bit of luck it might have worked. But he'd just gone blank and helpless, like that time in the other boat. Rather over-doing his lugubrious feelings of despondency and mortification, Peter told himself that it had been obvious from the beginning that he wasn't the right sort of person for the Navy. He'd just have to make up his mind to go to an ordinary school next autumn and do something else when he left. What that something else was going to be, Peter simply didn't know. He'd never considered anything but the Service.

After a bit, even Nicola found Ginty's grumpiness a bit damping, but she couldn't feel altogether quenched. She was in a lighthouse, the sun was shining, and there were seagulls floating past the window. Lots of yesterday had been pretty frightening—curiously enough, Nicola thought, it seemed more frightening now, looking back on it, than it had been when it had actually been happening—but it was practically over now, and it would be a tremendous thing to tell when they got back to school. She pulled her jersey over her head and galloped down the lighthouse stairs whistling cheerfully to herself. She dashed out, down the rock steps, and on to the little beach. The first thing she saw was Foley's back, as he leaned against a rock, his hands in his pockets, staring out to sea.

Nicola stood stiller than stone. She was just going to rush back into the lighthouse and warn the others, when he turned round.

"Hullo," he said.

"Good morning," said Nicola flatly. She waited a moment and then, as he didn't seem to be going to say any more, said tentatively, because after all, it was his lighthouse and she didn't want to be rude: "We thought—I mean—you said you'd be gone by this morning."

"So I did," said Foley. "But God disposes. Come here."

Nicola hesitated for a fraction of a second, then went towards him. He took her by the shoulder and twisted her round to face the place where the *Talisman* had lain. For a moment, Nicola didn't understand; and then a wave, screeching back over the pebbles, showed the fragment of keel which was all that was left.

"*Oh*," said Nicola appalled. "How—how *awful*. What happened to her?"

"What you see. The keel jammed between those rocks when we brought her in last night and the storm finished her."

Nicola said nothing. She stared at the place where the *Talisman* had been, with a choked feeling in her throat. For apart from anything else, the *Talisman* might almost be said to have been her first command: the first ship she had ever sailed——

Behind her, Foley began to whistle under his breath; she felt his fingers dig into her shoulder as he twisted her round to face him. "Now tell me," he said. "You turned her round on purpose, didn't you?"

Nicola's heart thumped. Foley had queer, rather nice, eyes; not quite grey as she had thought, but greenish, with darker flecks in them; she stared at them, while she said: "Yes, I did."

"I thought so. And what happened to the engine?"

Nicola's throat felt dry. Foley whistled softly between his teeth. "Come on. What happened?" And then his fingers tightened on her shoulder. "We know the same songs, don't we? 'Injuns on the railroad'. Isn't that what you were whistling when you came out?"

Nicola's cheeks flamed. "Y-yes."

" 'Sugar in the petrol'," said Foley softly, staring at her. "Well, I'll be damned. Of course. You said you knew Rob Anquetil, didn't you?"

"Yes."

Foley took his hand away. He said conversationally: "Now, I'll tell you something rather comic. I made up that song when Rob and I were kids. It commemorated a trick I played on a very unpleasant and influential relative. You know *Hamlet*, I suppose?"

"N-no," said Nicola, a little puzzled by what seemed an abrupt change of subject. "We don't do Shakespeare till next year. Lower Fourth, you know."

"So if I tell you that 'tis the sport to have the engineer hoist with his own petard, it won't be such a cliché to you as it might to someone better informed?"

Nicola flushed again. She looked at him, but he didn't seem particularly angry, so she asked curiously: "What *is* a petard?"

"A sort of limpet bomb. You remember during the war the frogmen used to attach them to the sides of battleships? Well, a petard was much the same thing, only it was used to break in castle doors and drawbridges and things like that. And I imagine", said Foley, "that I'm one of the few men in England who could give you that information off-hand. Why did you turn the *Talisman* back and sugar the petrol?"

He shot it at her. Nicola's cheeks felt as if they must crack, they felt so hot. Even though she wasn't particularly afraid of him any more, it took a fair amount of courage to answer at once: "Because we think you're a traitor."

He looked at her with a queer violent expression, as if he would have liked to hit her. But before she could flinch, his expression altered. He took out his pipe, filled it, stuck it in his

mouth and began to light it. Between puffs, he said: "Well, so
I am. A less honest person would probably quibble and ask
you what you meant by the word. But I'll accept the ordinary
definition."

Nicola gazed at him. It seemed very queer indeed that a
person should just admit something so—so awful as that. To
be a traitor—to be a spy—it was quite the most beastly thing
to be. And the odd thing was, he didn't seem to mind. She felt
his eyes on her, as if he knew her thoughts and was laughing
at her. He probably was, for he said in an amused voice:
"When you wrinkle your forehead like that, you look like a
spaniel pup I had once. As if you found life too puzzling for
words."

"So I do," Nicola burst out. "I mean—why are you a—
a——?"

"A traitor? Suppose I told you I wasn't? Suppose I told you
I was playing a lone hand to confound the enemies of this
realm? Suppose I told you I'd been patiently setting a trap
and that now it was baited and ready to be sprung? What
would you say to that?"

Nicola looked at him. His eyes, impish, teasing, looked back
at her. She said slowly: "I don't think I'd believe you."

"And you'd be right."

She felt sick with disappointment. She had hoped desperately that he would insist that that was the truth and—and
show her papers to prove it. She didn't want him to be an
enemy. She said: "But *why*——?"

"Oh, I don't know. Don't you get fed up, sometimes, with
all the smug dutiful people, all busily scratching their little
livings, all saying the same things, all professing the same be-
liefs in the same words that all the generations have sucked
dry before them? Ninety-nine point nine per cent don't even
know what the words mean. It serves them right if someone
chucks a bomb into the ant-heap occasionally. And besides,
there are some secrets that are too good not to tell—" He

broke off, looking at her amusedly. "You don't understand a word I've been saying, do you?"

"No," said Nicola, not quite truthfully, because though she disliked what he was saying wholeheartedly, she hadn't the least idea how to argue with him.

"Never mind." He put out a hand and ruffled her hair, just as if she *had* been the spaniel pup he'd been talking about, thought Nicola resentfully. "Let's go in and see about breakfast."

Ginty was already getting it. She and Peter had seen Foley and Nicola talking as soon as they came down; they had drawn back quickly into the shelter of the lighthouse, looking at one another with startled faces and wondering in low voices what it meant. It wasn't until Peter took down the shutters in the room where they had had supper the night before, and saw the scattered driftwood littering the beach, that he realized what had happened. When he told Ginty, she turned very pale and began getting breakfast in silence. But she wasn't quite as frightened as she had been; she had been scared stiff most of yesterday afternoon and evening and no one, Ginty told herself with some relief, could go on being frightened like that for ever.

As for Peter, when the first shock was over, he felt suddenly pleased. His spirits began to rise. If Foley was stuck here for a bit, with the place clear of fog, anything might happen. They might be able to signal a passing boat, the pursuit might catch up with them. . . . Peter began to whistle very cheerfully as he set the table and watched Ginty hunt among the tins for something suitable for breakfast.

Foley and Nicola came in just as everything was ready. As Ginty poured the cocoa into the cups and put the sliced ham and biscuits on the table, Foley told them what had happened to the *Talisman*. Peter shot a glance at Nicola. He had expected her to be looking rather triumphant that her plan had worked so well, but she wasn't. She was eating ham and biscuits in silence, as if she found swallowing difficult. After a pause, Peter asked: "What are you going to do now, then?"

"*We*," said Foley. "You can't go if I can't, can you?"

"Why not?" said Ginty in a quick, apprehensive voice. All at once, she was frightened again.

"Because it might occur to you to inform the police of my whereabouts, mightn't it, my pretty? And I never think it a good idea to accept paroles. I wouldn't keep one myself in the circumstances."

"But we can't live here for ever," burst out Ginty. For the moment she really thought that was what he meant.

"Heaven forbid. Not for ever—till Sunday morning."

"Sunday morning?" echoed Ginty horrified. Said like that, Sunday morning seemed almost as far away as for ever.

"That's only forty-eight hours, or thereabouts. Rather less. The U-boat will be lying off the eastern end of the island at 06.00 hours precisely. Then we shall catch the flood."

But Ginty wasn't taking in any details. She exclaimed: "But we can't possibly stay as long as that."

"Why not?"

"Because," Ginty supposed it sounded a kiddish thing to say, and began to stammer, but said it all the same, "because Mummy must be awfully worried by now as it is. If we don't turn up till *Sunday*——"

"I doubt if you'll turn up on Sunday," said Foley cheerfully, getting up and rummaging amongst the tins in search of marmalade. "I doubt if you'll be put ashore before Monday at the latest."

"P-put ashore? But aren't we staying here?"

"No. You're to be taken off in the U-boat too."

Ginty went white. She put down her knife and fork. "But I can't *possibly* go in a U-boat."

"Why on earth not?" asked Foley impatiently. He found a tin of marmalade and came back to the table.

"Because she can't," said Nicola belligerently. "She can't go in Tubes, even. A person who can't go in Tubes couldn't possibly go in a U-boat."

"Oh," said Foley. He looked at Ginty as if he felt rather sorry for her. But he said: "Well, I'm sorry, but there it is. I'm afraid you've no choice."

Ginty stared down at her plate, speechless, a lump of frightened tears wedged in her throat. Peter said quickly: "But why can't we be left behind, like you were going to do before? Why has that changed?"

It seemed a long time before Foley answered. Then he shrugged and said: "I don't know. Some other complication has turned up, I suppose."

It didn't sound especially convincing. Peter looked at Foley who was spreading his biscuits lavishly with tinned butter and marmalade. And knew the reason. Foley hadn't been meant to leave them behind the first time; only, because he was meeting the U-boat a long way off, it hadn't mattered; he had been going to tell some tale about having heaved them overboard. But this time the U-boat was coming in; the people on board would be able to see for themselves that—

That they were still alive.

Peter put out a hand and helped himself to a biscuit. Then he dug into the butter and the marmalade. He didn't feel in the least like eating anything, but he knew instinctively that if he didn't make himself behave calmly and ordinarily he would soon begin to feel more frightened than he could manage. He spread his biscuit with butter and marmalade and chewed determinedly, staring out of the window at the sea. He was staring so hard without seeing anything that it was Nicola who scraped back her chair with a jerk, and dashed through the door, crying:

"Destroyers! Quick!"

They all got up and crowded downstairs and out on to the cat-walk to look. Far out on the horizon (much too far out to see a signalling handkerchief) the ships of the Home Fleet went by. Peter counted five destroyers, an aircraft carrier, three cruisers and—so far out that she was only a shadow in the haze —the outlines of a battleship. The rest of the ships must be out of sight, over the horizon. Peter's heart thumped. He was still part of that company till the end of next term—or Sunday morning. And it struck him suddenly that that was why the U-boat was not putting in an appearance until 06.00 hours on Sunday. The exercise would not end until Saturday midnight. From now till then, it would be unsafe for the U-boat to be at sea. Illogically, for it didn't really help much, Peter felt more cheerful. It was always pleasant to know that the enemy had something to be afraid of, too. He leaned on the rail and listened to Nicola, excitedly identifying the destroyers.

". . . and that's a Battle class—and a Tribal—there, Gin— *there*, where I'm pointing. . . ."

"Not Tribal," said Foley, "one of the S class."

"Is it? I don't believe it is. It looks——"

"S class," said Foley firmly. But then he had the advantage of a pair of binoculars.

Nicola said no more. She wasn't going to argue with a naval officer; especially not one with binoculars. She hung over the rail, and watched the ships with what her brother Giles called her midshipman look. Peter glanced at Foley. He wondered how it felt, to be a naval officer watching those ships and at the same time knowing yourself to be a person who was doing his best to destroy them; it was queer how little people's thoughts showed in their faces. And suddenly he couldn't bear it. He couldn't go on standing beside Foley, knowing. . . . He spun round and walked blindly into the lighthouse. To Nicola and Ginty, who had been thinking along much the same lines, it was obvious enough why he had gone and they wondered uneasily what Foley might do; but, as he lowered the glasses, Foley didn't look particularly anything—not vengeful, not conscience-stricken, just mildly interested. He said: "Come inside, and let's finish breakfast. Is there a tin of sardines?"

"*Sardines?*" exclaimed Nicola scandalized. "*Now?*"

"Not for me," said Foley amused. "For the gulls. I always feed the gulls when I'm living in the lighthouse."

Foley fed the gulls. Ginty boiled sea-water, and she and Nicola washed up. Peter, having nothing to do, and not much wanting to talk, went down on to the little beach which was beginning to disappear again under the sea and threw stones in a thoughtful way at a piece of driftwood. Now that he was standing on the beach he could see that there was practically no chance at all of being able to signal a passing yacht from there, for, as Anquetil had told Nicola, a series of high, knife-edged rocks a few yards from the beach screened it most effectively from the open water. All the same, there must be *some* way. There must be *something* they could do. He scrambled on to a giant boulder at the sea's edge and found that even so, he could not see beyond the rocks. 06.00 hours on Sunday. And now it was half-past nine. That left forty-four and a half hours to think of a plan. It wasn't long, really, but he didn't feel quite as blank as he had done. Somehow the sight of the ships had made him feel more sure of himself, as if he were not entirely alone. If only he could get in touch with them—if he could signal to them, somehow. It would be dark when they came back, which was a pity. Otherwise—

Peter clutched hard on the stone in his hand. But that was what lighthouses were for—to signal in the dark. Suppose—

He fought down his excitement. He would have to be careful. If Foley suspected he was thinking of ways of escape, he would see to it that he had no chance to do anything so dangerous. It was probably only because Foley thought him a muff because of the boat thing that he was letting them have as much freedom as he was. He must be careful and not spoil that. Pretend that it would be rather fun to go in the U-boat . . . pretend he believed they would be put ashore somewhere, sometime on Monday. . . .

The tide swirled round his boulder. Peter jumped off and

shot a glance round what he could see of the empty, sparkling expanse of sea. Then he went soberly back to the lighthouse and asked if he could help Foley feed the gulls.

Presently the tide confined them. Foley produced packs of patience cards from a locker. It was rather like any wet day in the holidays, except that there was nothing else to do once patience became boring. Ginty laid out a patience too, and turned the cards over, but she kept missing moves. Peter looked up once at the same time as she did and caught the expression in her eyes. He supposed she was thinking about the U-boat, but for the moment there was nothing he could do about it. He couldn't even say anything reassuring with Foley sitting there, absorbed by the game of chess he had laid out for himself. Even a sign would be risky. So he pretended he didn't know what she meant and looked down again at the silly bits of pasteboard. He thought that if they got out of this safely, he'd never touch a pack of cards again.

. . . Somehow, he'd got to get up to the lantern and have a look round. It would be too risky to try it in the daytime; and as he had his torch, it didn't really matter too much. Very early in the morning would be better than late at night. Four o'clock, say: he must remember to bang his head on the pillow before he went to sleep. The light itself ought to be all right. It had been in working order during the Victory Celebrations, Nick had said, and that wasn't so awfully long ago. Suppose. . . . Peter went on chewing over the possibilities: for somehow his basic idea had got to be given outline and detail. Somehow, it had got to be made to work.

If you play it long enough, patience becomes absorbing. Peter went on laying out game after game in the hope of getting it out; and now, at last, it was coming. He looked up triumphantly to show Nicola, and caught the tail end of her expression of incredulous triumph as she stared across at the window opposite. Then she gave a muffled whoop, sprang to her feet and dashed for the stairs.

Peter had never seen anyone move as fast as Foley moved then. He seemed to see what Nicola had seen and to be after her almost at the same time. There was no chance of stopping him, for Nicola and Foley were on the same side of the table, the side nearest the door. There was a crash and a thump and then Nicola had been yanked back into the room, her arm doubled behind her back, and Foley's revolver pressing hard just below her collar bone.

"If either of you move or make a sound," said Foley, "I'll blow Nicola to pieces. I swear it."

There was no question that he meant what he said. Peter and Ginty sat as still as stone, and as silent, while the brown sail tacked to and fro just beyond the furthest line of rocks. To Nicola, with the pain in her doubled arm fast becoming unbearable, time seemed to go on for ever. The muzzle of the revolver dug into her back, but that wasn't nearly so bad. In a moment she would have to say in as steady a voice as she could manage: "Let go, please. You're hurting." But it would be kiddish to say it yet. Not till she'd counted five—and another five—and another—

Her knees had begun to shake and a horrible warm feeling was creeping down the back of her neck. And then, through a haze of discomfort, she heard Ginty say in a quick half-frightened, half-defiant voice: "Let her go. You're hurting her."

Foley let go at once. He peered down at her face and then said, in the sulky aggrieved voice that an older child uses to a much younger one: "Sorry. I didn't mean to hurt you. Why on earth didn't you say?"

Nicola said nothing. If she'd opened her mouth at that moment, she would have burst into tears. She leaned silently against the frame of the door, staring out at the staircase and the blank wall. After a moment she went out and sat on the stairs, because her knees were still inclined to tremble violently and they felt as if they'd be happier sitting down. The tears in her eyes wanted to fall quite badly, but she held her head so high that it was impossible for them to come out. After a bit, Ginty came out and sat beside her.

"Are you all right?"

Nicola nodded. She said shakily: "That was the *Golden Enterprise*. If I hadn't mucked it up, we'd be rescued by now."

Ginty stole a glance at Nicola's white face. She wanted to say: "If *I* hadn't mucked it up in the house yesterday we mightn't be here at all," but she found she simply couldn't. Her shame over that moment of panic on the stairs at Mariners was so real that it felt as if there was a lump of ice inside whenever she thought of it. She said: "Perhaps he'll come back."

"Oh, I expect so," said Nicola in a miserable, defiant voice. She raised her voice and said loudly: "I shouldn't think Mr. Anquetil would have come at all if he hadn't known we were here. He's bound to come back."

But she didn't believe it, and neither did Ginty; nor did Peter or Foley. Ginty went on sitting on the stairs, feeling that Nicola might be glad to have company even if she didn't say so. But they didn't talk any more; and presently Ginty got up and went back into the living-room, to hot up the tinned steak-and-kidney puddings she'd chosen that morning as the right things to eat for a celebration dinner. Even though it wasn't a celebration any more, steak-and-kidney puddings with tinned peas and tinned peaches to follow, were still quite good things to have.

[ii]

Anquetil sailed back against the wind to St.-Anne's-Oldport. He had taken the *Golden Enterprise* out that morning in a faint hope, which he knew was more than three-quarters fantasy, that he might sight the *Talisman*'s dinghy with the three children safely aboard. He had been a long way to the north when he had seen, through his binoculars, the tiny white blur half-way up the lighthouse; he had identified the blur as seagulls a split second before he remembered Lewis's habit of feeding them.

He tried every trick he knew, but it was a couple of hours before he was within hailing distance of the lighthouse, and by that time the tide was swirling three-quarters of the way up the rock on which the lighthouse was built. There were no gulls there now, beyond the few which always seemed to circle it, their wings fringed with light as they skimmed overhead across the sun. The *Golden Enterprise* idled to and fro in the clear patch of sea between the shoals and the rocks, while Anquetil raked the rock with his binoculars. But the lighthouse, black, towering and sentinel, told him nothing. Not a door, not a window stood open. No face appeared at the windows; only the gulls mocked him with sharp cries which sounded oddly human. A herring gull stood on the top of the rock and cocked its head at him, peering sideways; then it lowered its head and began to clean its feet. If it had not been for the cloud of gulls he had seen earlier, he would have sworn the lighthouse was deserted. And yet in a curious way, he had the feeling that behind those windows eyes were watching him. He didn't like it at all.

And then, just as he was deciding to give it up for the time being and return in a few hours' time, to see whether the lighthouse was ready to declare itself, he had an inspiration. He could have kicked himself for not having thought of it before. He sailed well away and anchored to landward of the lighthouse, where there were no windows, taking his time. If Lewis *were* there, there was no point in putting him on his guard by making an almighty row with the chain and anchor. Then he dropped into his dinghy, and rowed slowly towards the lighthouse, making for the little harbour on the eastern side of the island. If there were no dinghy there, it would still not be proof conclusive: but if there *were*—

He had never rowed in alone before; Lewis had always been with him. He felt a sense of betrayal, that he should be using the secret channel Lewis had shown him when they were schoolboys, to fight and defeat him. But Lewis was always putting one in these predicaments. He had done it when they were boys at school, cheerfully telling Robert all his intentions so that when the mischief was discovered, Robert always knew how and why it had been done. The worst of it was, thought Anquetil, that Lewis never asked you not to give him away; he always sat back with a grin and watched you make up your own mind whether you should or not; he was not in the least grateful if you kept your mouth shut, but equally, he bore no malice if you gave him away. Either way, he thought it extremely funny.

The dinghy scraped over rock. He was nearing the entrance to the channel. Anquetil shipped his oars and the dinghy floated on, into the narrow tunnel the sea had channelled through the rock. It was always cold and dank in here, and it smelled heavily of decaying fish and seaweed. You had to pull the boat along by grabbing at spurs of rock, all right if there were two, not much fun for one. But at length the tunnel came to an end and the dinghy shot out into the sunlight. Anquetil looked ahead. His hunch had been right. The dinghy was there.

His first impulse was to land, overpower Lewis, and take the children off. But overpowering Lewis might not be easy. They were much the same weight and they had both served in the Commandos. In the kind of fight which would develop, either could win; and in the circumstances, a fifty-fifty chance was not good enough. If Lewis killed him, Lewis would be very sorry—afterwards. But a dead Robert—even a badly hurt Robert—would accomplish nothing. It was no occasion for bogus, single-handed heroics. His duty, here and now, was to return to the mainland and report his discoveries.

He wondered whether he should stove in the bottom of the dinghy. But he decided he would do better to get away, leaving no trace behind him. The less Lewis knew, the less he could defend himself. In any case, he couldn't go far in that cockle shell. As he worked his way back through the channel, Anquetil remembered that Lewis had once called him, in puzzled criticism, a cold, calculating piece of goods. Lewis never calculated and was proud of it; Robert, as he pulled in his anchor and sailed away, wished that cautious common sense were not one of his virtues, either. Glancing over his shoulder, he saw that the lighthouse was already growing smaller in the distance. He wished with all his heart he could have stayed there.

9

*

"The Children are Expendable"

Anquetil found Commander Whittier in a moderately good humour when he reached the police station. Lawrie had come round just after Anquetil had left, and had muttered drowsily about Peter's Foley and a boat in the fog, before she dropped off to sleep again. Whittier listened to what Anquetil had to tell and then said: "Well. We've a reasonably sound foundation to work on now. It's still touch and go, of course, but we've a fair chance of taking them. You saw no actual trace of the children?"

"No."

"They may be dead, of course."

"Yes." For of course they might. It was unlikely that Lewis would have killed all three deliberately, but at the same time, if the *Talisman* had been wrecked, Lewis might have had no chance, or even no inclination, to save anyone but himself. "But I think——"

"Well?"

"You don't think Foley may have meant to go to the lighthouse all along? To lie low there, I mean, while we were beating up and down in the supposition that he would be trying to put as much sea between us and himself as he could? He could have kept the *Talisman* under cover—there are plenty of anchorages among those rocks where you'd never see a small boat from the sea—and then at night—or in another fog—say, in a week's time—he could have slipped out and sailed away at leisure."

"And the children?"

"By that time, surely, he could afford to leave them there. It would probably be a little while before they were rescued—unless they were very lucky or very resourceful."

"Yes." Commander Whittier who had been standing looking out of the window turned round and had a look at Anquetil. "Tell me. Are you telling me what you'd have done, or what Foley might do?"

Anquetil flushed. "I don't know, sir."

"Well, I do. That waiting, cautious game is all very fine, but it's not Foley. He'd never have the patience to sit down for a week on the perfectly good chance that we'd think he'd slipped through our fingers in the fog." And Whittier smacked the back of his head, a gesture which all his subordinates used when they wanted to make it quite clear whom it was they were imitating. "Now you—you'd have it all worked out. You know the coast, you'd reckon how long the fog was likely to persist, how long before the hue and cry was raised, how far your boat would go in the time at your disposal, and you'd decide that you'd stand a better chance sitting quietly in the one place that was so obvious we wouldn't be likely to look at it. And I'll tell you another thing. You wouldn't be such a fool as to feed a horde of seagulls and draw attention to yourself. But Foley," he walked back to the table, and, taking one hand out of his pocket, began to leaf over the file lying there, "Foley's not like that. I had the Admiralty dig out his service record before I came down. I've been reading it this morning. Very interesting and very revealing. Now here," he put a long elegant hand flat on the page, "here's a wild, slapdash young man, with a life-and-death temperament. Plenty of courage, but no discipline. No loyalty, either. No idea of working as part of a team. You remember Operation Fireweed?"

Yes, Anquetil remembered.

"The worst casualties of any minor raid we had. And why? Because when Foley landed, he suddenly had a better idea. So off he goes on his own, bags the Commandant and the samples and forgets that his job is to silence the listening-post. So eighteen men are killed, six are so badly wounded that they have to be left behind and the rest of you get away by the skin of your teeth. If I'd been his Commanding Officer I'd have had him shot."

"Would you?" asked Anquetil with interest.

"If I could have got away with it. I've no use for the death-and-glory boys. Not when they jeopardize other men's lives and the success of the mission. Take yourself—you could have hung around the lighthouse this morning till the tide went down, waited your opportunity and grabbed Foley without any trouble at all. Or so a good many people might suppose. But you had more sense," said Whittier, slapping the table emphatically. "You saw the perfectly clear possibility of failure and what that would entail. So you came tamely home and reported. And quite right too."

"I'm glad you think so."

"Why? Aren't *you* sure?"

"Yes, sir. Rationally speaking. But——"

"Well, I'm only interested in speaking rationally. Now. The position is this. We have information that echoes, probably those of a submarine, were picked up here the day before yesterday." Whittier put his finger on the chart lying on the table. Anquetil got up to look. "The Admiralty say that none of our subs were reported as being in that position at that time. Foley is in the lighthouse, with or without the children. And sooner or later, now that the *Talisman's* gone, he and the U-boat have got to make contact at the lighthouse if he's to escape and hand over his information. Sooner or later, then, the U-boat has got to surface off the lighthouse, *unless——*"

"Unless?"

"Unless they decide that the information he's got isn't worth the risk and that Foley is expendable. In that case, we go in and take him off ourselves."

"But I thought——"

" 'M?"

"I thought his information *was* valuable. I thought that was why——"

"Oh yes, it's vital enough. The only question is whether they realize its value, or whether they've already had it from another source. Or, of course, whether Foley has already communicated it."

"Lewis would never be such a fool," said Anquetil with conviction.

"So I think. So I'm working on the assumption that they know the value of his information and that they're prepared to take the risk. In that case, all we have to do is wait. How near and from what direction could the U-boat approach?"

"Only from the east. From any other direction she'd be ripped to pieces on the rocks. They're like a fence. And even from the east, she can't approach within, say, a quarter of a mile. It's too shallow."

"She'll have to surface, though, to take Foley off. How near can she come then?"

"Not much closer in safety. A few hundred yards, perhaps. Otherwise, she'd risk running aground. In any case, she'll have to come in on the flood."

"And at midnight, since she's going to surface. Do you think she'll risk coming in while the exercise is on?"

"I wouldn't. Besides, she probably knows that's how she was spotted before. And look here, sir. She probably knows also that this is another anti-sub trial. She can't risk it when all our people will have their anti-sub devices full on."

"True. Then that still leaves us with Sunday night as the most probable time."

Anquetil nodded; but after a moment he said, uneasily: "But look here, sir."

"Well?"

"Where the children are concerned—aren't we taking a great risk? I mean—we don't know what their plans are—Foley's and his friends', I mean. Lewis may leave them behind, but he may as easily be forced to take them with him. Or—there's nothing to stop that boatload of thugs killing the children at the lighthouse and leaving them there. Oughtn't we to make sure of getting them away before——"

"How?"

"There's only Lewis to offer any resistance at the moment. If you gave me a couple of men we could land at low tide this evening and take them all off. And then we can wait for the U-boat as before."

"Can you land on the island without being seen?"

"Almost certainly."

"Almost isn't good enough. You forget that the children will probably welcome you with open arms. If they see you, they'll most likely raise the roof. Which will give Foley nice time to barricade himself in the lighthouse and warn the U-boat. And besides——"

"Sir?"

"We don't know for certain that the children are still alive."

"No," said Anquetil, after a silence, in a voice which did not seem to belong to him. "But suppose——"

"Well?"

"If they are—is it absolutely essential that the U-boat should be destroyed? If we take Foley before he can pass on the information, even if the U-boat escapes, won't we have done all that's essential?"

"No."

"Sir?"

"We're fairly certain that, so far, the U-boat has only been used as a carrier pigeon. But that's not the end of her uses. Suppose they want to land agents in this country? Suppose they decide that a little sabotage or a few bugs might be useful? The thugs who crew her have nothing to lose but their lives. So we must destroy them. And if we let them slip through our fingers now, we may waste months before we pick them up again. I'm sorry, Anquetil, but the potential danger is too great. If we're to make sure of making a clean sweep of this particular crowd, we can't consider what may happen to the children."

Anquetil said nothing.

"You understand me, don't you, Anquetil? There can be no question of any premature attempt to rescue the children. Once the issue is settled we'll do everything we can. But until then—*until* then, the children must be regarded as expendable."

There was a brief silence. Whittier glanced at Anquetil and then down to the file in front of him. Momentarily, he was unsure of Anquetil's response: it was a hundred to one that he had no intention of doing anything but obey orders, but there was the hundredth chance: and so he went on, as if there had been no break in their talk: "I said Sunday night as the most likely time for the U-boat to put in an appearance, but of course, we can't take anything for granted. How d'you feel about standing a twenty-four-hour watch till then? I can give you a couple of men—Bill Anstey and David Freer, probably. And I don't need to tell you not to make yourself conspicuous."

"Yes, I can keep watch, of course. And the *Enterprise* isn't remarkable in any way." Anquetil sounded faintly relieved. It would be something—not much, but something—to be within hailing distance.

"And if the U-boat should pop up, wireless us, and do what you can. I'll have something standing by, by then. But don't ruin everything, Robbie, by dashing in prematurely. We'll have to take a chance over the children. They're not", Whittier stared stonily at Anquetil, "our first priority. Remember that, young man, and go on remembering it."

[ii]

Anquetil went up to the hospital. A telephone call had come through while he was still at the police station to say that Lawrie had recovered consciousness for the second time and would be allowed to talk for a little if it was really important. Whittier thought it might be. The child might have noticed or remembered something which might be valuable—they couldn't tell. But Anquetil was to say nothing of what he knew or suspected. As for the wreck of the *Talisman*, that was still known only to the coastguards and the police, besides themselves. So far as Mrs. Marlow was concerned, she was to be told that nothing definite was known, but that the search continued.

"If you don't think you can manage that," said Whittier, "I'll send up the police sergeant. But the child may talk more easily to you, if she knows you know her sister."

Anquetil agreed and went. But he didn't relish the idea of the visit. He felt so horribly responsible. If only he had been more definite with Nicola—and yet, if he had, he might only have roused her curiosity and the result might have been much the same. The only thing to do was to put out of his head everything he knew or judged to have happened since the children disappeared. He did what he had done a number of times during the war, when, operating in enemy occupied territory, he had had to assume another identity with a particular story to tell. As he walked he told himself: "I spent the night at the station. Early this morning I went to Mariners. Since then I have inquired from the coastguards and the local police, but they have heard nothing. My own people have heard nothing. It is known that the Marlow children were at Mariners and that the *Talisman* and her dinghy have gone. In the absence of other evidence, we are assuming that she is still at sea and the search is continuing."

By the time he reached the hospital, this story was part of him. He went upstairs and found Mrs. Marlow waiting for him in the corridor. She looked white and anxious and she said at once: "You've no news?"

"I'm afraid not. Nothing at all yet. . . . How is Lawrie?"

"Better than they expected, I think. They say that long spell of unconsciousness was the best thing for her. She came round a little while after you left, but only for a moment and she was very dopey, so it didn't seem worth while getting you back. She says she hurts all over, but she's being very good—so far. But they don't want her to talk too much and the doctor said I was to tell you that he wants her to have something to make her sleep again as soon as possible."

Anquetil nodded and they went into the private ward. Lawrie was lying propped on pillows, the cage over her leg humping the blankets. "Hullo," said Anquetil. "Feeling better?"

"No," said Lawrie firmly and rather faintly. "I feel absolutely awful. How d'you do? Mummy says you want to talk to me about yesterday."

"Yes. Now look. I don't want you to have to talk too much. I'll try to ask the questions so that you can just say yes or no, or something brief like that. I'll tell you what we know so far, and then you can tell me whether we've got it right or not. All right?"

Lawrie nodded and then looked as if she wished she hadn't.

"Head bad?"

" 'M. Beastly."

"Poor old chap. Well now, listen. And then you can go back to sleep. Now; you and Nicola and the other two went back to Mariners yesterday. Any idea what time you got there? Before lunch?"

"About twoish, I think."

"I see. And you ran into Foley at once?"

"No. We—we were looking——"

"You were looking over the house. You went up to the crow's-nest?"

"Yes."

"And did you stay long?"

"Till the fog."

"I see." Anquetil thought back. "That would be about an hour, wouldn't it?"

"I don't know. P'raps."

"And then you came down from the crow's-nest, and you looked over the house?"

"Yes."

"And then you went down into the wine-cellar?"

"Yes. How did——?"

"Finger-prints."

"Coo!" said Lawrie more cheerfully. "Really?"

"Yes, really." Anquetil explained. "Well, now. You were in the cellar—and Foley found you?"

"After a long time. We found—we found—" Lawrie shut her eyes and screwed up her face as if something were hurting her and then said in a sort of gasp: "a box of things."

"What kind of things?"

"Photographs. A—a torpedo."

There was a short silence. Robert, remembering that Mrs. Marlow knew nothing of Foley and his activities, made his face look puzzled. He said: "Photographs? Does Foley know you found them?"

"Yes. Binks—I mean Peter—gave them to him before—before we knew."

Anquetil went on looking puzzled, but his heart sank. "I see. Did he say anything?"

"No. I mean, he waved his revolver about and said 'Get weaving' and things like that, but he didn't *say* anything." Lawrie screwed up her face again. Anquetil looked at her anxiously.

"Don't try to talk too much, Lawrie. Just listen. Foley got you out of the cellar and into the park. And while you were going through the park, you managed to escape?"

"Yes. I——"

"Never mind just how for the moment. But tell me this. Have you any idea at all when the others were taken off in the *Talisman*? Or if"—a new idea struck him—"if they were actually taken off?"

Lawrie did not answer for a moment. The pain in her head was really hurting her rather badly, and she was beginning to feel very tired and far away. But after a few moments she collected herself and said faintly: "They went away in the *Talisman* at once. I went and looked. I looked"—her voice began to shake—"for ages. And then I ran away."

"Do you know what time it was?"

"Sort of sunsetty."

"And the whole time you saw no one but Foley? No one at all?"

"No. But I thought I should. I thought all the time I'd run straight into the Master Spy." And then Lawrie's face quivered and tears rolled down her cheeks. She sobbed: "I'm awfully sorry, but my head does hurt so."

Mrs. Marlow looked anxiously at Anquetil. Anquetil said quickly: "That's all right—that's all, Lawrie. Thank you for telling me so much. You've been a great help. You can go back to sleep now as quickly as you like."

Mrs. Marlow rang the bell and they waited in silence until the nurse came and (with an indignant glance at Anquetil) gave Lawrie an injection. But just before she slid off to sleep, Lawrie said drowsily: "When will they be back?"

"Very soon now," said Anquetil. "Perhaps by the time you wake up again." But Lawrie was asleep almost before he had finished speaking.

Mrs. Marlow walked with him down to the main entrance.

"Was she any help?" she asked as they stood on the steps.

"Quite a lot. It clears up the times for us. Things like that." Anquetil began to say good-bye; there was one obvious question to be asked and he wanted to get away before Mrs. Marlow thought of it.

But Mrs. Marlow had thought of it. "Mr. Anquetil—what did Lawrie mean about finding photographs? She said something about a torpedo. What is it they've run into?"

"I'm not sure," said Robert slowly. "As far as we know, Mariners is being used by a ring of dope smugglers. But the photographs don't seem quite to belong with that."

"No, they don't. Mr. Anquetil——"

"Yes?"

"Would you think me a perfect fool if I said it sounded more like spies than dope?"

"No, I wouldn't at all. But we should have to know more

about the photographs than we do now to be sure of that," said Robert boldly.

"Yes. I suppose—I mean—whichever it is—the children are —are in—" Mrs. Marlow collected herself. "I mean, wherever they are or whoever they're with, they're in a good deal of danger."

Robert saw no sense in denying this. "Yes. I'm afraid they may be. Mrs. Marlow—don't think I'm being an alarmist— but couldn't you get your husband over? It would be company."

"Yes, I know. But he's concerned with this exercise, and I don't want to bring him over just—well, just because I'm frightened out of my wits. I'm hoping the children will be picked up before the exercise is over, and then he won't have to be worried. Of course, if they aren't, then he must be told."

Anquetil nodded. He could not bring himself to say: "Perhaps he ought to be prepared." So he said instead: "Yes, I see. And of course we'll let you know as soon as there's any news."

"Mr. Anquetil."

"Yes?"

"You really have heard nothing?"

"Nothing at all," said Anquetil steadily.

"Because—if you think it may be bad news, perhaps my husband should be told now."

Anquetil's inside seemed to turn over. He was torn between a desire to be properly frank with Nicola's mother, and his professional sense that no one must ever be told more than absolutely necessary. He had to say: "I don't think so. As he can't come over till Monday anyway, I don't think there's much point in worrying him unnecessarily."

Mrs. Marlow looked infinitely relieved. "That's all right, Mr. Anquetil. I thought you might be trying to break something to me gently. But you will let me know the moment you do hear anything, won't you?"

"Of course," said Anquetil and went on down the steps. As

he went, Mrs. Marlow remembered that she hadn't asked him how he came to know Nicola. If he had been in the Navy it would have explained itself; but Nicola had never made friends with Scotland Yard before. But it was too late now, and it didn't really matter. She went unhappily upstairs to sit with Lawrie, and stare out of the window and wonder about the three who were lost, and tell herself that if only she had stayed at the hotel instead of going to Farrant, none of this would have happened. It seemed almost worse than the time her husband's cruiser had been bombed and she had waited to hear if he were among the survivors.

Anquetil walked down to the quay and went aboard the *Golden Enterprise* to check her stores and give her a complete overhaul. It wasn't a particularly cold day, but he couldn't stop shivering. What with one thing and another, he felt more wretched than he'd ever done in his life before. He took the engine to pieces and cleaned it thoroughly and then, when he had reassembled it, went ashore to buy two more spare cans of paraffin. The *Enterprise* would be less conspicuous without her sails and that was essential, even though he meant to lie well away from the lighthouse. It was going to be difficult enough as it was, keeping continuous watch without arousing suspicion.

When he returned it was nearly sunset. As he came aboard, someone called to him from the cabin.

"That you, Robbie?"

"Yes. Who is it?"

"David Freer. I've got Bill Anstey with me."

"We didn't wait on deck," said Freer as Anquetil ran down the companion into the cabin, "because we thought we might cause comment. You know Bill, don't you?"

"I think so," said Robert. "Yes, of course. Salerno, wasn't it?"

" 'S right," said Bill gloomily. " 'Scuse me not getting up, but your cabin roof's beastly low and anyway I feel sick."

"We had a party last night," explained David.

"And the last thing my tum wants to do is put to sea," added Bill. "I'd have told old Whittier so, but he's in such a crashing rage, that I just said 'Aye, aye, sir' and came away. What's the matter? Has everything snarled up?"

"Not that I know of," said Robert, surprised. "It was all ticking over quite nicely the last time I saw him."

"It's those children who are mixed up in it who are upsetting him," said David, taking his feet off the table. "He and their father were the same term. He began telling me he didn't know what he'd say to Geoffrey Marlow if anything went wrong and then he smacked his head and shut himself up. So I didn't say anything either. So I don't really know what's happening, except that we're to play being a one-man blockade. What is going on, Robbie?"

"I'll tell you while we have supper," said Robert. He lit the primus and opened the store cupboard, feeling suddenly happier. If Whittier were disturbed about the children too, it wasn't so bad. Even though nothing had changed, it was better than it had been when Whittier had said in that savagely emphatic voice: *The children are expendable.*

[iii]

In the lighthouse, the afternoon and evening passed quietly. No more boats appeared, the tides came and went, the shutters were put up and the lamps were lit. They ate their supper, cleared it away and got out the patience cards. After a while, Foley and Peter played chess. Peter was rather good at chess; for a time it looked as if he had quite a good chance of winning. Nicola and Ginty left their patience games half-finished in order to watch. Very soon, each of the four was thinking the same thing: if Foley won, so would the enemy; if Foley lost, somehow the enemy would be defeated.

Chess is a creepy game. The pieces are moved, not so much for what they may do now, as for the way in which they will affect the game three or four moves ahead. The pauses became longer and longer. Foley had his pipe to smoke. Peter twisted a piece of string round and round his finger. Ginty dug her nails into her palms, and Nicola clutched the knife in her pocket. For a long time the pieces were moved about the board, were lost, were crowned, and then——

"Check," said Peter, his voice shaking.

"Mate," said Foley, and slipped his bishop across in the move he had foreseen three moves back.

"Good show," said Peter automatically, as if he didn't care. But he felt sick with disappointment. He sat staring at the board, wondering how he could have been such a fool as not to *see*. . . . But it was no good now. Foley had won. Nick had flushed, Ginty had grown white, and Foley was leaning back, his pipe between his teeth, smiling to himself. There was nothing for it, but to say how late it was and that it was time to go to bed.

10

Peter Makes a Plan

[i]

Peter woke early, as he had planned, while it was still dark. Looking at the luminous face of his watch, he saw that it was just ten past four. It was raining and blowing hard, and he could hear the spray being blown like buckshot against the glass. That was all to the good, thought Peter, sitting up and groping for his clothes. With all that racket going on, there was much less chance of Foley hearing him moving about.

He dressed sitting on the edge of his bunk. It would have been easier if he could have switched on his torch, but he wasn't sure how much of the battery was left. In any case, it wasn't really so dark, once his eyes got used to it. The broken cloud, scudding across the sky, let through quite a lot of moonlight. When he was ready, he picked up his shoes and crept across the floor. He turned the handle carefully, closed the door behind him, and waited a moment. If Foley had heard and came out to ask what he was doing he could say he'd felt hungry and was coming down to look for some biscuits. But there wasn't a sound. He turned and crept up the stairs to the door of the lantern. He opened it, slipped inside, closed it behind him and switched on his torch.

Like the rooms below, the lantern was circular, but it was much smaller. Only the walls which faced the sea were shuttered, so evidently there was no glass on the landward side here either. The only thing in the room besides the lantern was a chest standing against one wall. He didn't bother with that for the moment. What interested him most was the lamp itself. It stood on a stone pedestal in the middle of the floor with a sort of canopy over it and it looked surprisingly old and small; so did the reflectors. It could not throw its beam very far.

Really, it seemed to be nothing more than a large kind of oil lamp with a glass flue. Peter stared at it rather blankly for a moment, and then told himself not to be such an ass. After all, Fabian Foley had used it for wrecking and it had been lighted again for the Victory Celebrations. So it must work. It was stupid to expect electric light as if he were at the Lizard.

But where was the screen? You must have a screen to make the pattern of flashes, and there was nothing here that looked in the least like that. Nor, now he came to examine it, did it look as if the light revolved. Well, of course, the early lights had been fixed; and they had cut off the light by putting some sort of cylinder over them. Peter eyed the canopy, wondering if that was what you lowered; and then he saw a lever on the other side of the pedestal. He pressed it cautiously and a cylinder creaked down from the canopy and covered the lamp. It was primitive and rather stiff, but at any rate it was easy to work. The only thing you would have to be careful about would be to make sure you didn't hit the glass and break it. Otherwise, the flame—

Peter felt as if someone had hit him in the chest. None of this would be any good at all unless there were enough paraffin to keep the flame going. There was a can downstairs in the storeroom-cum-dining-room, but there wasn't much in it. Peter remembered how Ginty had had to tilt it when she had filled the lamp last night. And even if it had been full, they couldn't have been sure of getting hold of it. There were plenty of cans

of petrol—he remembered unloading them from the *Talisman*
—but Foley had taken those into the wireless room and that
was the one room with a key. And even supposing he could
think of a way to get at it, he didn't think an oil lamp would
burn on petrol.

He stood staring despondently at the lamp, his hands in his
pockets, and he remembered the game of chess. Foley had won
and that was all there was to it. It had been a good idea if it
had come off, but the lack of fuel was something you couldn't
get over. They might try signalling with their torches, but it
was a dreadfully forlorn hope. And anyway, he didn't see
where you put the paraffin, even if you had it. . . .

There was a metal rod leaning against the wall. Peter looked
at it and back at the lamp. The rod looked a bit longer than
the pedestal. He went over, picked it up, examined it, and saw
that it was marked off for intervals of an hour. It was greasy,
too. As he came back to the lamp from the other side, he saw
a metal cap on the top of the pedestal. It was stiff, and for a
long time it would not budge, but at last it gave, and he unscrewed it quickly. As he took it off a familiar, heavy smell rose
from the hole. He did not dare to think at all. He slid the rod
down through the hole, felt it touch bottom, and brought it up
again. The rod was shiny and dripping along nearly three-
quarters of its length. There was enough paraffin in the pedestal to keep the lamp alight for nearly eight hours.

He stood there, grinning idiotically. Whoever had had the
filling of the pedestal for the Victory Celebrations, must just
have emptied the paraffin in without worrying about how
much longer the lamp would need to burn.

All at once he felt very calm and confident; he knew what he
was going to do and how he was going to do it. It was a lovely
feeling and all he had to do now was tell Gin and Nick. He
switched off his torch, opened the door, and found Ginty and
Nicola standing on the threshold.

It was greatly to their credit that only one of them (they

never found out which) gave the smallest squeak of surprise. Then Peter whispered: "Come in here. Don't make such a row," and they were all standing in the lantern.

"What are you doing?" whispered Nicola as the door shut.

"Looking at the lamp. Why did you come up?"

"We were both awake and we thought we'd better talk to you. So we looked in your room and you weren't there and you weren't anywhere so we thought you must be here. I say, Binks——"

"Do we have to whisper?" asked Ginty, whispering too. "Foley can't hear us from here, can he?"

"No, of course not," said Peter in his normal voice. "Sorry. I say. I think it's going to be all right."

"Do you?" said Ginty hopefully. "Why, all of a sudden?"

"Because of the lamp. We can light it. So we can send out a signal. SOS, SOS, till someone answers. And then we can tell them."

"Suppose no one does answer?"

"They must. Don't you remember? The exercise finishes to-night. All the ships will be steaming back like they did the other morning. One of them's bound to see."

"It would be a jolly poor effort if they didn't," said Nicola. "But, Binks——"

"What?"

"Do you think we shall be able to come up here just like that? I mean—it's sort of our last chance. Don't you think Foley may be extra-specially watching us?"

"Yes. That's why I think one of us had better hide here. So that even if the others are pinned down, that one's free. Me, actually, I mean."

"But, *Binks*——"

"No, listen, Nick. I don't mean just stay up here. That would be mad. Of course he'd look for me. But if you and Ginty take the dinghy out, *either* you can pretend I've gone and you don't know anything about it, *or* you can say that we all tried to get away, but that I fell overboard and was drowned, so you came back. Whichever you like."

They thought it over. "I think the second would be better," said Ginty at last. For nearly the first time since Foley had caught them in the cellar, her voice sounded gay and ordinary.

"Why?" said Nicola, not arguing, just wanting to know.

"Because if he's drowned he won't look for him. And if he's just missing we'd have to stop him looking by saying the boat was gone. That might look a bit suspicious, don't you think?"

"I could have told you I was going," suggested Peter.

"Ye-es. But it'll look heaps more likely if we come in soaked and shivering and saying poor Peter's drownded," said Nicola with relish. "We might even lose an oar. Ginty's very good at sculling over the stern. I remember Daddy saying so."

"Yes, and look," said Ginty eagerly. "If he thinks we're utterly crushed about you, he won't think of us having the energy to try anything more. He won't watch us half as much."

Peter conceded this. "Well, then, to-night about eleven you come up here. There's no point starting before that and we *can* begin a bit later. We'll want matches——"

"And something to eat," said Nicola. "We may be signalling for hours and I shall get jolly hungry. And so will you all day. We'll have to smuggle you up something."

"Chocolate then. That's easy."

"And drinking water."

"And a lantern in case my torch gives out."

"Only whatever happens he mustn't see us taking them. I know. You can come down and get them now. Don't you see," said Ginty urgently, "that would be much more convincing. Anything that's gone can be stuff we took with us in the dinghy —much better than if things keep disappearing all day."

"All right. Then look. To-night Nick and I will do the signalling because we both know morse. And you can stand guard. It'll be pretty putrid, but you can have a lamp. Well, can't you?" as Ginty didn't answer. "One of us has got to keep watch in case he comes. We don't want him just bursting in on us."

All the gay energy with which Ginty had joined in the relief of planning to get away was gone. "Oh, Binks, *no*."

"But why not? I know it won't be much fun, but none of it will be. And one of us has got to, and you can't do morse."

Ginty said something, but so indistinctly, that all they heard was "last time".

"What last time? There isn't a last time. We've never done this before," said Nicola impatiently.

It felt as if she were being squeezed slowly into a small cold box. "At Mariners," said Ginty huskily. "When I was waiting. I saw his legs and I—I——"

"Poor old Gin," said Nicola at length.

Peter said with a rush: "It isn't worse than a boat thing I did last term. It just happens sometimes."

"And even if you had warned us," added Nicola practically, "I don't suppose it would have made any difference. He'd have caught us just the same."

"And anyway, I should have thought he was all right and handed the stuff over," said Peter. "So it would *all* have happened just the same."

They were being very decent about it. Perhaps everyone would be. And that didn't make any difference either. If she knew what the boat thing was that Peter was talking about, she'd naturally be decent about that, but she'd very likely think him a bit of a dope all the same.

"Look here, then," said Peter. "We'll take it in turns. One of us will have to watch for the answering signal, and you can do that just as well as either of us, till the message starts. So you won't be out there all the time. And anyway, he mayn't come."

Ginty said no more. You couldn't very well say you wouldn't stand your turn. And suddenly there seemed nothing more to arrange. They stole downstairs and collected the things Peter needed—the matches, the chocolate, an opened tin of ham, some biscuits, a flask of drinking water, a lantern and some candles. They had better not risk anything in the way of chess or patience cards, they decided. It would be a dreadfully long dull day for Peter, but no one was going to believe they'd taken a nice game of chess to play in the dinghy going home. They helped him carry the stuff upstairs and Nicola nodded towards the chest.

"If Foley does come up here, you can hide in that, p'raps."

Peter nodded. He hadn't really thought what might happen if Foley came up to the lantern during the day, but that was a risk he'd have to take. He hoped this was the best plan and that they hadn't made it unnecessarily complicated, but it was too late to begin chopping and changing now. It would be awful to wait till evening and then find that Foley meant to tie them up, just to make sure. Only, if this *didn't* work, if Foley discovered him after they'd said he was drowned, then the whole thing would be blown sky-high. There were risks either way, and there was no way of telling which was worst. They would just have to go ahead and hope for the best.

Nicola and Ginty were ready to go.

"Take care," he whispered as Ginty opened the door, and Nicola gave him the V-sign. "Don't drown yourselves."

"Not us. Only you," whispered Nicola cheerfully. And then the door shut and he was alone.

It was just beginning to get light. Ginty and Nicola crept down the stairs in the grey, rainy light and out of the lighthouse. The tide was on the turn, and the noise of the sea covered the sound of their footsteps on the shingle.

"I say, Nick."

" 'M?"

"If we *could* get away in the dinghy—I know it would be awfully mean to leave Binks—but do you think we ought to?"

"Yes," said Nicola decidedly. "I'm sure we ought. But I don't think we could possibly row that far. I mean, I can't row at all because I've never learned, and you couldn't possibly row all that way by yourself. Besides, look at the sea. I should think we'd be swamped almost at once."

Ginty said no more. They walked out along the little causeway, got into the dinghy, untied her, and pulled in the kedge. Then—

"How do we get away?" said Nicola, looking round her.

They looked at one another in dismay. It looked as if they lay in a little lake.

"There must *be* a way," said Ginty, pulling herself together. "You can see the high-water mark. The entrance must be hidden, somehow. I'll scull round, and you look hard, Nick."

Nicola did as she was told, though she rather wondered whether it wouldn't be simpler to haul the dinghy over the rocks and launch her in open water. But as they passed it, she saw the mouth of the tunnel.

"There it is, Gin. Through there. You can see the light at the other end."

Ginty looked. For a moment she thought she was going to hear herself saying that she couldn't *possibly* go through there —not to escape, not to confound Foley, not for anything. And then she found she couldn't say that, either. Sometime she was going to have to shut up about being scared stiff or it would always be like that afternoon at Mariners. She turned the boat without a word and slipped through the entrance.

"I can't use the oars," she said in a choked voice which sounded hollow as it echoed along the tunnel. "We'll have to pull ourselves along by the rocks."

She heard Nicola say cheerfully: "What a perfectly stinking stink there is," but she couldn't answer. The walls and roof of the tunnel seemed to get narrower and closer as they went along, and every now and then a wave, pouring in through the seaward end of the tunnel, lifted them nearly to the roof.

Ginty's mouth was dry and her heart was pounding; in another minute she'd have to say they must turn back, that she couldn't stand this another second—but looking back over her shoulder she saw that the entrance was as far away as the outlet. They were at—what was it called?—the point of no return. Ginty swallowed hard, and pulled, grabbed at the next piece of jutting rock and pulled on that, saw a wave break before it ran foaming and swirling into the tunnel and lifted them up towards the roof—and then, suddenly, unbelievably, the tunnel was coming to an end and they were shooting out into the free air with the sky far above their heads. Ginty seized the oars as an incoming wave broke and carried them back towards the tunnel. There was a wild moment of flurry and struggle and then they were drifting in comparatively calm water in the shelter of the rocks.

"We look jolly wet and shipwrecked," said Nicola with satisfaction, looking at Ginty and herself and the water sloshing in the bottom of the boat. "What now?"

Ginty shook her head. For the moment she felt quite spent. She had shipped the oars and put her head down on her knees to try to get her breath back, as if it were the end of a race and everything was over. But Nicola's question reminded her that it wasn't. It was only beginning. They weren't getting away, they were only pretending to. They'd got to get back. . . . Ginty sat up.

"I think we'd better upset the dinghy and let her go," she said. "Then it'll look as if we overturned and Binks was swept away."

"All right," said Nicola. "And then we can get back over the rocks—I s'pose."

"How d'you mean—you s'pose?"

"Well, they all look so very steep and edgey. But I suppose it won't matter if we look a bit scraped. Look. If we climb on that rock, we can turn her over and give her a shove and she'll go off."

"She won't. She'll go quietly into that little bay. You go ashore, Nick. I'll take her out a bit and swim back."

"Can you?"

"Of course I can."

"Well, if you say so," said Nicola doubtfully. She climbed on to the ledge of rock and watched unhappily while Ginty rowed out into the open water where the waves were shorter and steeper. It was very lucky, thought Nicola, that their plan hadn't depended on being able to row away. Even with Peter in the dinghy, it obviously wouldn't have been possible. And it didn't look as if Ginty would have any bother upsetting the boat; she was going to upset by herself. And if Ginty took her out much further, she wouldn't be able to swim back. And Nicola couldn't help. She had only just learned to swim the width of the baths at the end of last term. Suppose it was going to be true when she got back that one of them had been drowned? Suppose she had to go scrambling back over the rocks by herself and tell Foley something that was to have been a useful lie and had now become suddenly and horribly true. Suppose——

Ginty was thinking much the same thing. The dinghy was becoming difficult to handle, and the rock where Nick was standing seemed a horribly long way off. Only it was no use upsetting the dinghy in a place where it couldn't float away; Ginty rowed another stroke or two, feeling the icy morning wind strike hard through her soaked jersey. For the first time at sea, the familiar feeling of panic was rising inside her, and she had a horrible feeling that in another moment she wouldn't be able to upset the boat at all. For the sea looked simply awful; not in the least like the friendly holiday sea Ginty loved; this one was dark green and solid and laced with foam as far as she could see. But there was no use thinking about it. If she did, she'd be so petrified that in another minute she wouldn't be able to swim a stroke. She shipped her oars and sat quite still for a moment, trying to calm herself. It wasn't any *good* thinking how cold the water would be and how strong the current and how likely it was she'd get cramp. Perhaps if she took an oar with her, she could swim and rest a bit if she had to, and swim and rest again—

She pulled one of the oars out of its rowlock. And as she did so, the current swung the dinghy round broadside to the breaking seas. The next moment she was gulping for breath beneath the surface.

Fortunately she had kept hold of the oar. It gave her a certain amount of confidence, which she badly needed at the moment. Streaking the length of the baths or wallowing for fun in a rough sea were entirely different from fighting for your life in icy water against a dragging current. Blinking the water out of her eyes, she could just make out Nicola crouched on the ledge of rock, gazing anxiously across at her. Ginty struck out with her legs, pushing the oar in front of her. She was making a certain amount of headway, but all the time the tide was pulling her sideways, in the same direction as the dinghy, towards the open sea. She struggled on, feeling the sea become steadily more solid-feeling and cold; perhaps it wasn't worth struggling; perhaps she should just let the current carry her where it would; perhaps—and what was Nick doing? Ginty, who was further in than she realized, saw that Nick was scrambling along the ledge as if trying to keep pace with her; and now she was letting herself down from the ledge and beginning to wade out. Ginty wished she wouldn't. Nick couldn't swim nearly well enough. If she fell in. . . . She struggled on furiously, watching Nick wade slowly forward, slip, recover and come on, and was so absorbed by her fear that Nicola might stumble and be swept away that she barely noticed how close in she had come until she felt an agonizing blow on her leg just below the knee. She cried out and sank. But as she did so, she put her feet down instinctively, and jarred them on solid rock. The next moment she was no longer swimming, but scrambling towards Nicola across the sharp, barnacle-covered rocks, slithering on the seaweed, but getting closer every moment. In another instant, Nicola had reached out and grabbed her hand. The ledge sloped gently here; they were able to stumble up a shallow rise and lie sprawled, dripping and shivering, out of the reach of the sea.

But it was bitterly cold in the wind. Nicola yanked at Ginty's arm. "We can't stay here, Gin. We must get back."

Ginty, who was lying face downwards on the rock, didn't answer. She felt too exhausted even to shake her head. She went on lying there until Nicola shook her arm again and then found voice enough to say: "I thought I'd never make it."

"So did I."

"It was awful." But the painful sensation of not being able to breathe was leaving her, and she rolled over rather slowly, so that she could look at Nicola. "If I hadn't crashed into that rock, I think I'd have been swept right past."

"I say, Gin! You *have* banged your knee."

"I know. Didn't you hear me yell? It was where the ledge

started under the sea, I think." Ginty hitched up her damaged leg so that she could have a look at it and said: "Golly, what a lot of bleed. But things always do when they're wet, don't they?"

"I suppose so," said Nicola doubtfully. "But it looks a nasty sort of cut, just the same. Gin, aren't you awfully cold?"

"I suppose I am. But I can't move yet. None of me wants to get up at the moment. Couldn't you go and have a look and see what's our best way back?"

Nicola got up. She felt pretty chilly herself, and tired too, which was absurd, because it wasn't as if she'd done any swimming. She'd only, she told herself severely, sat comfortably on a rock and watched Ginty. She felt sure they ought to get back to the lighthouse as quickly as possible. Ginty looked very queer and white and the cut on her knee was a bad one. As she scrambled to the top of the ridge, Nicola thought that perhaps they'd better tie it up, even though their hankies were soaked. Then she hauled herself up the last few feet to the top and stared about her. After a few moments, she climbed down again and went back to Ginty who was still lying flat with her eyes shut.

"Gin——"

"Hullo. I say, Nick. I feel rather sick. I think I must have drunk a lot of sea."

"Why don't you be sick, then?"

"It doesn't feel like *being* sick," said Ginty in a drowsy-sounding voice. "Only just sick inside."

"Oh. Well, look Gin. I don't think we can get back over the rocks. They rise up, quite steep. I don't think we could possibly climb them. And I don't expect I could swim enough in between. The sea simply swishes round them."

"What do we do, then? Stay here?"

"Oh, Gin, do wake up. Of course we can't stay here. We've got to get back because of to-night."

"Couldn't we signal a ship from here?"

"No, we couldn't. There are rocks in the way. If you sit up you'll see."

Ginty opened her eyes, and, with an evident effort, sat up. She looked about her and said: "Oh." After a moment, she said: "What are we going to do, then?"

"Well—I s'pose we'll have to wade back through the tunnel."

"Oh, Nick, *no.*"

"But, Gin, we must. It's not like a real tunnel. You didn't mind coming through."

Ginty looked at the sea. After a moment she said: "But how d'you know we can wade? It may be frightfully deep."

"I don't think so. I felt the dinghy scrape lots of times. But **if** you don't want to, you'd better think of something else."

"I'll go and look," said Ginty. She got up, and went off towards the ridge, limping rather. She felt odd and rather trembly, as if she had banged other bits of her, as well as her knee. And she did feel awfully sick. Her inside felt most peculiar. And suddenly she was extremely sick; once it was over she felt better.

But Nicola had been right. They couldn't get back by way of the encircling rocks. Unless—Ginty's spirits rose a little— suppose they went along the ledge as far as it would take them. They might be able to climb along the roof of the tunnel. It was worth trying. Ginty went back to Nicola and suggested this.

"All right," said Nicola, "I don't mind trying. But I bet it'll be the tunnel in the end."

The tide had gone down some way by this time. The lower ledge which had been covered when they first came out of the tunnel was now bare wet rock. The wind blew through their wet clothes and made their teeth chatter. But it was fairly easy going, and they soon passed the mouth of the tunnel. And then, as she walked confidently forward, Nicola walked straight into the sea.

It felt as if the whole of the sea was rushing up her nostrils and into her mouth. She came to the surface, choking and momentarily terrified. Then she felt someone grab at her arm and the next moment she was sprawling and scrambling back on to the ledge. She lay face downwards on the rock, coughing and choking and trying to breathe.

"Come on," said a harsh voice. "You're not dead yet. Get up."

Nicola went on choking. She felt so sore and shocked and uncomfortable, that for some moments she hardly realized what had happened. Then Foley bent down and yanked her to her feet. "You little fool," he said. "You might have been drowned. Where's Peter?"

"Peter?" gulped Nicola. For the moment she really didn't remember. It was Ginty, standing pressed back against the rock on the narrow shelf near the tunnel who said: "We think he—we think——"

"What?" said Foley, spinning round.

Ginty clenched her hands behind her. "We—he—when the dinghy upset——"

"What d'you mean?"

"He—we couldn't see him——"

She said it very well. Even Lawrie, thought Nicola admiringly, couldn't have said it better. Foley stared from one to the other and then past them, towards the sunrise, where the dinghy was slowly drifting, keel upwards, into the smother and roar of the waves breaking at the base of the rocks. It looked horribly convincing. Foley said slowly: "Where were you when it happened?"

Ginty pointed vaguely.

"He must have struck his head," said Foley, half to himself. "Otherwise he should have been able to make it."

Ginty said nothing. Nor did Nicola. She cleared the last of the sea-water out of her eyes and moved closer to Ginty.

"You don't think," said Ginty at last, "that he might—I mean——"

"I'm terribly sorry about it. But even if we had a boat," said Foley gently, "I don't think there'd be the slightest use trying to look for him. He must have struck his head and been carried out on the undertow." He looked at the two draggled children in front of him and said: "There's no use standing here. We'd better get back to the lighthouse and get you into some dry clothes."

He gave Nicola a gentle shove in the direction of the tunnel and she stumbled forward obediently. Ginty hung back for a moment, and then followed, the blood singing in her ears. The water was quite shallow now, barely as high as their knees in places, though now and then the rock sloped down until it rose to their waists. Nicola, dazed, soaked, chilled to the bone, her teeth chattering uncontrollably, still had room to feel triumphant: it had been a beastly, uncomfortable, frightening time, but they had brought it off; it was so far so good. But Ginty felt differently; she had had, on the whole, the more strenuous morning in every way, and Foley's gentleness had been the last straw. An enormous unhappiness, made up of fright and pain and anxiety, descended on her. Her knee was hurting her badly, with every step her terror at being in the tunnel increased, Mummy must be frantic with worry by now, they would never get home again, to-morrow she was going to be shoved into a submarine, and anyway they would never get out of this tunnel because every minute the roof was coming lower and the sides were closing in and there were odd, terrifying sounds in the rock as if it was beginning to break up. Ginty stubbed her toe in shallow water and went down on her hands and knees, grazing herself badly. She picked herself up and stumbled on, but her self-control was ebbing fast; and as they neared the end of the tunnel and the daylight showed along the walls, Ginty began to sob.

[ii]

The lighthouse seemed almost homely when they returned

to it after all the turmoil of the sea. Foley produced an old towel and a first-aid box, a couple of rough jerseys and two pairs of shorts from the sail locker which stood against the wall in the room in which they ate, and told them to go and get changed and bandaged. They went obediently, Ginty still sobbing helplessly. Unlike Lawrie, she cried very seldom. But when she did begin, it was a long time before she could stop. In the ordinary way, Nicola would have tried to do or say something to make Ginty stop crying so hard, but she felt so stupid and shivery herself that she couldn't think properly. And then, just at the most inconvenient moment, just as she had stripped off her wet clothes and was all cluttered up with towel, Foley came upstairs and, to Nicola's horror, went straight past their door and up to the lantern.

For a moment she stood petrified. Then she tore after him, tripping absurdly in the towel ("just like a *hen*", said Nicola, describing it afterwards) and calling loudly.

"What on earth's the matter with you?" demanded Foley, reappearing round the curve of the stairs.

Nicola clutched his arm and blurted out the only thing she could think of.

"G-Ginty. She's crying frightfully. I don't know what to do."

"Nor do I. Let go my arm, Nicola." He wrenched himself free, and said, not at all gently: "I'm going up to the lantern to see if I *can* see anything of your brother after all. He *may* be stuck on a rock somewhere. If he is, we'll have to think of a way of getting to him."

"I'll come too," said Nicola in a great hurry, her teeth chattering loudly.

"Don't be absurd. You can't caper about the gallery in nothing but a towel. You get some clothes on and tell Ginty to get a hold on herself."

He turned to go. And Nicola, who could think of nothing more to say to delay him, let him go. At the back of her mind she knew that the sensible thing to do would be to get dressed as quickly as possible, but she simply couldn't move. If Foley found Peter, towel or no towel, she'd have to go and help. She went on standing there, her bare feet icy on the stone stairs and her teeth chattering uncontrollably. She heard the door into the lantern open and close and after that a long silence. Then the door opened again and Foley came downstairs.

She stared at him dumbly. He glanced at her, hesitated, shook his head briefly and went on downstairs.

Too numb with cold to think coherently, Nicola went back to their room. She pushed the now sodden towel at Ginty, and, with hands which shook and stumbled, pulled on the shorts and jersey. They were several sizes too big, but at least they were dry. She looked at Ginty, told her gruffly to get a move on, and went downstairs.

Foley was just lighting the primus. Nicola sat down on one of the chairs, still shivering violently, and stared at his back. She still couldn't think properly, and when Foley said suddenly: "What on earth's that noise?" she gazed at him blankly.

Foley looked at her and said: "Good Lord, it's your teeth chattering. Can't you hear yourself?"

Nicola couldn't. Then she made an effort to listen, and found he was quite right. She tried to clamp her jaws shut, but she couldn't prevent them from coming loose occasionally. And then Ginty came in, tears still rolling down her cheeks and still wrenched with sobbing. Foley looked at her helplessly and then at Nicola.

"Can't you make her stop?" he asked in a curt angry voice. "She'll make herself ill."

Nicola shook her head. But she thought Foley had better know it was no use his getting furious with Ginty, and she forced herself to say after a moment in a husky jerking voice: "No one can when she starts. She just goes on till she stops of herself."

Foley looked at Ginty as if he didn't like her much, and then turned abruptly away and went on getting the breakfast. Presently Nicola found herself drinking cocoa which tasted of sugar and something else. After a bit, as the hot drink began to make her feel warmer and more sensible, she decided Foley must have put some rum in it. It made the cocoa taste beastly, but it did stop her teeth banging together.

She looked at Ginty, wondering if she was feeling better too. But Ginty, though she was drinking her cocoa, was still crying. All the same, though she couldn't think what had made Ginty start one of her crying fits, which always made Nicola feel squirmy inside even when they happened at home, she had to own that it couldn't, if you looked at it in one way, have come at a better time. Foley was bound to think it was because of Peter being drowned, and so there was no need for Nicola herself to do anything but be rather silent and miserable and—what was it she'd heard someone say in a bus when they were talking about a funeral? *"Dazed with the shock, my dear. Couldn't seem to take it in at all."* Nicola thought she'd be like that. Because whatever happened she wasn't going to say or do anything that would make Foley be sorry and kind. It was all right to tell him Peter was dead and get away with it if they could; Nicola thought a person must be pretty feeble-minded if they counted a lie told to a traitor as a real lie; but all the same she didn't want him to start comforting them.

But Foley had never been the kind of person who finds it easy to say comforting things, and like Nicola, he found the sound of Ginty's sobs thoroughly unnerving. And when, through the rest of breakfast and washing-up, Ginty continued to sob and show no sign of stopping, he suddenly remarked savagely: "If you can't control yourself you'd better go and lie down, and try to get some sleep. But I can't stand that noise any longer and I don't suppose Nicola can either."

Ginty was not surprised. It was the way people generally did speak to her after a bit. In fact, at home, Mummy generally sent her to bed as soon as she started. So she hiccupped her way upstairs to her bunk, rolled herself in her sleeping-bag, and after a while fell asleep from sheer exhaustion.

Nicola yawned. What with the rum and one thing and another, she wouldn't have minded a little extra sleep either. But she thought someone ought to keep an eye on Foley. Otherwise, thought Nicola sleepily, he might wander up to the lantern. And suddenly, as if someone had thrown a bucket of cold water over her, Nicola stopped yawning. For Foley had been up to the lantern. Ages ago, when she was feeling colder and more stupid than she had ever felt in her life before, Foley had gone upstairs and—And what?

Nicola stared at him across the table. He had lighted his pipe and was setting out the chessmen. She stared at the red knight and her imagination began to gallop. Suppose Foley had found Peter? Suppose he'd knocked him on the head and tied him up? Suppose he'd tipped him off the gallery into the sea? Suppose—?

Nicola clenched her hands and tried to think back. What actually *had* happened? He'd gone into the lantern and then—then nothing. Nothing for ages, till he came downstairs again. And then he'd just shaken his head and gone by. It might really just have meant he hadn't seen Peter anywhere; or—Foley might be good at telling lies too. A traitor would have to be, thought Nicola, her heart thumping at least as loudly as her teeth had chattered; it was a wonder Foley didn't hear it. But he only looked up and said: "Can you play chess? or is Demon your only game?"

"Yes," muttered Nicola. "I mean—no—I——"

But Foley didn't seem to care which she meant. He went on gazing at the chessmen, absorbed in the problem he had set himself. Nicola propped her chin in her hands and stared too, her thoughts racing. If only she knew how much Foley knew; the thing she most wanted to do was to dash up to the lantern and see what had happened. But she couldn't see how she was to get there. The lavatory was no good—it was on the floor below; and to be caught going secretly upstairs might be fatal; if Foley didn't know already, he might easily begin to guess. She *could* say she wanted to see how Ginty was—but suppose he came to look for her? If he found her in the lantern she could say she wanted to make sure Peter wasn't on any of the rocks. . . . It sounded awfully feeble, somehow. And if Foley *had* found Peter—if he knew all the time. . . . Nicola thought she knew just how a mouse feels when the cat sits crouching over it, pretending not to notice. . . . Besides, if Foley *had* found Peter, they would have to make another plan. At least—*she* would have to make another plan. There wasn't anyone else.

Nicola blinked at the chessmen. Then she found her eyes had closed and opened them in a hurry. But she could feel her lids dropping again . . . she came to with such a jump that she knew she must have been asleep. Perhaps it would be a good thing to put her head on the table . . . pretend to be asleep. . . . Foley might give himself away . . . or go down to the wireless room . . . or talk to himself . . . if only she could shut her eyes . . . just for a moment . . . you often woke up as soon as you tried to go to sleep. . . .

Nicola sat up with a start, her heart pounding, and Foley's hand on her shoulder. For one horrible moment she thought she had slept the clock round and it was morning.

But the lamp was alight and Foley was saying: "That was a fine sound sleep you've had. Shows what a clear conscience can do for you. But don't you think you'd be more comfortable in your bunk?"

It was half-past nine. Nicola got off her chair, feeling stiff and sleep-sodden. The fears and speculations she had gone to sleep with jostled in her mind: Did he know? had they failed?

She said "Good night" and so did Foley. It sounded ordinary enough. He added that she'd better take some biscuits in case she felt hungry in the night.

And that sounded ordinary enough too. Or did it? Did he

know they meant to sit up signalling and was he, like Miss Cromwell at school, being sarcastic and beastly?

There was no way of knowing. No way of knowing either what Foley might have done all day, while she was asleep like the dormouse in *Alice*. Nicola remembered a phrase Giles used sometimes and applied it to herself: she'd made a complete nonsense of the whole thing. She said good night again, and went meekly up to bed.

*

Mutiny in the "Golden Enterprise"

[i]

The weather was getting worse. Anquetil had closed the distance between the *Enterprise* and the lighthouse, but it was difficult to see much. Fortunately, the bad weather worked both ways: it cut down visibility, but it also made it unlikely that the U-boat would surface to take Lewis and the children on board. And in an hour or so the tide would have passed the flood and the likelihood of the U-boat surfacing would decrease until the next tide. All the same, it was just as well they were keeping watch, even though Bill Anstey didn't seem to be enjoying it much. If it came to that, he and David Freer weren't having too good a time, either. The smack's motion was always uncomfortable in a swell, particularly when she was hove to. Anquetil lowered his binoculars for a moment as the *Enterprise* dropped into the trough of a wave, lurched, and wallowed up again. He wished David would get a move on with that tea he'd gone down to make half an hour ago.

At that moment, the sliding hatch was pushed back and David's head appeared. He scrambled on deck and in another moment had dropped into the cockpit.

"Where's the tea?"

"Nowhere. I mean, I haven't made any. I've been mucking about doing things for Bill. You know, Robbie, I don't think he's just sea-sick. I think he's ill."

Robert stared at him. "How's he ill?"

"Well, he feels hot and queer. And he's got a pain, he says. A very bad pain, apparently."

"Bill always did have worse pains than anyone else. If he cut a finger, his arm was coming off."

"Yes, I know. I thought that at first. But he started to babble, a while back, and then he got quite sensible, and now he's babbling again. You know what I think?"

"I know what I think."

They looked apprehensively at one another.

"Appendicitis?"

"Could be, couldn't it?"

"One thing I'm not going to do," said David firmly, "is open Bill up with a penknife, while you stand by with a hurricane lamp. I know it's the best way to get our pictures in the papers, but I just don't happen to fancy it, somehow."

"Nor I. Poor old Bill. Well, we'll just have to make him as comfortable as possible, till——"

"Till when? Not till this trip's over. He could be dead by then."

Robert stared at the rain-blurred outline of the lighthouse.

"Robbie! You don't seriously think we can leave him down there for the next few days, do you?"

"Suppose we take him back? Suppose it's not appendicitis? Suppose while we're away the U-boat does surface? What then? It'll take three hours or so to get back to Oldport, and another three hours or so to return. A lot could happen in that time."

"Yes," said David, who had turned rather white. "Or we can stay and Bill may die."

"*Yes, I know*. But—forgive me, David—the other would be far more disastrous."

After a pause, David said in a calmer voice: "Look, Robbie. This watch we're standing is really only a precaution. Whittier doesn't expect anything to break until Sunday night—you said so yourself. Bill's illness is a certainty and the other's only a possibility. Look here—if you think I'm exaggerating, come down and see for yourself."

They went down into the cabin. It was obvious, as Robert saw at once, that Bill was ill enough to make a return to port the only feasible course—if only there were no other considerations. He said as much to David.

"But I keep telling you," shouted David. "The U-boat's barely a possibility at the moment. If you weren't so obsessed about those Marlow children we wouldn't be here now. Whittier said so."

"Said what?"

"That you had to be kept quiet and happy, and that out here you could have the illusion of being useful without making a nuisance of yourself. *Now* will you turn back?"

There was a short silence. Then Robert said, in a flat-sounding voice: "All right. As soon as the tide turns."

"How long is that?"

"About an hour and a half."

"And suppose that's too late? Look here, Robbie. Whittier knows as much as you do. If he's satisfied that nothing will happen till Sunday night, why are you being so fatuously obstinate?"

"Because there's always the possibility he's wrong."

"And you won't turn before the ebb?"

"No," said Robert, going towards the companion ladder.

David said no more. He too had been in the Commandos. He knew exactly how and where to hit a man so that he crumpled instantly and hardly knew he had been hit. As Robert put his hand on the ladder, David struck. Then he lugged

Robert on to his bunk, ran up the ladder, bolted the hatch, and turned the *Enterprise* towards St.-Anne's.

[ii]

Robert lay and stared at the cabin roof for some moments without quite knowing what he was looking at or where he was. His head was aching furiously and someone was banging a mallet or a chunk of wood somewhere quite close. It took him a while longer to realize that the noise was inside his head. Then, somewhere in the cabin, someone groaned. For a moment, Robert thought it was himself; then, as it happened again, found it wasn't. He sat up, swung his legs over the side of the bunk, felt his head spin giddily, saw Bill Anstey, and began to remember.

After a bit, he got off his bunk and stood up, clutching shakily at the table. The deck seemed to be lurching a good deal, but he got across and, with an effort, climbed the companion ladder. He tugged at the hatch, but found it immovable. David must have bolted it. He was about to hammer on it, when it occurred to him that this would be useless and not particularly dignified. David would only let him out when they were so near port that he could do no harm. He went back down the ladder and for the first time became conscious that the air in the cabin smelt stuffy and foul. It probably wasn't Bill's fault that he kept being sick, but that didn't help anybody much.

Robert opened a port-hole and stuck his head well in the line of air and spray. His head began to clear. To his surprise, the lights on shore looked very near. He looked at the clock and found it was nearly seven. So he had been out nearly three hours. David had been almost excessively thorough.

He decided it would be as well to clean the place up a bit. While he was doing so, he felt the keel scrape the shoal at the harbour mouth, and, after a little, felt the boat lose way. He could hear the familiar sounds of anchoring and tying up, and

then the hatch was pushed back, and David came slowly down
into the cabin. He looked at Robert as if he were about to say
something, thought better of it, and said instead: "How's Bill?"

"About the same, I think."

"Oh . . . I've sent a kid along to phone the ambulance. I
don't suppose they'll be long. You can turn her straight round
and go back if you like."

"I'm afraid not," said Robert politely. "I shall have to wait
for the tide. We scraped coming in, you know."

"Oh." David glanced at him uncomfortably. "Look, Robbie, I'm sorry about this. If anything happens about the other
—if anything goes wrong—I'll take the blame, of course."

"Oh yes," said Robert politely. "I'm sure you will."

"Why not say it, Robbie? You'll feel much better."

But Robert only eyed him blankly. There was no point in
cursing David; whatever the consequences, the thing was done
now; calling David every name under the sun would change
nothing. And besides, despite his manner, he felt so savage
with rage, that if he once gave it expression, he was not likely
to stop at words. As he very well knew, he had a temper as
murderous as Lewis Foley's if he once let himself go.

In the distance the clanging of an ambulance bell made itself heard, came rapidly closer, and stopped. David ran up on
deck and in a few moments the ambulance men came aboard.
In a very short time, Bill was lying on the stretcher and being
carried on deck.

"I may as well go with him," said David. "And then I'll go
and report to Whittier. I'll be back before the tide."

Robert merely nodded. When David and Bill and the ambulance had gone, he finished the cleaning up, left the port-
holes and the hatch open and went ashore. He thought he
might as well get some supper, and he thought it would be as
well to have it in company. It was useless to sit glowering in
the cabin, thinking of all the violent and painful deaths it
would be pleasant to watch David die. He nodded Hullo to

Ginger and Jackie Peterson, the young sons of one of the local fishermen, who were hanging about the quay, and went on towards the shore.

He found himself yawning. It occurred to him that he had had no sleep for the last thirty-six hours, nor very much to eat either. His head was still aching from David's blow, too. Still, hot food and plenty of it would probably put all those things right. And it was quite true that after a large plate of steak and chips and a double whisky at the pub at the end of the hard, he did begin to feel more like himself. He was just lighting his pipe, when he heard a shrill voice yelling his name: "Mr. Bob! Mr. Bob! Come quick!"

He was out of the pub in an instant. Ginger Peterson grabbed his arm.

"Mr. Bob, the *Enterprise*! That motor-cruiser's drifting down on her! Jackie's yelling at them, but they don't take no notice."

It was going to be too late. Robert could see that as he began to run. He could hear Jackie's shrill little voice as he capered anxiously on the edge of the quay and Ginger Peterson still panting out his story as Robert left him behind. He was still only half-way along the quay when the *Fair Wind* struck the *Enterprise* and drove her against the quay with an agonizing, crunching, splintering sound.

The *Fair Wind*'s owner was volubly apologetic. He came aboard the *Golden Enterprise* and accompanied Robert on his despairing tour of inspection. It wasn't as bad as it might have been, but it was bad enough. If the rudder had been undamaged, Robert might still have managed to put to sea. As it was, it was hopeless.

As earlier with David, Robert was extremely polite. He would have liked to bawl and shout, but where was the good of that? The damage was done and it had been an accident. The *Fair Wind* had come in with too much way on her, overshot her mooring, and smashed into the *Enterprise* before the Thorpes had realized what was happening. It might have been due to bad, landlubberly seamanship, but it was no good starting a brawl about it. Robert looked at Mr. Thorpe's round, red, good-natured, distressed face and said with a shrug that nothing could be done till morning.

Mr. Thorpe was chiefly concerned about Robert's insurance. If there was anything to pay—if Robert needed the money advanced—if there was anything at all that he could do——

It was on the tip of Robert's tongue to ask for the loan of the *Fair Wind* for a few hours. He needn't explain much; he could pitch a yarn about smugglers—Whittier would back him up in the role of excise officer—it would probably go down all right. And then, as if a voice had spoken in his head, he heard Lawrie saying: "I thought every minute I was going to walk into the Master Spy." Robert stammered and was silent. Suppose—just suppose—that Mr. Thorpe, for all his redness and roundness, good nature and distress, were concerned with the U-boat? Suppose, after all, the accident were no accident? Suppose they suspected they were being watched? Suppose. . . . Robert asked in the politest, most disarming fashion if he might look over the *Fair Wind*.

He was welcomed with open arms; he was taken all over the little ship. He admired the engine, the neat, luxurious cabins, the electric light, the gadgets of every description (though really Robert despised gadgets), the arrangement of the lockers, the gleaming, polished galley, and he saw nothing whatever to justify his suspicions. And yet—his suspicions persisted. Was his welcome too hearty? Was he being shown too much? Was Mr. Thorpe's accent a little too broad to be genuine? By the time Robert was back on board the *Enterprise* he was nearly sure Mr. Thorpe was not to be trusted.

Down in the wrecked cabin, Robert put his elbows on the table, and shoved his aching head in his hands. He wondered if he were making an almighty fool of himself. Whittier evidently thought so for one. What was it David had said? That Whittier had sent Robert out in the *Enterprise* to keep him quiet and happy? Well. That might be true or it might not; even if it were, Whittier was not infallible. Certainly the ultimate blame or credit in the affair would fall to Whittier, but in a job like this neither praise nor blame mattered very much. The thing was to get it done. And if you broke a few rules doing it—well, if you pulled it off no one cared, and if you didn't, nothing anyone could say would be worse than the failure itself. Robert made up his mind and immediately felt much better.

He set about tidying up the mess and litter in the cabin. After a while he heard footsteps on the deck overhead and went up. It was David.

"I say," said David. "I just ran into a child called Jackie Peterson. This is a piece of sheer foul luck, isn't it?"

"Yes," Robert nodded, sucked at his pipe. "How's Bill?"

"Just being shoved into the operating theatre when I came away. I've seen Whittier."

"Oh yes?"

"He didn't approve of my methods," said David candidly. "He said so very loud and clear, too. But I gather he agreed with me, more or less. Said he thought a good night's sleep all round would be the thing, but he didn't press it. But, of course, he didn't know about this. Looks as if our good night's sleep was going to be forced on us, doesn't it?"

Robert agreed. Yes, it did.

"What will you do? Sleep on board?"

"Yes, I think so. The cabin's quite habitable."

"Tell you what. I'll see Whittier again and tell him what's happened. Then he can commandeer something by the morning and we can get back on watch. O.K.?"

"Good idea."

"Well, I'll push off then." But David hesitated. Anquetil,

leaning against the coaming, gazing at him thoughtfully as he drew on his pipe, seemed a bit too calm to be true. David, who had known Anquetil for some years now, knew that if once Robert was pushed beyond a certain point, he was apt to become, not wild, exactly, but unpredictable. "Look here," he said uneasily, "why don't you come back with me? Wouldn't do you any harm to sleep in a bed for once. You look pretty cheap, you know."

"Oh, I don't think so. I'd rather stay on board. Perhaps when I see the damage in daylight, it may not be as bad as I think."

There was an underlying bleakness and obstinacy in his casual-sounding voice. David, contemplating him uneasily, felt fairly certain of three things: one, that Anquetil was considering a particular course of action; two, that David was to be told nothing; and three, that if David interfered, it would be David who would be hit over the head this time. So he said:

"Good night, then. See you in the morning."

"Good night. Oh, and David. Tell Whittier to get whatever craft he gets hold of round by five-thirty at the latest. We don't want to miss the tide."

"Right," said David, relieved. Whatever Robert was up to, it didn't look as if he was going to be up to it to-night. He said good night and took himself off.

He might have felt less certain of this if he had been able to watch Robert's behaviour fifteen minutes after he had gone. When he had shut the hatch and port-holes and checked the riding lights, Robert went ashore. He walked along the quay, calling good night to anyone who passed, and even stopped one or two people to tell them of the accident. Then, at the end of the quay, he stopped as if to light his pipe. As soon as he was satisfied that no one in sight was looking in his direction, he ran like a shadow down the wooden stairway to the beach.

A pile of barrels and a dinghy made a convenient hiding-place. He could just see the cabin light in the *Fair Wind*. She drew a slightly shallower draught than the *Golden Enterprise*. With luck, he should be able to sail shortly after midnight—provided the Thorpes, who were only dining on board because they would have been too late for the hotel meal, didn't change their minds and decide to sleep there too. They had invited him to join them, but Robert had old-fashioned ideas: he didn't think you ought to eat a man's bread and salt and then make off with his ship, all in the same evening. After all, he had no proof that Thorpe was mixed up with Lewis's gang. It was only a hunch.

It was cold on the beach. The barrels and the dinghy gave a certain amount of shelter, but the pebbles themselves were cold as sea-water. Anquetil shivered, put his pipe in his pocket, and began to recite Greek irregular verbs to himself. He always did this when he had to wait for an indefinite time under conditions of some discomfort. Greek verbs were pleasantly impersonal. They seemed to take some of the edge off the situation.

But at last the cabin light went out. Anquetil saw the Thorpes come on deck, and, in a few minutes, heard the splash of oars. Then, after a while, he saw them strolling along the quay. He counted them: Mr. Thorpe, Mrs. Thorpe, the two grown-up daughters, and, after an interval, the long, gangling shape of Johnnie Thorpe. There was no one left on board. They climbed into their motor and were gone.

Anquetil looked at his watch and waited twenty minutes in case one of them had left something behind and came back for it. But nothing happened. The quay was empty, the water chuckled and gobbled against the sea wall, and the lights were reflected in long, gleaming lines across the water. Anquetil got up stiffly, thankful that the scurrying rain clouds covered the moon, and went softly along by the wall. He slipped off his canvas shoes and slung them round his neck by the laces. Then he waded into the sea, gasping at its coldness, and struck out in the direction of the *Fair Wind*. It was a longer swim than he had thought. He was chilled and numb by the time he climbed aboard.

He did not want to light a lamp in the cabin in case someone else had seen the Thorpes leave and came to investigate. But he had taken particular notice of the large torch which stood on one of the shelves in the cabin and now, drawing down the blind, he laid it on the deck. It gave plenty of light to see by as he stripped off his sodden garments and rifled the Thorpes' lockers for towels and dry clothes.

He had just fastened the belt of his borrowed trousers when he heard the splash of oars alongside; the next moment some-one climbed aboard.

Anquetil switched off the torch and stepped back through the galley which lay between the two cabins. Standing well back in the darkness he heard someone come down the com-panion and then the light went on. It was Johnnie Thorpe.

Anquetil glanced at his watch; but for this interruption he could have been making ready to sail. If young Thorpe had come back to fetch something, well and good. But if not— Anquetil did some rapid calculation concerning tides and speed and decided to give young Thorpe exactly fifteen min-utes.

But Johnnie Thorpe showed no signs of leaving. He seemed in a cheerful mood, whistling to himself as he moved about the cabin, occasionally breaking into a mock operatic solo, com-bined with a double-shuffle, and then guffawing gently to himself. The minutes crept by, while young Thorpe rifled a biscuit tin and put a saucepan on to boil. It was painfully obvious that he was going to spend the night on board.

Anquetil considered. It would be quite simple to put young Thorpe to sleep, much as David had dealt with him earlier on. On the other hand, if Thorpe would, he could help a lot. As crew he would be invaluable. Anquetil was quite prepared to take the *Fair Wind* out single-handed, but a little help at the right moment might come in very handy. Suppose he pitched

young Johnnie the smuggling yarn, only the other way round
—said he had to rendezvous or something of that kind. . . .

Only, if the elder Thorpe were mixed up with Lewis's lot,
how much might Johnnie be expected to know about it?

Anquetil made up his mind. And at that moment, Johnnie
came through the galley and into the sleeping cabin.

He looked very young and startled and speechless at the
sight of Anquetil standing there in the middle of the cabin.
But at last he said, in a voice which wavered rather: "Look
here! I don't know what you're doing here, but this boat belongs to my father."

"Yes, I know. I was here earlier this evening."

"Oh! Was it your boat I wrecked?"

"Yes, it was."

Johnnie crimsoned. He said, his voice very deep in his boots: "That was my fault, actually. I didn't cut the engine in time. Dad pitched into me like stink afterwards. He said I'd have to see you and—and apologize. But look here——"

"You'd like to know what I'm doing here?"

"Well—er—yes, I would."

"The trouble is, my lad, that you smashed my boat at a very inconvenient moment," said Anquetil severely, not because he was particularly annoyed with Johnnie any more, but because he believed in keeping the war in the enemy's camp. "And it's essential I should be at sea to-night."

"Fishing?" said Johnnie doubtfully. "Well, I don't know much about it, of course, but I shouldn't think the *Fair Wind* would be much use as a fishing smack." He got very red again. "I mean—if it's a—a question of compensation——"

"I don't want to use her as a fishing boat."

Johnnie looked pardonably bewildered. "I'm afraid I don't see—and anyway, why didn't you ask Dad? He's pretty decent about things. I'm sure he'd have lent her to you if you'd asked him."

"I couldn't very well do that. If I were to be caught, and he'd lent her to me, he might get into trouble too."

"What on earth d'you mean? I say! You don't mean——"

"Yes. Smuggling."

A large curling grin spread over Johnnie's face. "A smuggler! I say! Are you really? What d'you smuggle?"

"Brandy, mostly." Anquetil looked at his watch. "Look here. Time's getting on, and I've got to keep a rendezvous. Now listen. I'm going to use your father's boat to-night. If you like you can give me a hand. Or, if you'd rather not be mixed up in it, I'll knock you out and truss you up and you need never know anything about it."

"Suppose," said Johnnie thoughtfully, "I didn't want to do either? I mean, suppose I say you can't use the boat?"

"*Are* you saying that?"

Johnnie looked at him warily. "Well, I said *suppose*——"

"You mean you'd like to know if I can make you?"

"Well——" And then Johnnie, who had been thinking he was doing rather well, broke off with a gasp. He stood staring at the short-bladed knife in Anquetil's hand.

"All right," he said after a moment. "I only wanted to know. You can put it away now."

"And which are you going to do?"

"Oh, I'll help," said Johnnie, grinning broadly. "I wouldn't miss a chance like this if you offered me a new motor-bike. Smuggling!"

"It's time we got under way, then. Where d'you keep your oilskins?"

"In this locker." Johnnie pulled out a couple and chucked one to Anquetil. "I say. Are those Dad's trousers you're wearing?" And when Anquetil nodded, he began to grin like the Cheshire cat. "I say! It's really smashingly funny. You know —not funny, exactly, but masses of dramatic irony."

"What is?"

"You in Dad's trousers and going smuggling. You know who Dad is, don't you?"

"No. Who?"

"One of the chief blokes in Customs and Excise. And now you're going smuggling in Dad's boat and trousers and oilskins and I'm helping." And Johnnie Thorpe guffawed loudly as he scrambled up on deck.

"Oh, Lord," thought Anquetil following. But it was too late now.

The anchor came clanking up and the engine began to turn over. As the boat began to move, a voice hailed them across the water.

"That you aboard, Mr. Thorpe?"

Anquetil held his breath. Johnnie called back:

"No, it's me, sir. I'm just taking her out for a spot of night cruising. I'll be O.K."

"Going to be a bit of a blow, sir. Sure you can manage on your own?"

"Yes, thanks," called Johnnie. "I'll watch out."

He waved cheerfully. The next moment the *Fair Wind* was motoring gently through the harbour mouth, her course set towards the lighthouse.

Johnnie turned to Anquetil. "Jolly lucky I was with you, wasn't it?" he remarked complacently. "And if anyone asks any awkward questions, I can always say I had your knife jabbed in my ribs, can't I?"

And he guffawed happily at the notion, evidently finding it very amusing indeed. The next moment he said: "I say! I hope we're not going to run out of gas. I think we're down to the last two cans."

12

*

Foley's Folly Light

[i]

It had seemed very silent in the lantern that morning once Nicola and Ginty had left the lighthouse. Peter, packing his stores neatly just inside the chest so that they would be out of the way if Foley came up, wished he could have gone with them. Ginty was pretty handy in a dinghy, of course, but Nick knew nothing about it and she couldn't swim much, either. He began to wish he hadn't had this extra idea. It would probably have been quite safe to bank on Foley behaving just as usual, and not to have bothered with all this nonsense of pretending he was dead. Suppose the dinghy overturned in earnest? Suppose one of them were really swept away? Suppose——?

Peter made himself stop supposing. If he did manage, somehow, to stay in the Service, this sort of thing was going to happen all the time. All his life he was going to have to be prepared to make plans which would risk other people's lives as well as, or even instead of, his own. And the older he got, and the more important, the more it would happen to him. Besides, thought Peter, not exactly comforted, but a bit relieved all the same, it wasn't as if the alternatives at the moment lay between danger of their own making and eventual safety at Foley's hands. If they waited, they were almost certain to be killed when the U-boat's crew got hold of them. And besides—Peter blushed rather, for it sounded pretty pompous as soon as you put it into words—it was probably a thing they ought to do—to do everything they could to prevent that oilskin package falling into enemy hands. And you couldn't fight the enemy without taking some risks.

If only he could know how Nick and Ginty were getting on. His torch was beginning to give a yellowish sort of light, as if it wasn't going to last much longer. Peter rummaged in the chest, lit a candle, and walked over to the shutters. Some were just shutters, but the middle one had a handle sticking through. Peter turned it, and heard the catch come back, stiffly, as if it were covered with rust. He pulled cautiously, inch by inch, holding his breath as the hinges squealed, and found that he was looking out on a gallery about three feet wide with a two-strand guard-rail circling it. Far below, the sea showed white edges of foam round the bases of the rocks.

Peter gulped. Somehow, he hadn't realized how high the top of the lighthouse would be once you were looking down. But his anxiety for Ginty and Nicola drove him out. He pulled the door to behind him, wedging it with his handkerchief in case the lock stuck, and then edged slowly along, keeping well back against the lighthouse wall, until he was looking down on the part of the beach from which they must have left.

For the moment he couldn't see them at all. The gusts of wind hurled themselves against the lighthouse from the south-west, and he could feel the gallery quiver under him; and there was a beastly swaying sensation, as if the lighthouse were a gigantic pendulum. Spread-eagled against the wall, Peter stared grimly out to sea. The sun was just up among the bruised-looking clouds on the horizon, and shafts of light were striking gleams out of the tumbling, snail-coloured sea. It was beastly cold. Peter shivered; and then, out of the corner of his eye, he saw the dinghy, looking unbelievably small, shoot out from behind a rock.

He felt tremendously relieved. He edged back round the side of the lighthouse, so that he could watch what happened next.

To Peter, watching, none of it seemed nearly as alarming as it did to Nicola and Ginty in the thick of it. For one thing, the distances looked so much smaller; Ginty, for instance, seemed to have hardly any way to swim at all. And he couldn't make out what they thought they were doing all the time they were lying around on the rocks. He wished they'd get a move on and get back to the lighthouse. Really, his worst moment was when he saw that Foley had come out and was standing on the beach.

This happened at the moment when Ginty grasped Nicola's hand and stumbled up and out of the sea. Fortunately, Foley seemed to simply stand and stare round for a bit, as if he were looking at the weather. Once, as he stood at the edge of the sea, he turned and looked up at the lighthouse and Peter froze against the wall, his heart banging against his ribs, thankful that he had moved out of the sunlight to the shadowed side of the wall. The moments passed, while Foley still stared up, and then he turned away. Peter found that he had been holding his breath and let it out in a long sigh of relief. The next moment Foley, wandering round the beach, discovered that the dinghy had gone.

Even foreshortened, with his back turned to Peter, he looked as if he were standing stiff and still with fury. Then he kicked off his shoes, rolled his trousers as high as they would go, threw off his jacket, and waded into the water. The next moment, so far as Peter could see, he had walked straight into the rock.

He was glad to see that Ginty and Nicola had stopped lying down and running about in that aimless sort of way by now. His legs had begun to ache, partly from excitement, partly from cold, partly because he was standing so stiffly pressed back against the wall, and he decided to sit down. Then, because he couldn't see what was happening if he sat with his back against the wall, he sprawled cautiously on his stomach, holding grimly on to the lower rail. He got himself settled just in time to see Nicola about to step off the rock straight into the sea.

He yelled frantically. Fortunately, the wind shredded his voice away and no one heard him. And in a moment it was all over. Nicola disappeared; Foley thrust past Ginty, flung himself flat on the rock and grabbed Nicola as she came splashing and thrashing to the surface. The next moment Nicola was lying sprawled on the ledge and Foley was bending over her.

Peter found that he was shaking all over. He hardly took in what happened next, though he saw Ginty point in the direction of the upturned dinghy. Then they all disappeared into the rock again, and he was lying on his stomach, far up in the air above an empty sea, with a cloudy, rainy sky gathering overhead.

And he couldn't move. He simply *couldn't* let go the rail and stand up. Now that nothing else was happening, he was only too conscious that once he took his hand away, there was nothing to stop him rolling under the rail as Nicola had done on the morning of the thunderstorm, and falling . . . falling . . .

He gulped and shut his eyes. He had to let go and he had to get back into the lantern. It didn't matter that the gallery quivered with every new gust, and that his inside was churning about in the most peculiar and horrible fashion. The thing to do was not to look at the sea, but at the floor of the gallery. Slowly, Peter brought his head round, away from the sea. Then, very slowly and with an enormous effort, he got himself on to his knees. For a few moments, that was as much as he could do. Then, not daring to move his eyes from the floor in front of him, he unclenched the fingers that were gripping the rail, and squirmed himself over as near to the wall of the lighthouse as he could. Then he began to crawl. Deep down, a part of his mind kept telling him how jolly silly he must look, crawling painfully along a gallery which Nicola, for instance, would simply have run round. But he couldn't help it; nothing on earth could have got him to his feet at that moment. After what seemed so long a time that he was sure he must have passed the door and be crawling round and round, he came on it. He pushed it open, crawled over the sill, and fell in a heap on the floor of the lantern.

He still went on shaking and shivering for a bit in what he felt was a perfectly idiotic way, but after a while he began to feel more like himself. He climbed to his feet, closed the door, and relit the candle which had blown out. He ate some biscuits and chocolate because he suddenly felt enormously and ravenously hungry, and then remembered that he hadn't looked properly inside the chest.

He looked at it a bit apprehensively, because after all, chests were well known to be most useful and usual hiding-places for bodies. But he lifted the lid quickly, before he had time to be too alarmed by the idea, moved his stores, and found that the rest of the chest was full to the brim with old split sails, some Victorian books for boys and some other oddments. Peter turned these over curiously: a pair of heavy gloves, a leather-covered book filled from cover to cover with a neat tiny script, and a most curious-looking thing made of black gauze. Except for the colour, it looked exactly like the thing his mother put over her head when she went out to the bee-hives. He supposed it must have something to do with working the light, but for the life of him he couldn't think what. He pulled out the sails, put back the oddments, and stuffed them behind the chest; with only the books at the bottom, there was plenty of room for him as well, if Foley should suddenly decide to have a look round. He had a look at the books, but most of them he had read already. He chose one he didn't know called *By Watch and Ward: a tale of Nelson's Days* and put it handy in case he felt like reading later on. He thought he'd probably have to feel like reading; it would be too awful to do nothing but sit and think, and wonder and worry from now till eleven o'clock at night.

After a bit he put a layer of sails on top of the books, climbed into the chest, and made himself as comfortable as he could. There was just enough room for him to lie down and close the lid if Foley should come up unexpectedly and it was easier than having to scramble in from outside. It would be awful if Foley lifted the lid and looked inside, but for the life of him (so Peter tried to persuade himself) he couldn't see why Foley should want to look at a lot of old sails and equally old books. Except, of course, that if Foley didn't believe he was dead, it was probably one of the first places he *would* look to see if he were hiding. Peter tried to tell himself that this wasn't likely and then gave it up. He scrambled out, and stuffed the sails back into the chest as nearly as possible as they had been before. It was no use funking it. If Foley came up, the only really safe place to hide was on the gallery.

And at that moment he heard Nicola's voice on the stairs.

He shot through the door and out on to the gallery without giving himself time to think. Instinctively, he edged round until he had put plenty of space between himself and the door. He remembered from games of 'he' how, if you had a good solid tree or a table between you and the person who was 'he', you could dodge round, practically speaking, for ever. Besides, Foley might not come out here at all. He might simply open the door of the lantern, look in, and go away again. Peter thought furiously. Had he left anything in the lantern that would show he'd been there? He didn't think so. The only possible thing was the candle, and that he'd pushed into the chest, well under the pile of sails.

Inside the lantern, he heard the door open. He waited to hear the sound of the chest lid being lifted up, but instead, the striding feet walked straight across the room and he heard the door opening.

Peter moved fast. He put the full diameter of the lantern between himself and the door and then stopped to listen. He wondered desperately which way Foley was coming, and even as he did so, saw the rail vibrate on his right hand, as if someone had put their hand on it. Foley was walking widdershins.

But very slowly. Peter couldn't think what he was doing. He went on walking round, matching his own steps to the sound of Foley's which he could just hear, very faintly, as an extra vibration. Slowly the two of them circled the lantern and then, to his infinite relief, Peter heard the door close, the footsteps cross the floor, and after, the sound of the other door closing. He waited for a while, in case it was a trap, and then walked back to the door. For an instant the handle stuck and for one horrible moment he thought Foley had wedged the door from the inside, but the next moment it turned and he stepped back into the friendly darkness of the lantern.

It was only then that it occurred to him that he'd walked twice round the gallery and never even thought about it. To be sure, it was probably because he had been in such a panic in case Foley caught him that he hadn't had time to think about it, but all the same—Peter began to giggle, his hands stuffed against his mouth. Somehow, the memory of himself crawling painfully round the gallery in an absolute bleat of terror, seemed one of the funniest things he had ever heard.

And then, all at once, he found he could hardly keep his eyes open. He was so weary that he could have lain down on the floor and slept where he lay. All the same he knew he couldn't do that. If Foley came up again and found him lying there, it would be the end. Peter stuffed some of the sails under the chest, got inside, propped the lid open just a chink with a wodge of paper torn from one of the books, and the next moment was fast asleep.

But he slept neither long nor soundly. Something inside him kept jolting him awake or calling up the most real-seeming nightmares in which Foley opened the lid and stood peering in at him, his voice booming like the sea, or else crept stealthily round the lantern towards a Peter who shrank away and always ended by falling into the sea. After a succession of such nightmares, Peter decided it wasn't good enough. He got out of the chest, lit the candle, and tried to read *By Watch and Ward*.

But it didn't really hold his attention. He kept listening for the sound of feet and voices on the stairs. If Foley were to come up again and if this time he didn't have enough warning to reach the gallery in time—Peter didn't care to contemplate what might happen then. For the first time he began to imagine what would happen to them if the plan failed. For it might. If no one saw their signal—if no ships passed within range of the light—if—Peter stared into the candle-flame, his eyes so dark a blue they looked nearly black.

He wished there were something he could do *now*, instead of just sitting here. It might almost have been worth taking down the shutters and trying to signal to a ship in daylight. But even if someone did see him waving, how were they to know he wasn't waving quite cheerfully? And if Foley were to wander out of the lighthouse and see him, that would be the end of everything. All the same, he hesitated, until the sound of rain on glass and a buffet of wind put an end to the idea. If the weather had closed in, no one could possibly see him.

A worse thought came to him. Suppose, to-night, there should be fog?

Peter swallowed hard and sat up. It was no use sitting around doing nothing and working himself up. He would just have to try to find something sensible to do and, so far as to-night was concerned, hope for the best. Was everything ready? He thought so: the light, the fuel, the matches—

The message.

Peter felt a bit inclined to giggle again. Here he was, fretting himself frantic in case no one saw his signal, and he hadn't even decided what message he was going to send if a ship did answer.

He fished in his pockets, found a stub of pencil, and tore out one of the blank pages at the end of *By Watch and Ward*. It wasn't easy to say everything he had to say concisely as well as clearly, and he had used up all the end pages of *By Watch and Ward*, as well as those belonging to two or three other books, before he got the message more or less as he wanted it. Even then, he wasn't really satisfied. He thought it sounded dreadfully melodramatic. But he didn't see how he could help that: the whole thing *was* melodramatic. He read the message over again:

"*From V.P. and N. Marlow. We are being held prisoner*—Peter scowled and crossed out *prisoner*—"*at Foley's Folly Light by*

Lieutenant Lewis Foley, R.N., a traitor." Peter hesitated, crossed out *a traitor* and substituted *an enemy agent.* "*A U-boat will rendezvous at 06.00 hours to-morrow Sunday to embark Foley, ourselves and documents containing secret information.*"

Peter sucked his pencil. Did it sound responsible and sensible, the sort of message someone would act on even if it was the first he or she had heard of their disappearance? Or would it be dismissed as just children playing at pirates? With luck it would be one of the ships of the Fleet, who would check up, even if they didn't altogether believe. But it might just as easily be seen by some terrible drip of a week-end yachtsman. So he added: "*Inform Admiralty immediately*", then crossed out *Admiralty* and put *Police.* Somehow, *Police* sounded more solid and down to earth than *Admiralty.* Even a drip wouldn't think that children playing pirates would want the police called in; and probably a drip wouldn't know how to get in touch with the Admiralty, anyway, and a sensible bloke would do it without being told.

So that was done, and now he had to think of something else to do. Then he remembered the leather-covered book, the one that looked like a diary. He dug down under the sails, groped a bit and found it. He turned to the title page and read: "*Fabian de Noyes Foley: his book: March 7th 1833——*": there was no second date.

Peter put a sail on the floor, lay down on his stomach and began to read. He read a page or two, sat staring in front of him for a moment and then went on again. He didn't want to read it, and yet he had to, held by the same hateful fascination which Ainsworth's *Tower of London* had had for him when he was younger. It was horrible, and he hated it and yet he had to read Fabian Foley's record of his wreckings, even though they were written with a cheerful relish in destruction which turned his stomach. And though this record of broken ships and drowned men had nothing whatever to do with their own predicament, still, in a curious way, more clearly than ever before, he began to understand what he and Ginty and Nicola were up against. He read on and on until the tiny, faded script began to jump and dazzle before his eyes.

Peter started awake in complete darkness. Something cold and harsh-feeling was pressing against his cheek and he could see no chinks of daylight behind the shutters. For a moment he knew what real panic felt like: he even wondered if he had been carried out of the lighthouse and dumped into the U-boat. Then he caught sight of his watch and saw that it was nearly half-past seven. He had been asleep for hours.

The matches were in his pocket. He struck one, and saw that the candle had burned itself down to a pool of grease. He lit another and decided that if it were dark outside there could be no harm in taking down the shutters.

The night sky was so full of moon-whitened clouds that it looked as if it were paved with them. He put the shutter down gently, feeling quite shaky with relief, for even through his nightmares the thought of fog had persisted. But it was all right, after all. He took down the other shutters, opened the door on to the gallery, and stepped out into the gusts of wind. It felt wonderful after the dead air inside. He stood snuffing the wind and watching the distant loom of the shore lights. It would have been lovely to light the lamp now and take a chance on its being seen. But only too likely Foley would see it too. They had to wait.

He leaned against the rail, feeling the swing of the lighthouse, and knowing that he didn't really mind it any more. He could stay here, watching the sea and the sky as long as he liked. He thought he would like. He couldn't have said quite why, but whenever he thought of Fabian Foley's book, it seemed better to be out here in the wind, instead of shut up inside the lantern. It was very odd, thought Peter, but that book had made him feel so absolutely furious that if it hadn't belonged to someone else, he would have dropped it over the rail to be pulped and pounded to pieces by the sea. Which was idiotic, really, when the man who had written it had been dead more than a hundred years, leaping to his death from the roof above Peter's head. Peter grinned to himself and said aloud in a stage voice: "So perish all traitors!" and felt better. And presently the wind freshened still further, the moon was covered by a blanket of cloud, and, out of the darkness, first in a scatter and then heavily, it began to rain.

It was nearly eleven o'clock. Peter closed the door leading to the gallery, tiptoed across the floor and, very cautiously, opened the door on to the stairs. He couldn't hear a sound, except for the noises of the sea and the wind. He wished Nick and Gin would hurry up, and he wondered for a moment if he should go down and try to find out what was keeping them. But whatever the reason, the risk simply wasn't worth taking. He listened again, but no one seemed to be stirring, so he closed the door, went back, and lit the lamp.

It seemed very brilliant inside the lantern after so much darkness. He blinked, getting his eyes accustomed to the light; it was going to be an awful nuisance, looking into that glare all the time one was signalling . . . and then, with a sort of chumpish feeling, he realized what that black gauze bee-skep thing was for; he had just got it out of the chest when he heard a soft scratching at the door, the handle turned, and Nicola and Ginty crept in. He wondered why Nicola looked so enormously relieved at the sight of him, but there wasn't time to ask.

"Hullo," he whispered. "You're awfully late."

"We couldn't help it. Foley seemed to be packing up for ages. We weren't sure what he was up to, so we thought we'd better wait for a bit. But he seems to have settled down now. Have you begun?"

"Not yet." He lifted the cylinder and they all blinked. "Is it safe to begin?"

"Safe as it ever will be," said Nicola with a grin. "Who's going to do what?"

"I'll start the signalling and you can watch for an answer and Gin can watch the stairs. All right?"

"No, bags me watch the stairs," said Nicola quickly, making a secret face at him. Peter looked at Ginty, saw that she had been crying, and said: "All right."

Nicola lit one of the lanterns and went out. Ginty moved over to the window and stood staring into the darkness. Peter pulled the bee-skep over his head and pressed the lever. Short, short, short: long, long, long: short, short, short. Pause. Short, short, short: long, long, long: short, short, short. Pause.

The black gauze took the glare from the light, but it soon got pretty warm. Peter took off his coat and got on with it. Short, short, short: long, long, long: short, short, short. Pause. He said to Ginty as he began again: "How did you get on all day?"

"All right," said Ginty, after a pause. "I mean it was all right about you being drowned. He believed that. But the tunnel was absolutely awful." Her voice trembled suddenly. "I wouldn't have gone for a million pounds if I'd known." There was a silence. "I say, Binks."

"'M?"

"Do you—do you think this is going to work?"

"Hope so."

"S'pose—s'pose, though, it doesn't?"

"Dunno," he grunted. He pressed the lever again. Short, short, short: long, long, long: short, short, short. Pause. He wished Ginty wouldn't say things like that. She knew quite well what would happen if it didn't work. So did they all.

Time passed. Ginty went out to sit on the stairs and Nicola did the signalling. Then Ginty took a turn and Peter went out. Then it was Peter's turn to signal and Nicola went on watching because Ginty said she felt so hot. They none of them

talked very much. There was only one thing that was important now, and that was whether anyone was going to see their
light. Even Ginty felt she couldn't ask again whether anyone
ever would. The real trouble was the weather. The panes of
glass were thick with rain and spray. Through all that rain the
light would carry a much shorter distance than on a clear
night. They all knew it and they were all—even Ginty—careful not to mention it. Nicola rubbed the steamed-up window-
pane clear and dug into her pocket for some chocolate. And
then, as she did so, she saw the lights far away to the east.

"Binks! There they are!"

He couldn't help it. Just for the moment he left the light un-
covered and dashed to look. She was right, of course. Dipping
and disappearing, as if they were wallowing in a head sea, the
lights of the Fleet shone out, tiny and remote. He rushed back
to the light, and began to signal fast and desperately: three
short, three long, three short; three short, three long, three
short; three short—— Why didn't Nick call him? They must
have signalled by now.

But Nicola was silent. She stood, staring through the glass
and occasionally rubbing it clear, and then, at last, not even
doing that. He had to say it, even though he knew what her
answer would be.

"Didn't they answer?"

"No."

"Not at all?"

"No."

There was a silence. Peter went on sending out his signal
automatically. It didn't seem any use any more, but to stop
now seemed not only feeble, but an admission of disaster so
great as to be unbearable. At last he said gruffly:

"Perhaps they've detached a destroyer. They might have
seen something but not been sure what."

After a moment, Nicola said in a careful voice: "Yes."

Peter said no more. He knew she was only just not crying

and that if she had to talk she might not be able to keep it in. He was glad he had the gauze over his head, because the muscles of his face kept twitching into odd grimaces he couldn't control. At last Nicola spun round.

"I'll go and send Ginty in," she said in a husky, not quite even voice. "Only I don't think we'd better tell her. She's in an awful state as it is."

The night wore on. The turns worked round again and then again. The rain had stopped and it wasn't blowing so hard. Nicola stood staring out to sea, watching the panes grow dry and clear and thinking sleepily how much better it would have been if only this had happened a couple of hours ago. But she felt so sleepy that she couldn't mind anything very much any more. She just wanted to lie down somewhere and sleep. She even felt she could be like Napoleon and sleep standing up. Her eyes closed for a moment, and it felt wonderful. It was an enormous effort to open them. Much pleasanter to close them . . . much easier . . .

Nicola clutched at the glass, her heart thudding fast as it always did after the falling nightmare. She felt very shocked and wideawake, and she stared into the darkness, hoping Peter hadn't noticed. She yawned hugely, looking at the sea. The moon was down. In an hour or so it would be getting light. It was Sunday. And on Sunday, at 06.00 hours. . . .

And then a light shone from the sea. For a moment she couldn't believe it. Long, short, long; long, short, long: invitation to transmit—

"*Peter!*"

"What?"

"A light—they're here—*quickly*——"

Peter came wholly awake. For a long time now his signalling had been pretty erratic, a muddle of dots and dashes and only an occasional S O S. But he was very much all there now. He dug into his pocket and brought out the scribbled message.

"Here, quick. Read it to me while I send."

He was signalling the preliminary call even while he fumbled in his pocket. Nicola grabbed the crumpled paper and dashed back to the window.

"From V. P. and N. Marlow. . . . We are being held . . . at Foley's Folly Light . . . by Lieutenant Lewis Foley, R.N. . . . an enemy agent . . . a U-boat will rendezvous at 06.00 hours. . . ."

Suddenly the door burst open and Ginty stood there, stammering something in a high, frightened voice.

"Shut the door," snapped Nicola. "We're sending. They've seen."

Ginty stood white-faced in the doorway for a moment; then she vanished.

". . . to-morrow—*to-day*, Binks—Sunday . . . to embark Foley . . . ourselves . . . and documents containing secret information. Inform police immediately. End of message."

Almost at once the light from the sea blinked again, rather slowly, so that it was easy to read.

"Repeat time and day of U-boat's arrival," said Nicola.

"06.00 hours, to-day, Sunday," signalled Peter.

The light winked again in the "Message received" signal. "R" it said. And that was all.

For a moment they looked at one another, triumphant and relieved, but a little dashed all the same. Somehow, they had both expected something more heartening: "The Navy's here"—"The Fleet's lit up"—something of that kind. And then, outside the door, they heard someone cry out, and then there was a clatter and a tinkle, and a slithering, bumping sound as if someone were falling downstairs.

It had been quiet, sitting at the top of the stairs in the friendly circle of light thrown by the lantern. By the time the last watch came round, Ginty had got fairly used to it. She sat hugging her knees and staring down the darkness of the stairs, and shivering rather, partly from the cold and partly from her thoughts. It hadn't been so bad when they had first started signalling; she had felt keyed-up, but not particularly frightened any more. She had thought, with enormous relief, that she must have cried out most of her fright during the day, but now, during the last hour or so, she had felt it all trickling back. It hadn't been so bad when she had been inside the lantern with Nick or Binks for company, but out here alone with nothing to do but think, it was different. And she was sure something awful must have happened, just before Nick came out to relieve her once. Ginty hadn't asked, because she hadn't wanted to know for certain, but it didn't need much imagination to be pretty sure that a ship had passed and hadn't seen.

Ginty put her head down on her knees. She felt horribly tired and horribly wideawake at the same time, and her thoughts frayed inside her like ropes dragging against a jagged edge. The thought of the submarine was at the back of her mind all the time, but she tried not to think about it too much, because it frightened her so dreadfully that when she did she couldn't stop shivering at all. So instead, she thought of all the other things which might happen: suppose *all* the ships that passed never saw them at all? Suppose in the morning they were lined up on the beach and shot? Suppose they were carried off to Siberia? Ginty began to remember all the things she had ever heard or read or imagined about prisoners of war and concentration camps. Suppose——?

And then, far below in the lighthouse, she heard a series of scraping sounds. It was Foley taking down his shutters.

She must warn Peter and Nick. She scrambled to her feet as the door below banged open, and dashed into the lantern. She said in a shaking voice: "Foley's coming up. I can hear him," and Nick spun round, her eyes blazing, and said: "Shut the door. We're sending. They've seen."

Ginty found herself standing alone with her back to the closed door, her heart pounding to the same rhythm as Foley's

230

feet as he came racing up the stairs. In a moment he was going to come round the curve and he would be on her. . . . Ginty clutched the handle of the lantern in her hand, wishing she had a stick, any sort of weapon, to hold him off for just a few moments. She never doubted he would overwhelm her in the end, whatever she did, but she might have been able to hold him off, just long enough for the others to get the message through.

And then, fully dressed, he came tearing round the curve of the stairs. For a moment Ginty stood staring at him, paralysed with fright and helplessness. And then, as he bounded up the last few stairs, she flung the lantern as hard as she possibly could.

It caught him full in the face. He sprang back, covering his face with his hands, missed his footing and fell, rolling over and over down the stairs. Ginty, her hands clenched, waited for him to get up and come for her again. But he crashed against the wall, and lay still, sprawling across the staircase with his head turned away from her.

Ginty began to go down the stairs and then found she couldn't. Suppose he was dead? Suppose he was dead and she had killed him? Ginty hung on to the rail, gulping, and staring appalled at Foley's sprawled shape. The door of the lantern opened hurriedly.

"What's happened? Gin, are you all right?"

"Y-yes. Binks, have I killed him?"

"Killed——?" Peter and Nicola came slowly down the stairs until they stood beside her. Then, after a moment, Peter went on down. He hesitated, and then bent over Foley, who made him jump by groaning suddenly.

"No, he's alive all right. What happened?"

Still clinging to the rail, Ginty told him. When she had finished, Nicola said approvingly: "That was jolly bright! It would have been too awful if he'd stopped us in full spate."

Ginty felt rather better. She said: "Isn't the first-aid box in

our room? And oughtn't we to get him on to a bed or something?"

"I don't see how we can manage the bed, but you can get
the first-aid box if you like. No, Nick, you go. Gin, come and
help me turn him over."

"Turn him over? But we oughtn't to, ought we? We might
damage something. Inside him, I mean."

"Can't help that," grunted Peter, tugging. "We must get—
that package. Oh, Gin, don't just stand there. Come and
help."

Ginty clenched her teeth and came. Together, though Foley
moaned and frightened them badly, they got him over. Peter
slipped his hand inside the inner pocket to which Foley's hand
had always wandered, fumbled for a moment and then looked
up triumphantly. "Here it is."

"Good." But Ginty looked, and sounded, more worried than
a good counter-spy should over an enemy agent who has been
put out of action. "Binks, I'm sure he's badly hurt. D'you
think he's going to die?"

"Might be a lot simpler if he did," muttered Peter.

Ginty looked thoroughly miserable. Now that Foley's face
was visible, she could see how badly the oil from the lamp had
burned him, and there was a long gash down his right cheek
where he had been cut by the breaking glass. Fortunately, at
this moment, Nicola returned with the first-aid box.

"You two see to him," said Peter getting up. "I'm going
down to smash the transmitter. It would be the end if he
warned the U-boat now."

"Couldn't you send a message?" suggested Nicola.

"Who to?"

"The Admiralty. Someone like that. Just in case whoever
was signalling doesn't get through in time."

Peter considered this. "I don't see how I can. I don't know
what the Admiralty wavelength is. And suppose the U-boat
picked it up? What then?"

"All right. Not a good idea. Just smash it, then."

Ginty was already cleaning Foley's face with a wad of cotton-wool. Nicola winked at Peter, a comforting sort of thumbs-up grimace, and he went off downstairs. He would wreck the transmitter and then have a good look round to see what he could see.

He had never been in the lowest room. He stood in the doorway for a moment and looked round at the mass of charts and books which littered the shelves and the floor. He saw a short iron bar in the corner, which would be just right for smashing something; when he paused, laid the oilskin package on the table, turned and dashed upstairs again. Ginty had just unstopped a bottle of smelling salts.

"Wait!" cried Peter, flinging himself up the last few stairs. "Don't bring him round for a second."

Ginty watched impatiently while he rummaged through Foley's pockets. "What are you looking for?" inquired Nicola at last.

"The key of the downstairs room. I thought——"

"So did I," said Nicola complacently. "Here. Catch."

"Thanks," said Peter and tore downstairs again. He did not bother to go in. He simply turned the key in the lock. It was a thick, heavy door. Even an uninjured Foley would never have been able to break it in. There might be stuff in there which the Admiralty would find very useful. Even the transmitter might be valuable if Foley ever talked to other people besides the U-boat. The room, the oilskin package—what else?

Foley's revolver. It hadn't been on him, Peter was sure. He unlocked the door again and went in. The revolver was lying on the table, holding down one corner of a chart.

He picked it up gingerly. He knew how to use one, more or less, for his father had shown him, but he wasn't too keen on them all the same. He set the safety-catch and then broke it, to make certain it was loaded, and found that all six chambers were full. Rather soberly, he slipped it into his pocket. He didn't particularly want to shoot anyone, but it might be very useful to have if any of the U-boat's crew came ashore before their rescuers——

A sudden thought stopped Peter dead in his tracks. They didn't know that there were any rescuers: they didn't know who had read their signal: for all any of them knew, it might have been the U-boat herself.

13

*

Ships in the Bay

Peter swallowed hard. Whatever happened, he couldn't tell Nick or Ginty that. He had to go upstairs and behave as if he were still certain the Navy was on its way. He dashed upstairs before he could think about it again, and found that Foley was just coming round.

He was sitting with his back against the wall, his face a greenish-white on one side, and an angry, burning red on the other. He looked up, seemed to focus his eyes with a great effort and recognized Peter.

"I thought you——" and then he stopped short as if something were hurting too badly to let him go on.

It was Nicola who answered, in a very matter-of-fact explanatory voice. "Well, we had to tell you that, to make sure of being able to signal. That was why we were on the rocks yesterday."

Foley shut his eyes again, as if this was all too much for him to take in.

"Is there any drinking water?" Ginty asked Peter.

"I expect so. D'you want some?"

"I thought p'raps he'd better have some sal volatile. There's a bottle of it here."

235

Foley groaned loudly. But not apparently in pain, for in another moment he opened his eyes and said: "There's a flask in my hip pocket. I'd like that much better."

"I don't think you ought to," said Ginty worriedly. "I mean if you've got internal injuries brandy's the very worst thing."

"It isn't going to matter," said Foley. "Really it isn't. Be a good child and get that flask. I can't twist myself round, I find."

It was Nicola who found the flask and unscrewed the cap. Ginty made no further protest, but she watched anxiously while Foley swallowed the brandy, tilting the flask to get the last drop. A little colour came into his unscarred cheek. After a moment he said: "That's much better. Help me up, will you?"

"I was going to put a dressing on that burn," began Ginty.

"Burn?"

"On your face."

"Oh. Is that why it feels so peculiar? No, don't bother. It doesn't matter. What burned it?"

"The—the lantern. I threw it at you," said Ginty apologetically.

Foley looked at her, bewildered, and then an expression of comprehension crossed his face as if he were remembering, and understanding what he remembered. "You were signalling."

"Yes," said Peter.

"Get any answer?"

"Yes."

"Who from?"

Peter did not hesitate. "The Navy. The *Samoa*."

"How d'you know? Did she identify herself?"

"Yes."

There was nothing friendly about Foley any longer. With his scarred face and furious eyes, he had suddenly become a very terrifying person to be with. Instinctively, they all moved back a little. He did not ask for any more help. He put out his

236

hand, grasped the rail, and, with a painful, agonized effort, got himself to his feet. He stood still for a moment, his unscarred cheek greenish-white again, his eyes shut, looking as if he were about to fall.

"I'll get some water," said Ginty anxiously.

"Shut up," snapped Foley under his breath. His right arm dangled uselessly from the shoulder; Peter, remembering his accident at prep school when they were playing football, thought Foley must have broken his collar bone, which was probably rather lucky; otherwise he might have been much more violent. But as Foley began to move slowly down the stairs, it became clear that there was something else that was damaged, something the matter with his side that kept making him catch his breath if he moved suddenly. Ginty, watching him, felt dreadfully guilty about it. But even she couldn't help feeling it was all for the best.

It was just five o'clock and beginning to get light.

Foley, his face very white and drawn, was sitting on the locker in the living-room, trying to make a sling out of an old burgee. He wasn't succeeding very well. Silently, Ginty took it from him, folded it with nervous fingers, slipped it under his forearm and knotted it round his neck. When she had finished she stepped back quickly, out of range. Foley did not thank her. He got up, rather slowly, and moved across to the window. The wind had died and the sea was flat and dull. He said, without turning round: "You may as well make some coffee. We've nearly an hour to wait."

As soon as he said that, time seemed to come to a stop. Peter and Ginty kept looking at their watches, and the minutes seemed to pass more slowly than a procession of snails. Nicola, who had no watch, slipped unnoticed out of the room and dashed upstairs and out on to the gallery. She walked all round, scanning the sea to the horizon, but so far as she could see, it was empty of both smoke and sail. Even the U-boat, which she had thought she might have been able to see, lying underwater like a great fish, was invisible. Perhaps, thought Nicola hopefully, it wasn't even there.

A cat's-paw flawed the surface of the grey, oily sea. Nicola went on watching the horizon for the first smoke of the destroyers or M.T.B.s or whatever the Navy decided to send, but nothing showed itself. There was a brown smudge all round the horizon and the sun, hanging low in the sky, just above the smudge, looked like a red plate. Nicola looked at it, not really seeing it, because she was staring so hard for her first sight of the ships. Then it struck her that she couldn't see as far as she had done; the outlines of the Limpet far away to port looked quite fuzzy. Nicola blinked and rubbed her eyes, but the Limpet was still fuzzy-looking. And then she remembered how the sea had looked the other day ("Goodness," thought Nicola, "only *Friday*") when they were up in the crow's-nest at Mariners. The fog was coming back.

Nicola watched. The sun grew smaller and paler, until, from being a red plate it became a white saucer and then just a bright spot in the mist. Then it disappeared altogether, and the fog, thick, white and wet, closed over the lighthouse. It was impossible even to see the rocks directly below. She made her way round to the door, stepped into the lantern and heard Ginty calling. As she went slowly downstairs, she couldn't decide whether the fog was likely to be worse for the U-boat or the destroyers.

But as time dragged past, it soon became certain that nothing was going according to plan. By half-past seven the fog was still so thick that they would see nothing from the windows except the rail of the cat-walk.

Ginty had made two lots of coffee by then, but they could none of them eat very much. Foley ate nothing at all. He gulped half a cup of black coffee and then sat staring moodily at the table-cloth. The fierce, malevolent expression on his white face reminded Nicola of a leopard she had seen once at the London Zoo who, according to his keeper, was suffering from a raging toothache.

Suddenly, Peter saw him begin to make his habitual gesture towards his inner pocket. Then his right hand fell back uselessly into the sling, and, with a small grimace of pain he felt in the pocket with his left. Peter held his breath. For a moment Foley was silent, as if he couldn't believe it; and then, making them all jump, he shouted:

"What have you done with it?"

Peter clenched his hands under the table. "I threw it in the sea."

Foley went on pressing his hand over the outside of his pocket. He said more quietly: "And the key of the room below?"

"Yes," said Peter, huskily, his heart thumping hard.

Foley stared at him so fiercely that it felt as if Foley were looking through the fabric of his jacket, into the pockets, and seeing the key bulging there in full view. He remembered that the revolver was bulging his pocket too, but that was no comfort. He'd never be able to shoot Foley, not in cold blood, nor in hot blood either. Somehow, at that moment, it was no reassurance to remember that Foley was badly hurt, and that Peter would probably only have to shove hard to get away from him; sitting there, he looked taut and hard and horribly strong; as if he could break Peter into little bits with one hand tied behind him.

But Foley made no move towards him. After a few dragging moments he said: "Much good may it do you," and got up. Rising, he moved too quickly; he had to stand still for a moment before he could walk to the door. Then he said: "Not that I believe you. I'm going to search your rooms. And in case you think of being brave boys and girls and trying to stop me, remember I still have this knife."

They looked at the short, strong blade and said nothing. Foley left the door open, and they could hear him going slowly —with occasional pauses—up the stairs.

Ginty's face quivered. "Oh, Binks. What *is* going to happen?"

Peter pulled himself together. "I don't know. Nothing, I expect, until the fog lifts."

"It's thinning now," said Nicola, looking out on to the fog, which had turned quite bright and milky in the last few minutes.

"If nothing's going to happen until it lifts, I wish it wouldn't," said Ginty in a shaking voice.

"You want to be rescued, don't you?" said Nicola sternly. "Very well then. It's no good crying in case it does."

"I'm not crying."

"Well, don't then."

They sat and listened to the thuds and thumps overhead. Presently they heard Foley coming slowly down the stairs. He did not come in, but went on down, and out through the main door of the lighthouse.

"What's he doing?" whispered Ginty.

"Nothing, I shouldn't think."

"He may be. Oh, Binks, do let's go and see."

But Foley was, as Peter had said, doing nothing. He was standing by the rail, staring into the fog. The tide was falling and there was a clear patch of beach at the foot of the steps. After a while, Foley limped slowly down. The fog was perceptibly thinner now; the sun was visible as a white saucer again, and they could see the outlines of the first line of rocks. Foley shouted suddenly.

It made them jump, but there was no answer. The sea splashed round the rocks and a gull cried overhead and nothing happened at all.

There was a lot more beach showing now. Foley was sitting on a lump of rock, staring into the fog in the direction from which the U-boat must come. Nicola had wanted to go down too, but Peter had held her back.

SHIPS IN THE BAY

"We'd better wait here," he had said, thinking, though he didn't say so, that if the U-boat's crew came ashore to take them, he could hold the head of the steps for six revolver shots. Not so many, perhaps, if the crew had revolvers too; all the same, they had a better chance here than on the beach.

"What's that?" said Ginty sharply.

They all heard it. The creak and splash of oars came through the fog, muffled but unmistakeable. The children scrambled to their feet and Foley stood up, the knife open in his hand. The boat was still some way away and her crew seemed to be making heavy weather of it. There was a crash and a splintering sound and a good deal of shouting, and then the sound of oars came across the water again. Peter gripped the rail, his cheeks scarlet. Beside him, Ginty had turned very white. Abruptly, Nicola dashed into the lighthouse and emerged again with two knives.

"Here," she said to Ginty with a relishing piratical look. "Just in case."

Ginty stared at the knife in her hand without any relish at all. It was quite plain that whatever sort of a fight Peter and Nicola intended to put up against the U-boat crew, Ginty meant to go quietly. But they none of them had much attention to spare for one another. They were all staring into the fog. It was clearing quickly. They could see the outlines of the boat quite plainly now as the wind carried the fog towards the mainland. In another moment the bows were grinding into the shingle, a man had jumped ashore, and Foley, his knife sheathed, had gone to meet him. They were his friends.

Ginty made a small strangled sound and shrank back into the lighthouse. She sat down on the stairs, and put her head on her knees and her hands over her ears; she simply wasn't going to see or know anything until they came to take her. Nicola moved closer to Peter, her knife gripped firmly in her hand. There was a lot of talk going on down there on the

241

beach, but they couldn't follow what was being said. It sounded like a lot of questions (not very amiable questions) and some equally hostile answers. Though he couldn't have said why, it reminded Peter of his interview with Foley after the boat thing; only now it was Foley who was in Peter's place. Somehow, from the look of his back and the set of his shoulders, Peter got the impression of his own angry, shamed feeling. It occurred to him, quite irrelevantly, that he'd probably been pretty rude; perhaps that was why there'd been such a tremendous row; perhaps that—

But he couldn't think about that now. He put his hand into his pocket and felt the key as well as Foley's revolver. He wished now that he'd hidden the key somewhere else, except that wherever it was hidden they could probably have made him tell. If the worst came to the worst he'd just have to chuck it into the sea. He shut his teeth tightly together because they badly wanted to chatter, not so much from fright as from the same uncontrollable excitement which was making him shake all over.

At last Foley and the other man seemed to reach some sort of agreement. The man turned towards the lighthouse. His voice carried easily, like the voice of a man accustomed to shouting against the wind.

"Now! You children! You will all three to come here, please!"

The moment had come and he wasn't really afraid. He looked across the beach at the man walking slowly, negligently towards the lighthouse and shouted back: "No!"

The man stopped dead, as if in sheer astonishment. Then he came on.

"We will not argue. You will come yourselves or you will be brought. As you please."

"No," said Peter again. The man was so close now that there was no need to shout. "Get back to your ship."

Afterwards, Nicola said she had been sure the man was going to pop with rage. But he said in a cold, level voice that was quite at variance with his purpling face: "Little boy, we shall have to teach you a lesson. Many lessons, from all I hear."

Peter's face flamed. He pulled out Foley's revolver and rested the muzzle on the rail. As he did so he caught a glimpse of Foley, half-sitting on a rock, and apparently surveying the scene with some amusement. He said: "I don't

suppose I can stop you leaving, but we're not coming with you. And if you come any closer, I'll fire."

"Will you?" said the man. He was standing at the foot of the steps by now. "But perhaps I shall fire too." He pulled a revolver fitted with a silencer from his holster, and levelled it, not at Peter, but at Nicola. "So. Now you will come down the stairs and there will be no more talk of shooting. Yet."

He thinks I won't, thought Peter, staring down at the brown face and the opaque blue eyes below him. He thinks I won't, but if he comes any nearer I shall. He felt very calm and cold and certain, and his hand had stopped shaking. He said: "We're not coming. Get back to your ship."

Something like a wasp flew past his cheek, and the bullet struck the lighthouse wall just behind his head. "There will be no more nonsense, please. You will come down here and at once."

Don't pull the trigger, Daddy had said, *you'll jerk it off the target if you do; just squeeze it gently.* Peter squeezed it gently. The next moment the report flew echoing among the rocks, and the man was lying face downward at the foot of the steps.

Peter gulped and stared, wondering, with a rather sick feeling at the pit of his stomach, if he had really killed him. But he hadn't time to think about it. Someone else had leapt ashore from the boat—no, several people, one of whom had begun emptying his revolver wildly in their direction. "Get back into the lighthouse," shouted Peter, trying to get the range of five targets at once and not succeeding, and knowing that Nicola had not moved. "Get *back*, Nick."

But Nicola was tugging at his arm and shouting, stammering so much that in the end she had to point instead. Peter looked, and was suddenly aware that the beach was filled with sunlight and shadow instead of a shadowless mist. The fog had rolled away inland and the whole sea was clattering with light. And then he saw what Nicola was pointing at: the long shape of the U-boat low on the surface beyond the rocks, and, far over on the port bow, the destroyer motionless as a lance in rest, a wisp of smoke floating from her funnel, her bows pointing towards the U-boat. And beyond her, two more. The Navy was making sure.

There seemed to be an instant of complete motionless silence. And then the scene broke up in tumult and confusion. Black smoke poured from the destroyer's funnel and a bow wave appeared on the sea in front of her. She heeled over and steamed straight for the U-boat.

The men on the beach were running to their boat. Foley, limping badly, caught his foot on a boulder and fell sprawling. Peter couldn't bear it. He tore down the stairs, leapt over the man's body, tore on across the beach and grabbed Foley by his good shoulder.

"Get—this sling—off me," panted Foley.

He was very white. Peter struggled clumsily with the knot and got the sling over Foley's head. "Thanks," said Foley, getting to his feet. "Here—take this. Souvenir of a crowded week-end."

And then he was gone, running down the beach as if pain were no longer a hindrance. The next moment he had plunged into a clear patch of sea and was swimming in the direction of the U-boat. As Peter watched, Nicola dashed past him and into the sea.

"No, don't," she shouted. "Come back! It's too late! Come back!"

What did Nick mean? wondered Peter, dazed by Foley's words and the knife in his hand and the speed with which things were happening. And then he saw, as Nicola had done, that the U-boat was crash-diving. The men in the boat were pulling hard and the coxswain was waving and yelling, but the U-boat's decks were awash already and the destroyer was coming up fast. Almost at the same moment there was a tremendous explosion and the sea spouted as if a whale had blown. Peter shouted "Nicola!" and began to run and then the blast of the explosion knocked him off his feet. For the moment he was winded; then, as he scrambled up again, he saw Nicola wading back through the swirling water.

"Oh, Binks," she said half-sobbing. "Why didn't you stop him? He'll be killed, I know he will."

"He'd rather be," said Peter, grabbing her, "I should think. Get down, Nick. They're firing."

Nicola, however, put her head up. She was still, though she hadn't the least idea of it, sobbing in a breathless way because

Foley was dead, or about to be, but at the same time she was intensely interested in what was going on. The men in the boat had given up trying to reach the U-boat. They were pulling desperately now in an effort to get clear of the destroyer. The U-boat's conning-tower disappeared below the surface just as the destroyer rammed. The ship jarred along her whole length, came momentarily to a stand, and then swept round in a curve. As she did so, six small black objects appeared in the air astern of her. There was a moment's pause and then the sea exploded.

The U-boat was lifted clean out of the water; she hung in the air for a moment and then fell sluggishly back beneath the surface, disintegrating as she did so. The sea boiled, and a surge of water drove up the beach to pour around and over Peter and Nicola. Then it receded. The sea was still boiling and swirling in little whirlpools, and the destroyer was steaming slowly back on her course. But there was nothing to be seen but oil and wreckage and something which might have been a man lying face downwards in the water.

The boat's crew were taken aboard the destroyer long before the children. Nicola, leaning on the rail of the cat-walk, a blanket draped round her, watched them paddle alongside and slouch grimly, but without fuss, up the companion, all except one man who sprang into the sea at the last moment and never came up. Nicola hugged the blanket more closely round her, and turned away, pretending she hadn't seen. A lump still seemed wedged in her throat whenever she thought of Foley, and this, thought Nicola, was really pretty futile, all things considered. Now that it was all over, she wished the Navy would buck up and take them off. But it seemed a long time before they were sitting in the ship's boat being taken back to the destroyer. Before that happened, a number of quiet, official-looking people had come ashore and asked a great many questions of all of them. Peter had handed over the key of the lowest room, and two or three civilians were still there, when at length the children were taken off, still going methodically through the books and papers. Two naval ratings were posted, one at the foot of the steps, and one at the entrance to the room itself. It all looked very business-like.

In the boat, everyone was very kind and cheerful and told them several times that they'd soon be home now. More blankets were produced, and they were promised dry clothes (of sorts) as soon as they were aboard. The odd thing was that none of them, Ginty in particular, seemed able to do anything but talk. It was almost as if it seemed so unreal to them to be safely among friendly people, who did ordinary naval things, that they had to talk a lot to make sure. But everything had been so odd and violent and suddenly changed for so long now, that for Nicola it was only an oddness among a crowd of other oddnesses that Robert Anquetil should be one of the people waiting for them when they came on deck.

As soon as they had changed into dry clothes—all several sizes too big, for even the smallest midshipman was a good head taller than Ginty—they had to tell their story all over again to Commander Whittier. He heard them through and then asked his own questions—rather different questions from those which the civilians who had landed at the lighthouse had asked. The *Talisman*—had she seemed to be specially fitted out in any way?—what time of day had it been when Foley had got in touch by radio?—had Foley said anything at all about his organization?—had he mentioned any names? . . . and all the time they were steaming back towards St.-Anne's-Oldport with the coast in plain view. They kept glancing at it through the port-holes.

"And Foley himself," said Whittier at length. "Any idea, exactly, what happened to him in the end?"

It was like looking through the wrong end of a telescope, remembering. Nicola found she could speak of it quite easily without any unnecessary and idiotic lump wedging itself in her throat. She said: "He tried to swim to the U-boat," and then remembered that Anquetil had been his friend. She glanced at him, but he was doodling carefully, his face rather tired-looking. Nicola, who had been going to say *"But I think the depth-charges blew him up"* altered it to "But I don't think he can have got there".

"Was he the man who dived from the island?" asked Anquetil, still doodling busily.

Nicola nodded.

"No one else?"

"No. The others all went in the boat."

"Then he was still in the water when the depth charges exploded," said Anquetil stonily to Whittier. "I was watching through the glasses. I saw someone swim away from the island, but at that distance I couldn't be sure who it was."

"Then he's accounted for," said Whittier briskly. "A pity we couldn't have taken him, but I daresay he wouldn't have told us much."

Anquetil said nothing, and there was a short silence.

"Let me see," said Whittier at length. "Anything else? Oh, yes. You won't have heard yet what happened to your sister, will you? A nice time you've given us, all of you, one way and the other." And he gave them a brief account of Lawrie's accident.

"Daddy will be *furious*," observed Nicola when he had finished. "Has he heard yet?"

"I should think he might have, just. Why will he be so furious?"

"Well," said Nicola, who was beginning to feel moderately at home, "because it's an unnecessary one. I mean, *I* see that Lawrie had to get away so she didn't look, but I bet Daddy won't. He'll say——" Nicola paused to consider, and Whittier watched her with some amusement.

"What'll he say?"

"How much more useful she'd have been if she'd had her fare with her and she hadn't been knocked down," said Nicola at length. And, as a matter of fact, shorn of embellishments and some pointed remarks about safety on the roads, that was very much what Commander Marlow did say, as soon as Lawrie was well enough to hear it.

Whittier grinned. "That sounds like Geoff Marlow. Oh, yes, I know him. Now, about this business. Your parents have been told the full story as we knew it this morning, and Lawrie knows the beginning; so they can hear anything else you like to tell them. But so far as the rest of your family and friends are concerned," he paused and then said emphatically, "you've got to forget the existence of spy rings, U-boats and all the rest of it. Your story will have to be that you were taken off for a sail, and that you were wrecked and that at last you managed to attract the attention of a passing destroyer. And don't even talk about this affair much amongst yourselves. Then you're not likely to let anything slip to other people."

They promised soberly.

"Of course, there's one other person who knows more than he should and that's young Johnnie Thorpe." Whittier looked at Anquetil, and Anquetil looked up briefly with an expression which conveyed that he had already heard Whittier's unvarnished opinion of *that* excursion. "But he's been told that he's not to discuss the affair with you at all, under any circumstances whatsoever, and that it'll mean the block on Tower Hill for five if he does. So you three and Lawrie just remember that too."

"Coo!" said Nicola. And then she remembered something. "Sir, who *was* it who saw our signal?"

"Anquetil." Whittier eyed Anquetil again. "He can tell you that story himself later."

Nicola felt her cheeks grow hot. But it was quite obvious there was a grandmother and a grandfather of a row on, so she said sturdily: "It was jolly lucky he *was* there. 'Cos we were signalling when the Fleet passed and they never saw a thing."

Whittier looked at her. Nicola met his gaze, but she could feel her cheeks growing scarlet. He went on looking at her in silence, and she stared stubbornly back; and at length he said in quite a friendly voice: "Then I must agree with you; it was most fortunate. My apologies, Robbie."

Suddenly the wardroom was a friendly place, and they were all grinning at one another in a cheerful and idiotic fashion. Whittier lit a cigarette and Anquetil sucked a match-flame into his pipe, saying: "We'd have been there earlier, only we were short of petrol and I had to nurse her." It was a glorious morning, they were making thirty knots, and home was coming nearer every second. "Time for grub," said Whittier suddenly, sounding and looking, thought Nicola, exactly like Badger in *The Wind in the Willows*. And she realized suddenly that for the first time in her life she was at sea in a destroyer, that she was sitting in the wardroom, and that she wasn't feeling sea-sick in the least. At that moment life, to Nicola, seemed almost too glorious to be true.

She spent the rest of the voyage on the bridge. Peter and Ginty were being shown over the rest of the ship by the small-est midshipman, but Nicola, having reached the bridge, de-cided to stay there. There would be other times in her life, during a Naval Week in Portsmouth, for instance, when she could see over as many naval vessels as she liked; but probably she'd never again be able to be on the bridge of a destroyer while she was actually at sea. The captain, a cheerful young Lieutenant-Commander, who knew Giles, said he saw her point. And having said that, he left her to it, beyond giving her an occasional friendly grin. He didn't, to Nicola's immense relief, take her for the kiddish sort of person who would think it an enormous treat to be allowed to give orders down the voice pipe. And he, on his side, was glad to see that she wasn't the sort of child, who, having been given one favour, expected half a dozen more. They shook hands with one another an hour later when the destroyer dropped anchor outside St.-Anne's-Oldport and said good-bye with increased liking and respect.

"By the way," said Whittier, who had come on deck to say good-bye and was leaning over the rail as Peter began to go down into the ship's boat, "what was it you said to the man you shot?"

Peter thought back. "I think I said: 'Get back to your ship.' Why? Shouldn't I have done?"

But Whittier was grinning. "Certainly you should. One should always make the most of one's opportunities. But it'll be a long time before you strike one like that again. Know who he was?"

Peter shook his head.

"Well, I don't suppose his name would mean much. But during the war he was *ein Kontenadmiral*." The German syllables rolled grandly. "That's the equivalent of a Rear-Admiral. So just remember, when some haughty sub in your first ship is telling you what a low form of life you are, that you once gave a Rear-Admiral his marching orders."

Peter grinned broadly. Whittier left the rail. Peter scurried down the companion and dropped neatly into the boat. The events of the morning were very clear and distinct, but they seemed to have taken place simply ages ago. As the boat bounced across the harbour he grinned at Nicola and Ginty, who grinned back, though Nicola looked a bit rueful. She was wishing this part of the adventure need never come to an end as it was obviously going to do quite shortly. But Ginty couldn't have looked happier; she didn't mind how soon they got ashore. As soon as they reached the jetty, she scrambled out and stood, safe and sound, on the firm hard blocks of concrete. It was a glorious afternoon, and people were just beginning to come out and stroll beside the sea in a perfectly ordinary Sunday-ish way, wearing gloves and their best hats. It seemed impossible to believe that only that morning they had been on a small rocky island in a fog, having revolvers fired at them. Ginty decided she wouldn't believe it. Or at least, not more than she could help. And then a motor drew up at the end of the quay and someone got out and waved and began to run. So did Ginty; she flung herself into her mother's arms and hugged her hard.

"Oh, *Mummy*," said Ginty fervently, "you can't *think* how glad I am to see you. I don't know about the others, but I simply loathed every minute of it."

In her bed at the hospital, Lawrie, very clean and brushed and bandaged, lay and waited for them. There was a vase of wallflowers on the dressing-table and some daffodils in another vase on the bed-table. She felt a good deal better than she'd done when she had talked to Robert Anquetil, but she still got tired rather quickly if people talked to her for very long at a time. So Lawrie meant to tell her story first. Whatever had been happening to the others, Lawrie didn't think it could have been nearly as impressive as what had happened to her. Fractured bones, broken bones, concussion—Lawrie felt they would have to produce something pretty remarkable to compete with that. She lay and watched the clouds floating past outside in the blue sunny sky, and rehearsed her story carefully.

"Well, it seemed pretty feeble just to go and all of us get captured, so I lay down flat and waited till you'd gone. And then. . . ."

There were steps outside the door. Mummy came in followed by Peter and Nicola and Ginty who looked at her carefully and then looked as if they were rather relieved by what they saw.

"Hullo," they all said. And then they all looked at one another as if they hadn't the least idea what to say next.

"Have some barley sugar," said Lawrie, at last, offering th

tin beside her bed. "And if you don't mind my saying so, those are some very peculiar clothes you're wearing."

Nicola and Peter and Ginty looked at one another. They supposed, now they came to think of it, they did look a bit odd. They each took a piece of barley sugar and promptly became more speechless than before.

"All right," said Lawrie, tucking her piece into her cheek and speaking fairly distinctly. "Then I'll start. Now listen. *This* is what happened to *me*."